DOGS IN THE DISTANCE

by

Kevin Leicinger

FIRST ONE HUNDRED BOOKS

Copyright 2014 by Kevin Leicinger

ISBN 9780692345054

CHAPTER ONE:

Anyone who described it as ballet didn't have any sense of grace. The police arrived loudly. At least three different agencies. It was all urgency and chaos. Sirens and yelling everywhere. Nobody was quite sure who was in charge.

A man had called in from a liquor store in Clackamas. He had found the woman we were seeking. A woman in her thirties, maybe forties, matching the sketch of "Natasha." He had called it in from the safety of his cage. A wall of thick, clear plexi. She hadn't caught on that he had made the call until she tried to pay for her fifth. He had seemed a little jumpy and a little too friendly. Natasha tried to run.

It just so happened there was a black and white, a local patrol, right down that very street. By the time Natasha figured it out they were already there in the parking lot. Guns drawn and waiting for back up.

There was a moment of fear that Natasha would panic and try to harm hostages inside. They didn't know if she was armed or not. The store clerk hadn't said. They just knew that she had already killed.

By the time I got there with Gillian, the whole circus was in full swing. The tactical detail had arrived. Quasi-military in style. Oregon's version of SWAT. They took their positions and waited. There was still some question of command.

Arguments ensued right on the spot about who had authority over the scene. It was a glory moment, or maybe more of a glory hole, for any cop wanting some fame. Arresting a serial killer was big news. Something that would stand out on your record. No man wanted to give up their piece of the pie. Inside, Natasha just waited.

Crowds gathered and news vans arrived. Local stations cut away from syndicated talk shows. Helicopters circled. Flies buzzing over a carcass. There was almost a collision. The TV choppers were ordered to stay away. Natasha was never going to get out of this one. At least not alive.

"Has anybody tried to talk with her yet?" I asked Gillian. "Beats the fuck out of me." His disdain for the FBI started on cue. Fuckers in Blazers. The "so-called-experts" were probably waiting for some negotiator to be flown in from the moon. His tirade didn't make sense but I got his point. The Task Force had taken control. They had evaluated the situation and assumed there were hostages. They needed to play it by the book. They'd take their time and wear her down. Eventually, she would have to give in.

The reporters were left with too much time to kill. They kept saying the same things over and over. A few stations cut back to their regularly scheduled programming but most stuck with the show. A man arrived in a black suit and slacks in the backseat of a government-issue sedan. The negotiator. A PHD. He had experience with these delicate situations.

They called the store but Natasha wouldn't answer. She wasn't in the mood to talk. The troops circled the noose and took closer positions. She wasn't going to be an easy target.

The crowd got bored. This wasn't what they had hoped for. A scene from Michael Man or John Woo. Instead it was sitting and waiting. Nothing much happened. Some admitted that it was really kind of dull. Few, however, would risk leaving. What if they missed something important?

Over an hour passed and contact had yet to be established. Some suspected that Natasha had managed to escape. We learned later what she did. How she used that time. She was very methodical in her ways.

She deleted all the information from her cell phone. Then she stomped on it until dead. Plastic remains littered the floor. The only witness to her actions was the lone clerk in his cage. That and the cameras that monitored the store. High-angle images from multiple views of Natasha burning the contents of her wallet. She was determined to get out even if she couldn't escape. It was as good an ending as any.

The police saw the fire and became concerned. It was small but what if it spread? The order was given to take the store. Concussion grenades were thrown in to confuse. Assault troops barged through the doors. It turns out they weren't really needed. They swooped in to take her but she was already half gone. Natasha was unconscious and bleeding on the floor. She had taken a broken bottle and done it right. Two slits. One on each of her wrists.

Blood had poured from her but she had mistimed the deed. She never should have started that fire. She was kept alive by the paramedics. She was soon stable. At least as far as the blood. Natasha Kruger was wheeled out on a stretcher. The killer had been caught. A victory for law enforcement everywhere. Grudging credit to the Portland PD.

And all the time you were laughing.

CHAPTER TWO:

Somewhere in my mental rerun of times gone by, the music I was listening to became a part of things. I saw a half dozen uniforms in their ponchos, waddling around aimlessly like mutant penguins. It's all as it was down to the nitty gritty. But it started to blur with memories of the music video. Nirvana, "Smells Like Teen Spirit." High School kids. The Janitor. I even pictured the Anarchist Cheerleaders performing in the alley. Black uniforms with nice, short skirts. The anarchist "A" symbol across their chests. Slowly, it became one big musical number. Flashing lights from cop cars and lovely young things cheering and dancing to grunge in the rain. "Entertain Us" indeed. It was all just a big, God damn show put on for your viewing pleasure.

And it was all in slow motion. The pissing rain caught, just so, with elaborate lighting rigs which defined each and every acid sting. The cold breath of the officers standing by the warehouse wall. The intense beams of the flood lights blasting down on the crime scene like the eyes of God himself.

Right on cue I saw myself strolling through the scene. Out of the car and past the cheerleaders. Out of the darkness and into the light. A present awaited me. The closed garbage bin a gift box for the trinket within. I saw my hand reach out.

The dramatic pause. Then, in a single gesture, the lid of the dumpster was flipped open to reveal my prize.

The music reached crescendo. Malicious guitars and violent drums as I stared down at him. He was seventeen. A seventeen year-old kid naked and trussed up like a turkey. His wrists had been bound to his ankles. And there wasn't a stitch of clothes on him. His pale skin glistened in the rain. A single drop fell from his hair. The poetry of death. And all I remember thinking was that even dead the kid looked pretty.

I stirred from the silence. My alcoholic daze disturbed by the playlist ending. Time to go to bed but I resisted. I was enjoying the self-pity and delusion too much.

Each conversation played in my head like snippets from a tape recording. I swear I almost heard tape hiss as I recalled the exact words that had been exchanged. First there was Johanson, the uniform. Twenty-years old and pleased as punch to be there. The rest of us wanted to be home in bed. But Johanson was on the trip of his life. Eager. Inquisitive. Excited. What could be better than this?

"You think he was a rent boy?" Johanson asked. "You mean a male prostitute?" "Yeah, whatever" he said dismissively. "Nobody calls them rent boys anymore." "You know what I meant." "Yeah, I do. And yeah, it's a possibility. But if he was one, he was either brand new to town or expensive." Johanson looked up at me. "How do you know that?" he asked. I pointed to our watery find. "Look at him. Not one sign of a rough life on him. He's a fucking Adonis. His teeth alone probably cost fourteen grand to make that perfect."

Hiss. Pop. Crackle. The great man had spoken. Senior Detective John Dudek of the Portland PD was already expounding wise to the naïve, young followers there to suck up every morsel of profundity.

I then talked to the homeless guy who had found the body. Maybe he was a messenger sent to guide me but I just couldn't hear his tune. St. Reeks Like Piss delivering the gospel. Hiss. Crackle. Crackle. "So, you called 911 right away?" I asked. "Yes Sir" St. Piss responded. "On what? Is there a phone around here I don't know about?" "On my cell phone." "You can afford a cell phone?" St. Piss looked at me and smiled.. "Pre-paid minutes." Hiss. Pop. St. Piss didn't have that much more to tell me. He was looking for bottles and anything else he could sell and found the kid. I believed him when he said he didn't touch the body. Unless he had stripped the corpse clean, there wasn't a whole lot to take.

I sat up in my chair a bit higher. Ikea crap falling apart at an accelerated rate. Dinner was sitting badly. I slowly took the headphones off and stood up. I felt grounded but had to concentrate a little to make my way across the hardwood floor. Maybe it was the memories of the saint, but I suddenly needed to take a leak with great urgency.

I faced myself in the mirror in classic, washed up detective fashion. With total seriousness I said the words. Those deep, painful words which gave insight into my inner turmoil. "Pre-paid minutes."

I smiled at my own ridiculousness and found some chips in the cupboard. I thought about grabbing a soda. Instead I grabbed another beer. I was having too much fun to let things end.

More words and memories were retrieved. Recollections of that night in the rain. "I'm not in advertising, I'm in design." I hated that guy. He was my age but trying to look twenty. His clothes cost hundreds of dollars and were hand-tailored to look used. Or "distressed" as they say.

Rewind tape. Cue here. White noise memory hum. "What were you doing down here at three in the morning?" I asked. "Working. We have a big pitch tomorrow. I'm a Senior Designer at Visionaire." "Where exactly is that?" He gestured vaguely down the street. "Twenty-one Ash. The granite and plywood building. I have a corner space that looks right onto the street." "Did you see anybody else down this way, earlier?" "I saw a grey SUV go by around eleven." I made note of his answer. "Can you describe it for me?" "Graphite. Chrome details. Medium sized." "Chrome details? You mean, like custom trim?" "No, the usual garish stuff" he said. "The same as on all of them." "Was there anyone else working at the ad agency with you tonight? He looked at me with indignation. "I'm not in advertising. I'm in design." "Right. Was there anyone at the design place with you tonight?" "No, I sent my junior home at ten. I've been alone since."

I remember thinking how it might be amusing to tell Johanson to send out an APB for "an average looking, average sized, SUV in grey with the usual garish looking trim." My guess is that he would have done it, eager puppy that he was. The thought seemed less funny now.

Lest the night should come to a close before its due, I forced myself to focus further. The scene was not yet complete. There was that moment. That golden moment when I learned the news from Tina, the forensics lead. I tried to make my fuzzy brain remember her exact words. It didn't come easily. Could be the beer. Could be exhaustion. More likely I was just old, tired and more than a little fucked up. But I got them. I got down into my little brain and retrieved those bits of conversation past. The little snippets that were the first clue that I was well and truly screwed.

Cue misery. Crank up the volume. Embrace the final cut. I approached Tina and wondered why there were so few forensics people on the scene. "So, where's the rest of your team?" "You're kidding right? You been in a cave all night? she said. "I was home. Then I was here." "You might try staying in touch with the world now and again. Might do you some good." "Might depress me, is what it might do. So, what the hell are you talking about? She looked at me in disbelief. Apparently I'd been out of the loop. "A family of four was down from Seattle to see the Blazers play. Someone decided to shoot them while they were going back to their car." "A robbery?" I asked. "Could be, but they went after them all. Even the kids. Three dead at the scene. The media is already on it like rabid dogs." "I bet" I said. "Which means the Mayor and the Chief..." "I get the picture" I said. And sadly I did.

Fade up mental image of his eminence, the Mayor, aglow from the light of TV crews as he gave a hasty press conference. Behind him stood The Chief of Police and my boss, The Chief of Detectives. Begin slow motion! Bring on the Anarchist Cheerleaders! Fine, young things with long, lean legs saluting all that is evil and all that is chaos! "Here we are now/Entertain us/I feel stupid/And contagious/Here we are now..."

CHAPTER THREE:

I needed to reach out for a beer and the smile that came with it. A kind look from a girl and it would be alright. It would drive away the voices in my head that kept wearing me down. A little conversation went a long way. And it sure as hell beat reflecting on the past.

It was a near enough destination that I could always walk. There was already a crowd which didn't make me happy. I wanted to be the only one. I took my usual seat at the bar and saw her in the back. There it was, the glance and the smile. I was already starting to feel better. I nursed my beer as I came back to life. Awakened by the sound of her voice.

"Hey, how have you been?" Emily said as she poured. "Hanging in, you?" "Busy. Hang on." She walked away to a booth and recited the specials of the day. True to its name, the Pig and Porter delivered both with aplomb. Braised pork belly with cabbage and pigs feet with beans. Listening to her made me realize how hungry I was.

I tried not to stare but couldn't seem to help it. The blond hair and body were magnets for men's eyes. Something Emily discovered long ago and now just accepted. They're like hookers who flirt but never deliver. Female bartenders traded on loneliness and lust. For the price of a pint you could pretend you had a connection. In Japan it's big business, far more formal than here. The game is the same in any language it's played. And it's still cheaper than strippers.

All of which made Emily that much more amazing. Sure, she traded a laugh for a twenty-percent tip. But somewhere along the line the illusion became real. At the very least you could call us friends. It had probably started when I helped her out with a DWI. Some cowboy in blue wrote her up for riding on her scooter drunk. It wasn't smart but I got involved. Reduced charges satisfied everyone.

Since then we had spent some time together, in the bar and out. I even knew a little about her. She was already worried that life had past her by. I suppose at thirty-three it kind of made sense. Her looks wouldn't last forever and she would have to adjust. And her degree in classic literature hadn't exactly prepared her for life. Words can only tell you so much.

She wanted to get into non-profit work and save the world. Nobody was hiring. A return for her Masters was in the cards but she had her doubts. Too many of her peers had such degrees and were still out of luck. They asked her to get them jobs at the bar.

Emily was a girl I could love but it was a one-way street. She had her guy and had been with him for years. He was the lead singer in an indie rock band. Good looking already, with a guitar in his hand he was crack to a junkie. I hated him all the more when I finally met him. He was a really nice guy. Modest. Talented. And very much in love with Emily. They were such a fine couple, it made me ache.

So, I took what I could get and we became friends. It was a fine arrangement as long as I didn't go off the deep end. She knew I wanted her but understood I knew better. She even offered to hook me up with her friends.

"What am I getting?" I asked without shame. "Pork Belly and Russian River." "Done." "You look like hell" she said. "I'm going for that world-weary, haggard look." "More like shit on a stick."

The harassment was concern which bothered me even more. Almost as much as if she didn't bother to say anything. I watched her walk away to tend to another. My eyes moved up and down her with every step she took. I was starving by the time my food arrived. It's the sort of meal that would kill you but I didn't seem to mind. It was rich and tasty and the beer was just right. Its bitter edge cut right through the fat.

Time passed as I had a couple more. I wobbled a bit as I got up to piss. I hadn't had much but had even less sleep. My mind was susceptible to persuasion when I was this tired. If I stayed longer, I was going to have to be careful not to overdue it. "What are you doing Friday?" she asked. "I don't know. Why?" "Billy's having a show at Dante's. You should go." I considered the offer but got sidetracked. "It doesn't sound right, you know." "What? Going to the show?" "Billy and Emily. Too many "eee's."

"Are you drunk? You didn't have..." I tried to get my shit together but it was a losing effort. "Just tired." "So, is that a yes or a no?" "Yeah. Sounds good." I was let off the hook, at least for being stupid. "Billy's got to go early to set up. So, why don't you meet me here at eight and then we'll go together." "Ok."

We said our good-byes and I called it a day. At least as far as more drinking was concerned. It was grey but not raining. One of those in between days you're not sure how it will fall. I walked to a park and sat on a bench. It was peaceful enough but I got up quickly to leave. The place reminded me far too much of a cemetery.

CHAPTER FOUR:

Rewind. After the trash. Before the beginning. The time of John Doe/Adonis.

The Mayor liked little girls. He liked to touch them. Hold them. Love them. These were the rumors taken as truth by those who believed in death panels and WMD. Any excuse for moral outrage and indignation would do.

Portland's posturing as a progressive town was undone by the cries of the overtaxed and overburdened. The economy was dying because of the Liberal Socialists. Taxes were too high. The government too inefficient. It was time for a change. Reduce waste. Cut the taxes. Kill the poor. Or at least make them get off their asses and get a job. And what's this with the Mayor and young girls?

The scandal was too much. A recall was declared. He had to go.

The Mayor had won but the cost had been high. Revelations were made and facts made clear. Mr. Mayor didn't like little girls but his taste in playmates was enough to cause concern. He was a sugar daddy who liked to dispense lavish gifts. Gifts given to pretty young women who thanked him in kind. Embarrassing details were printed. Like Bill sharing a cigar with Monica, it was made all too real.

And out of that mess the Mayor emerged and stood in front of the cameras. Damaged, bruised and burnt he was hanging on by a thread. And now this. A family of tourists murdered after a game. Portland was a nice place. We didn't do murders here. That was for places like Los Angeles. We might have Meth labs and petty crime but murder was not in the cards. Especially Downtown. Portland was a progressive, modern, safe city after all. A place people aspire to. A nice place to raise kids.

Roll tape as the press conference begins. Another memory distorted by disgust and hindsight. The Mayor and his minions feeding the beast. "It is with great sadness that I have to inform you that Sara Radovich died this morning as a result of her wounds. There will be a later press conference at OHSU to provide the details. In the meantime, I would just like to express my sadness and my determination to bring Sara's and her family's assailants to justice."

Animals at the trough. A feeding frenzy. The reporters jostled for position. A young guy from Channel Nine was the first to be heard. "Has there been any progress in the case so far?" The Police Chief took the question. "At this time we are pursuing several leads. It is too early in the case to get into any details regarding the course of our investigation."

Another reporter pushed his way forward. "Were the victims shot in the actual parking lot of the Rose Garden? Wasn't there security? Weren't there witnesses, given the large crowd?" The Mayor took the question himself. "Contrary to the misinformation given earlier, they were not parked in the actual lot but in the street about a block away." Another reporter. Further questions. "Can you tell us anything about the family? What were they doing in Portland?" The Mayor once again took the mic. "They were down from Seattle for a long weekend. We believe they were staying at the Marriot downtown and spent the day going to the art museum and shopping before going to the game." "Do you think this was a robbery that got out of hand?" The Mayor stepped aside. The Chief was better able to answer this one. "That is one of many avenues we are currently exploring."

The most telling of all was the final question. It was asked by a young woman from Channel Eleven. "Is it true there was another murder last night on the East Bank?" The Mayor and the Chief exchanged awkward glances.

Silence.

Silence.

Silence.

You're fucked John Doe/Adonis. Nobody cares.

Eventually, the Chief stepped up to the cameras and saved the day. All the right gestures. All the right phrases. "Unidentified person whose cause of death is currently unknown." "Every effort is being made." "No, despite the recent cuts in manpower due to budget shortfalls we have all the resources we need." It was a skillful performance and one full of lies. Not that anybody would be too concerned about such things.

One step inside The Cube and the truth was more clear. My home away from home. The Cube. Police Headquarters. A building so efficient it won praise and so green it won prizes. It was bundled up tight from winter rain and summer heat. Too bad they forgot to let us breathe.

The state of the art H/VAC failed every day. Windows didn't open. We were sealed inside our box. Rows of fluorescents illuminated the grey cubicles below. The resulting pallor reminded me of cancer. The dying and the already dead. Sometimes I swear I could even smell the rot and decay. But it was usually just the defecation backing up in the high-efficiency toilets.

Within this magnificent palace the troops were amassed. Detectives from Person Crimes gathered around a white board. The C of Ds gave the pep talks and assigned all the teams. The Radovich case would be solved no matter what the cost.

I sat alone in my cubicle thinking only of you, John Doe/Adonis. My ignorance remained. My calls unanswered by those that probed your body looking for answers. The Medical Examiner had other priorities. Even in death you went to the back of the line.

I killed time by pulling up all the missing persons files. Mothers, wives, husbands, daughters, lovers, sons, grandchildren, parents. They were all somebody to somebody who had bothered to report them. How many were "missing" and how many just didn't want to be found?

Fathers walked out the door and never looked back. Wives felt trapped and took the next flight out. So many people were just looking to escape.

As a rule, nobody bothered looking for the adults. If they wanted out and didn't say goodbye, that wasn't a crime. The kids though. The kids were the ones that got to you. Some may have been lost but most ran away. Fathers that raped them and mothers high on meth were none too deserving of their return. Yet, the streets were no place for them, at least not for long.

I had made the mistake once of getting close to a couple of the street kids. I didn't mind the way they thought nothing of using me for whatever they could get. I didn't even mind the stupidity of their false bravado. It was the knowing that in spite of all the people that wanted to help them, all but a lucky few were going to come to a very bad end.

I still remember Tiffany, age fifteen. A bright girl from Boise preferring a sleeping bag under a bridge to sharing a bed with her father. The "nasty cold" she refused to see a doctor for was T B. She was found in an SRO her friends had chipped in for to keep her out of the rain.

Give me the already dead anytime. The journey is less painful for all concerned.

I narrowed the search but came up with nothing. More time had been wasted. I didn't even have that most basic of basics. I didn't know yet who the victim was.

I gave into assumptions and started down the path. You were a gay prostitute. Pretty. Expensive. Disposable. It was a supposition that seemed logical and gave me something to do.

Patiently, I waited for the briefing to come to an end. The manpower was impressive. The determination to close the case fast even more so. I wondered if the Radovich family realized how much money they were costing the angry tax payers.

I got a hold of Gillian, a guy who knew vice. If there was someone to give me some direction, he was my man. I described a male prostitute who was young, fit and costly. A real high-end date for those with the means. I asked where I would look for him if I were in the market for such a thing. Gillian steered me to a web address but it came with a warning. "If he was really top-shelf you're not going to find him on any website. It's all about who you know."

It was all I had. So, I went at it with gusto. I typed in the address and lost myself in a world I had been blissfully unaware of. It wasn't what I expected. This was no little personals site. This was e-commerce. The men were listed by type and preferences. There were customer ratings after each and all of them. Five stars. Three-and-a-half stars. Pity the poor service worker that only got two.

And then there were the customer reviews. A few were short. "Best time I've had in years." "Gracious. Polite. Satisfying." "Highly Recommended." Most, however were an excuse for bad porn. Gifted wordsmiths these writers were not. I never realized how many ways there were to describe an orgasm. I also hadn't come to terms with how diminutive my genitalia were compared to these horse-like men who seemed to make up the bulk of the reviewers. I wasn't bothered by any of it, just bored and irritated. It was all such a waste.

I got heckled by anyone that happened to walk by. "Hey Dudek, looking for a date?" "I didn't know they had a site for Polock Porn. "I know that site. I think I saw your dad on there." Cop humor. Not funny but needed. Keep it light and connect with your brethren. They were all you had.

My web tour yielded nothing. I got more specific preferences. Age 18 (and younger, it implied). Tall. Athletic. Into: Bondage. A heckler's delight. "I never knew you were that kinky, Dudek." "Boys and bondage. I should'a guessed from that shirt you were wearing." The list narrowed but was still rather vast. I went through them all looking for you. I came up empty.

CHAPTER FIVE:

My memory was still playing tricks on me. In life as we know it, the medical examiner's office is a bland, busy space. It's an unambitious strip mall kind of a building on the far side of nowhere. A nineteen-eighties era design of beige, brown and grey with a public seal affixed to a cheap façade. It's a place of business and lacking in comfort. But that's not how I see it when I remember things.

Instead I see you lying flat on a slab. Fuzzy and yellow like an Atget photograph of a tomb in a Cathedral. All the more intriguing because the image isn't very clear.

You had been slit clean open. Your skin had been folded down like delicate wrapping paper as they emptied you out. Your brain was inspected for damage. Your heart weighed precisely. You were poked, prodded and analyzed by every means. It left you hollow. But they sewed you up well and made you presentable.

I still hear the Medical Examiner's words over the image. A long string of damage done and clues to nowhere.

"He died from asphyxiation. From the marks we found, it looks like a plastic bag put around his head. Somebody held it there with their hands nice and tight. A bad way to go but aren't they all? Probably a good three minutes before he actually died. Marks on his wrists and ankles from the rope. It doesn't look like he struggled much though. Maybe tied at gunpoint? I don't know. That's for you detectives to figure out. There were no fibers on the rope and the rope itself is the most common brand in the country. Chinese stuff you can find at any big-box retailer or mom and pop store. It's everywhere. Nothing else interesting with that. There were signs of anal penetration. No tearing or bruising. So, I assume, voluntary. Not a person. An object. A sex toy of some sort. Probably plastic. He clearly ate very well. By well, I mean properly, not fancy, necessarily. His teeth had been worked on but it was top quality. Mostly cosmetic. His insides though were like that of an old man. He tested positive for heroin, coke and speed. Also THC. The tox screen read like a pharmacy shelf. This kid was an omnivore when it came to pharmaceuticals. Uppers. Downers. Steroids. Viagra. Hallucinogenics. Also, he broke his ribs once. Probably when he was young. Like five or six. That's all there is."

I drove back from Clackamas, none the wiser. The 205 was stacked bumper to bumper with people getting a jump on traffic. Demands were being made for more highways to be built as people swore to themselves about road construction.

I arrived back at The Cube over an hour later. The floor was almost empty because they had been put out on the streets. School photos of the Radovich kids had found their way to the news. Cries of vengeance and calls for justice were in the air. It stank like mold. The building was rotting. Recycled insulation couldn't keep the damp out.

"The boss wanted to see you" Gillian said with a grin. He gestured to the office in the center of the cubicles. The Chief of Detectives sat behind his desk. He listened, waited and nodded on cue. All I could see of his assailant was the back of a head. Grey hair, unadorned. A female I think.

I walked down the aisle and got a better look. A woman in her late-fifties wearing a sweater and long skirt. You could almost hear the crunch, she looked so granola. Profiling habits didn't rest easily. Suburu. Lesbian. Shares a hundred-year-old house with her long-term partner. Gardens. Raises chickens in the back. Recycles tin-foil and tea bags. Turns shit into compost.

The C of Ds gestured for me to come in. "Detective Dudek. This is Maria Walker. She's the President of the LGBT Alliance" the Boss Man said. She put out a withered hand as I tried to remember the letters. Lesbian. Gay. Bisexual. But the "T" caused me trouble. I took a seat as I finally remembered. Transgender. Such a catchy name for people fighting not to be labeled.

Ms. Walker well knew that her people had clout. What they lacked in numbers they made up for with precision. Turn up the heat and get the message out loud. Ignore at your peril. As the mayor and his staff understood quite well, first and foremost it was about winning the primary.

Trivial mental exercises gave way to the beat down. A verbal assault spoken ever so softly. The smile of an assassin ready to finish the job. The C of Ds had enough of being on the wrong end of the stick. It was his time to shine and mine to remain silent.

"I was just telling Ms. Walker that you were the lead detective on the East Bank case," he said. His show was cut short before he even got started. Ms. Walker wasn't ready to relinquish the stage. "Detective, we were all deeply saddened at learning about the death of the young man on the East Bank. We were even more concerned at the way this department seems to be treating the case. Is there some reason one murder deserves five detectives assigned to it and one murder deserves only one, lone detective? I would hate to think that it has anything to do with the victim's sexual preferences."

Refusing to be pushed aside, The C of Ds set me up with the pitch. "I was explaining to Ms. Walker that the detectives in our department often work on multiple cases at one time." The cue given, it was my time to go. "You must have gotten inaccurate information, Ms. Walker. I'm the lead detective on the case but I am certainly not the ONLY detective on the case. In fact, I just came back from a meeting with county investigators. We have a great team on this."

I glanced down at her pearls and awaited a response. A knowing look and handshakes. Success all around. The lies were not lies but code for the game. She had gotten what she came for, the point had been made. Men would be reassigned. Resources re-allocated. John Doe/Adonis would finally get the attention he craved.

It was as I was gloating that the dagger was put to my neck. "Detective Dudek, maybe you can explain to me how a newspaper story got out about your victim being a male prostitute?" I had forgotten all about it and reeled from the blow. I mumbled an answer but knew I was done. "It was one of the uniforms. I made the mistake of answering a couple of his questions and..." "That's right. YOU made a mistake. Not me. Not this department. You. And YOU are going to fix it."

I shifted in my chair waited for the rest. A silence designed for my discomfort ensued. It worked as planned. I finally caved in and took my due. "And how am I going to do that, sir?"

"I'm glad you asked, detective. You are going to fix it by quickly solving the case and bringing the killers of this fine, young man we found dead to justice. And although you obviously have all the manpower and resources you need, you are going to find it more efficient to work on your own and taking your own initiative no matter how much overtime you have to put in or how many meals you need to skip. Isn't that right, Detective Dudek?"

More words followed. I just nodded and took my beating. "That will be all, detective."

CHAPTER SIX:

The dogs clamped their jaws and tried to rip him apart. The victim was flat on his back and flailing around in a panic. A fierce-looking German Shepherd pulled on his leg as the other bit into his wrist and pulled the other way. They shook and tugged with all their might. A third dog appeared and went for the groin.

The victim rolled over and tried to get up. A dog went for his neck but couldn't quite get to it. Their target was running around like his skin was being burned off. Terror and pain confused every step. A dog took his legs out from under him. He went down again. A fourth dog was released and then a fifth. They too wanted to taste blood and flesh.

And all the time people were laughing.

There was something clown-like and clumsy about the way the victim moved. Like some over-sized toddler. An infant being mauled by wild dogs.

FAST FORWARD

You could see the fear on his face. He didn't know what was coming but knew it was going to be bad. A crowd gathered to watch. A countdown began. "One. Two. Three."

And then he felt his insides exploding. He'd never felt anything like it. A truck running him over and then backing up to run him over again. He bent over but still stood. His muscles were convulsed so tightly they felt like they might shred. He was frozen. A sick marionette at the end of a five-hundred-thousand watt string.

And still he heard laughing.

He waited for it to be over but it didn't let up. He began to worry about the cardiovascular strain. His heart could stop at any second. Finally, it ended. Laughter and applause. But there was still more to follow.

REWIND

Poor Johanson didn't even realize that I was behind his torture. The police force was a fraternity and hazing was the price of membership. Even I had gone through my share of physical pain and harassment after coming out of the academy. But kids like Johanson were a special breed. Some of the other cops called them "Labradors" but, personally, I found this insulting to the dogs. Either way, the meaning came across. Eager. Stupid. And willing to do anything to please.

Johanson would have gone through enough based on that alone. But after I learned about his impromptu press interview about my case, I made a call to his sergeant. Unfortunately for Johanson, it was Tim Gage, the closest thing I once had to a friend on the force. We had been tight when we were both uniforms but since I had made detective we had drifted apart. All the same, once I had explained the situation with Johnason, he had been happy to oblige.

The time-honored and highly unpleasant hazing rituals were all upgraded on my behalf. Instead of wearing the padded suit and being attacked by one German Shepherd, Johanson was attacked by five. Instead of being zapped with a current issue Taser, he was jolted with an older, and much nastier, Stun Gun. Every discomfort was upgraded to non-lethal pain. Best of all, every moment of it was recorded and sent to me over the web for my viewing pleasure.

I cued up my favorite part again.

PLAY

Johanson was being pulled by one dog in one direction and by another in the opposite. The third dove for his balls. Even in a padded suit that clenching and tearing was going to leave a whole lot of bruises and aches. He'd feel like he'd been used as a piñata by the time things were over.

The toddler dance. Pretty puppy wants to play. And eat your intestines like sausages. And puppy brought friends! But best of all was the very end. The K-9 trainer called off the dogs. Instantly, they complied and disappeared from the screen. Johanson just lay on the ground. "You alright Johanson?" The trainer asked. The cops were still laughing. Johanson sat up with some effort but remained seated on the ground. "Johanson?" the trainer asked again.

Johanson took off the heavily padded helmet he'd been wearing. His hair was so wet it looked like he stepped out of the shower. His face was covered with sweat and he was panting heavily. He finally answered. "Yeah. I'm good." "Good. Because after we give the dogs a couple minutes to rest, we're going to go again. You Ok with that?" Johanson forced a wide smile across his face. "Sure. Anytime you're ready."

CHAPTER SEVEN:

I walked to my car and drove to The Pig. It was pissing down rain and seemed to be getting harder. I'm hoping Emily's waiting because there wasn't a place to park. The assumption had been made that I would drive. I didn't protest. I watched her run out and step into a puddle. It was deeper than she thought. Her canvas sneakers got soaked and I heard her curse through the glass.

She got in still swearing. We didn't hug or kiss. Jokes were more the song of the hour. "Have a nice swim?" I asked. She was too pissed to answer which was kind of a twist. Usually, I was the one sulking.

She tended to her shoes and then decided to give up. I asked her if she wanted to change. "No, thanks. I'm good. How are you this evening?" she asked with a smile. That warm smile heroin that kept me coming back for more. I knew what I was doing but I couldn't seem to quit.

She was in a mood to be sure. Tips had been decreasing. That night was pathetic. "Nobody uses cash anymore. It's all debit. So, instead of a dollar a beer I get fifteen percent." "Is that a huge difference?" "Hell yeah." "Maybe it's the economy." Portland's always been a cheap town but it was getting worse. The younger they are, the more they don't like paying. Even drunk, people were getting stingy.

We drove down MLK past the scene of the crime. It wasn't quite in sight but still too close for comfort. I didn't want to think about it. At least not right then.

We crossed the bridge and arrived at Dante's. Even in the rain there were crowds outside. Some were trying to get in. More than a few were just smoking. I wondered which they needed more, the tobacco or the conversation.

It took some circling but I finally found a space. There was something on her mind but I wasn't sure that I should ask. "You alright?" "Yeah, why?" It was a smile back but it wasn't the right one. I knew something was wrong. I didn't push my luck and decided to drop it. I didn't want to know if it was something about me. Let me at least have this night before we have that talk.

Everyone knew her and we're let right in. But we were too late to get a seat at a table and stood in the back. I always liked this club because you could sit and relax. That night, I'd end up aching from too much standing around.

The lights grew dim as a band began to play. It wasn't her boyfriend. He's the main act. Instead it was white lights and fog machines accompanied by a haunting score. A throwback to the old days but highly effective. Shadowy figures emerged in silhouette. It really was a vision to behold.

They remained frozen like statues in a thick layer of fog. One moved forward and commanded your attention. A boney figure, distorted by disease and ready to break. It wasn't anorexia but something worse. He's milked his malady for all it was worth. He was even wearing a dress.

The effect wasn't funny or ironic but more like a shot from "Vampyr." Keyboards and synths built the ominous sound. The stick figure singer added his distorted whisper to the scene. It wasn't my kind of music but I was entranced. It was the best show I'd seen in a long time.

After three encores, the house lights went on. Everyone present still seemed in awe. "Wow, that was great," Emily said. Her mood had improved and I spoke before thinking. I made the mistake of referring to a concert back in the eighties. Another charismatic singer had made the same impression. Psychedelic Furs lead Richard Butler. I might as well have put a label on my head with my age on it.

I saw a group of pretty young girls. "Are they legal?" I asked. "To drink or to sleep with?" I wasn't sure if she was serious. So, I declined to answer the question. "The show is 18 and over. So, the answer's yes to at least one of those." I regretted bringing it up and dropped the topic. We're comfortable enough with each other that there was no need to talk just to fill space. There was something on her mind but she'd tell me when she was ready. Until then I could only wait.

The crowd thinned out. I wondered if they would return. "Is Billy screwed?" I asked. She looked at me oddly. "What do you mean?" "Because he has to follow such a good performance." I wasn't certain but I swear I saw relief in her eyes. "No, he probably loved it. He'll be fine."

By the time he took the stage everyone was back in their seats. Accordions and acoustic guitars weren't my thing. It was the Portland sound, circa Twenty-Twelve. But Billy had a voice, there was no denying that. I had no doubt the kid would be a star. He had the perfect face for magazine covers.

I wondered who decided to have these bands play together. One or the other would have been perfect. Having both in one night just seemed a little weird.

CHAPTER EIGHT:

"Detective Dudek" he said in an accusing way. Every syllable was loaded and aimed right at me. "How is your case coming?" When I told him how little progress I had made, I was met with a glare. John Doe/Adonis remained unknown and unclaimed. I was already angry and frustrated that I couldn't get out of the gate. The C of Ds prodding wasn't helping the cause.

He listened coldly as I explained what I'd done. The doors I had knocked on to find further witnesses. The badgering of the forensics team to run further tests. It had all led to nothing and I was still grasping at straws. He walked away unimpressed. No more threats had to be made. They would have been redundant.

After my badgering, I got back to it. I went off the physical, at least it felt more solid. The kid worked hard to keep his body like that. Especially, if his life was about living fast and profiting young. If he was a prostitute, it made sense for his trade.

I made a list of local gyms and started at the top. A high-end place for high-end people. The kind with four-thousand dollar teeth. I already dreaded the legwork I was going to have to do. Gyms didn't suit me. Too much sweat and too much attitude. I'd rather go for a walk and grab a beer. But it had to be done. I went for the big one. The grand-daddy of them all. I'd probably be scolded for inappropriate attire.

The Athletic Club. A city institution for the Portland elite. The dues were high but the cost was worth it. It was all about business. Maybe John Doe/Adonis had met his customers there.

For all its exclusivity, the building was a disappointment. Concrete and glass, it was close to non-descript. I had expected so much more. Limestone, marble and paneling would have seemed more in line. But that was probably too Harvard Club and intentionally shunned. Subtlety was more the Portland way.

The crowd on the treadmills was surprisingly young. Not as young as John Doe/Adonis. But just out of college. I couldn't help but stare at an ass. It was round, sweet and branded. A mascot across it. Sweatpants with university labels were all the rage. The girl with the duck ass must have seen me looking. Her response wasn't scolding but more of a grin. It was almost enough to make me a fan.

The fun ended quickly as I approached the front desk. Ken and Barbie incarnate sat there smiling. Their expressions changed as I pulled out the photo. As fit as John Doe/Adonis might have been, looking at death wasn't pretty.

They had nothing useful to say but sent me to the trainer. The conversation yielded nothing but tips on my posture. I would have been insulted if I didn't know that he was right.

I looked around the vast space. More equipment than people. I noticed a man passing through who looked mighty familiar. It was the guy from Channel Seven who talked about restaurants. I always wondered how food critics managed to avoid getting fat. I thought maybe they just never finished a meal. Maybe like wine snobs they even spit up their food. Silver buckets provided to catch the cud. It bothered me that I even knew who he was.

I saw a man in a grey suit with his hair still wet. A quick work-out at the gym and back to the office. He was being hounded by another man in his fifties. This guy had dark skin and a ponytail. He would have been more out of place if his clothes hadn't been made of money. Custom-tailored or bespoke, as they say. He was wearing two months of my salary.

A blue-jacket type approached me then. He was the manager of the club, or so he said. Ken and Barbie had called and given him the skinny. He was none too pleased that I was in his place of business talking about murder. I took out my ID to remind him who I was. His tone changed considerably and he became almost helpful. Too bad he had nothing to say.

The search continued at gym after gym. Steroid insane jocks and sorority girls seemed to be the order of the day. I wondered where all the old people went.

It occurred to me that I had the hours wrong. I was going to have to do this all over again. Early morning was probably more their speed. A workout before breakfast at six AM. I hated early risers and never understood why the workday started so soon. Maybe someone should have told them they weren't farmers any longer and the chickens could wait. They were already plucked, packaged and waiting at Trader Joe's.

In spite of my pain, I made the rounds all over again. I showed the photos and left my information. It reminded me of a bad job interview. They'll call if they're interested but don't hold your breath.

CHAPTER NINE:

I stood there feeling more stupid than drunk. A woman from Intel was going on about White Space changing the future. Analogue bled too much. Digital was now the standard. Spectrums were being auctioned off and things would soon change. We would communicate through unused space.

Eventually, I figured out that it had something to do with television, Wifi and computers. Older television channels tended to be messy. Space was left around them to keep them contained. But digital channels are sharp and neat. White Space will exploit this bandwidth and revolutionize communication. Intel was already banking on it.

This woman, Wendy, was designing the chips. A whole new generation of WiFi would travel faster and farther through the purchased frequencies. She was proud of herself for her skills and her knowledge. She would be bringing us the brave new world.

I excused myself from Wendy and went to take a leak. Why the fuck did Gillian invite me to this thing? It was a party given under a tent in the rain. A celebration to unveil his latest home-brewed beer. A hobby that he dreamed would one day be his escape. He had offered me an early taste. I don't think

Gillian even liked me but we both liked the beer. I guess that was enough.

I couldn't help shaking a haunting thought. That I was the kid at the party that the parents had invited. None of the other kids wanted me there but their mothers had insisted. I was probably just projecting. I felt way out of place. It was all couples and kids for the middle-aged set. Even on paper, I was a bad fit.

The beer was good, although quite sharp. It was a double IPA, hopped up to the extreme. It blew out my taste buds. Everything else tasted like water after that.

I stood sipping a pint, watching a child of five. He was playing with his favorite toy, an iPhone. He laughed and laughed as he watched a short film on the screen. It was of cars standing on their noses. They were rigged and fell like dominoes, one into the other.

The kid watched it over and over again. It never got stale. Gillian approached me and we talked about his brew. Grand plans were in the works to develop a full line. Being a cop had gotten far too dull. He wanted his life to be pilsners and porters not violence and stupidity. If I had any money, I would have offered to invest.

The Radovich case was going about as well as my own. A fast track to nowhere under the public eye. The one angle that made the most sense was being quietly buried. A random act of violence that had no rhyme or reason. A junkie who freaked or someone just in a bad mood. Such things weren't shocking to cops anymore. Just a pain in the ass.

It was the worst possible answer for such a horrible crime. It was always sex, money or revenge. Those were the rules. If everything happens for a reason then there is nothing random. That's just the way it is. But such a poor answer would have meant the end of big plans. Safe, clean and quiet, random murders in Portland don't fit the bill. Especially now.

A massive development project was in the works. A modern complex of hotels and casinos. It would be bigger and better than anything before. Millions had already been spent wooing and courting. Soon Portland's South Waterfront would be a tourist destination beyond compare. The city needed the win.

It was no wonder that Gillian was ready to retire. Solving the crime by reaching the wrong answer was a paradox that would not be accepted. Correct but incorrect, he was left with nowhere to go. He took another sip from his glass and tried to move on.

He took comfort in my tale, as I wasn't doing much better. John Doe/Adonis was stuck in the mud. I described my adventures in futility down to the most mundane. His mood improved with every agonizing detail.

Gillian introduced me to his wife. She was beautiful but exhausted. Her career as an RN had given way to tending to two kids. Both boys, ages five and eight. They ran around like speed junkies, hitting each other over the head with cardboard tubes. The remains of wrapping paper which proved more entertaining than the gifts. She excused herself to chase them and tried to put an end to the carnage. Harsh words and warnings led to tears and pouts. His wife took them back into the house. "They're just tired," Gillian said.

We made more small talk about life in The Cube but it soon wore thin. Then he told me that I should buy a house. It was a good time. I couldn't argue his point but I still resisted. Buying terrified me. I was always a renter. All the same, I knew he was right. If I didn't purchase soon, I would be priced out of the market.

CHAPTER TEN:

All roads led to nowhere as I tried to figure out who you were. Questions about John Doe/Adonis were met with polite answers and modest nods. There were a few who were charming and even more that tried to impress. I cared about your world only for where it could take me. A sad few took pride in being extreme. The more they tried to shock, the more bored I became.

But then your death proved most rewarding. Cash for anyone with a solid lead. It wasn't my idea. In fact, I railed against it. For fifty-thousand dollars, people had seen things they deemed worthy of payment. Thanks to the benefice of the LGBT, the phone banks were flooded by the stupid and greedy. Sometimes I wondered if that was the point. Obfuscation by volume to keep things quiet.

The best was a man who turned himself in. Poor but not homeless, he was none too bright. He went by the name of Arlen Downs. He was probably only thirty but looked fifty-six. He stank of the cheap wine and reminded me of St. Piss. But compared to the saint, this man was a lizard. His reptilian brain was clearly the size of a pea.

The video tape rolled as he gave his confession. I sat out of frame amused by his act. "So, you killed him?" I asked.

"Yes, Sir, I did." "How did you do that?" "I hit him" Arlen answered. "With your hands or with something?" "With a wheel barrow." I needed to make sure that I heard correctly. "You hit the victim with a wheel barrow?" "Yes, Sir."

"Where did you get the wheel barrow?" "In my yard. That's where I killed him." "And this is at your house on Stark?" I asked. "Yes, Sir." "Why did you kill him?" "He was peepin' at my gal." "He was in your yard, trying to spy on your girlfriend? "Yes, Sir." "Was she in the shower or something?" "No, she was cookin' waffles."

I did my duty and followed it through. At least it continued to be amusing. "The body was found over thirty blocks from your house. How did you get him there?" Arlen answered without missing a beat. "In the wheelbarrow."

Eventually I'd had enough and decided to wrap things up. I laid it out to Arlen. "This is my problem. At this point, I'm pretty sure you didn't kill him." "But I did. I swear to it. I murdered that man." "OK. Let's just say you did." "I did. I killed that man. When can I get my reward?" "Arlen, let me ask you something." "Yes, Sir." "How are you going to spend your money if you're in prison for murder? Arlen thought about it long and hard. But I should have known better than to think he was stumped. "I didn't murder him. It was an accident." "You accidentally killed him with a wheel barrow for peeping on your girlfriend making waffles?" "Yes, Sir. When can I get my reward?"

If only that had been the worst of the nonsense. Aliens had been involved and witches had done it. It was burning up time and using up my reserves. All the while John Doe/Adonis remained unclaimed. It was the sort of fate that old men dread. You were dead but nobody seemed to miss you.

CHAPTER ELEVEN:

Emily said she had something to say. I knew from her voice that I didn't want to hear it. I waited for the talk that I knew would arrive. On time as scheduled, I thought, as she prepped me with the words "It's about Billy." I tried to ignore that we are doing this at The Pig. I was insulted by the setting and was hoping for something more private. I just prayed nobody else would walk in. I was already wishing I wasn't there.

She looked at me with sadness. A face full of conflict and sorrow. Funny, since I was the one about to be the victim. "Is he more jealous than you thought?" I stupidly said to move things along. Her confusion couldn't have been greater.

"No. Billy doesn't get jealous. You know that." And I did. It was something that angered me for reasons I can't quite explain. Aren't I worthy of a bit of petty rage? I shoved my ego aside and listened to what she said. All the time my guts got sore. Some things just weren't meant to be.

"He asked me to marry him." Not quite what I was expecting but along the same path. Our friendship must end and not for the right reason. It's all just too complicated and it was time for her to move on. I heard it all in my head before she said another word.

"Congratulations" I said, "when's the big day?" And then I realized my supposition might be wrong. She wasn't wearing a ring. "I said no." Thoughts got jumbled as I tried to reconfigure. I wasn't naïve enough to think it was about me. That was a sucker's bet that wasn't going to happen. All the same, I was waiting for more.

"I just couldn't go through with it. For years I dreamed of him asking me and then..." Tears filled her eyes. Once again, I regretted the setting. As empty as it was, this scene deserved better. Orders for fries and another round just didn't suit the occasion.

She tended to a table and returned to the bar. I asked her to keep going. I asked her to explain. She said she didn't really know. "I guess it just doesn't feel right." I could tell from her face that it was only half-true. Being a cop had its drawbacks when you'd rather buy into the lies.

I finally convinced her to take a break. We exited the building and found cover from the rain. She slowly got to the point. "It's just such a bad time. He just signed a record deal. Major. They're talking tours in Europe and Japan. I would never see him." I wondered what she wanted from me but I already knew. "Say yes and go with him. I hear Tokyo is lovely this time of year." She smiled a bit but still seemed quite troubled. "No. I can't see it. Following him around all over like that. I want to be his wife, not his groupie." "So, you're not going to marry him because he's become too successful? There's something pretty fucked up about that."

She kept arguing but I can tell that she wanted to be swayed. "You're just scared." "Of course, I'm scared. My whole life would change and what..." she ended mid-sentence. "What, what?" I prompted, wanting her to voice her real fear. "What if he leaves me? If he becomes a star everything will change. I'll become that clichéd ex-wife dumped for some super-model." Before I realized what I was saying, I said something dumb. "Then I'll marry you after the divorce." She laughed but it was a laugh that hurt us both. There was nothing funny about it to either one of us.

"Billy is a great guy and you're fucking this up because you're scared. You love him, he loves you, you both want this. You're just being a chicken shit." She stared at her Keds, wet from the rain. She was thinking of Billy and the new life on offer. Finally her eyes returned to me.

"Maybe you're right. I still don't know." She hugged me tightly like she never had before. She whispered in my ear a simple thanks. We both knew I really didn't have a choice. We got back into The Pig and didn't discuss it any further. I pictured her in a wedding dress and know she'll be happy. In spite of knowing better, I let myself fall into my beer. I became filled with regret and wondered how it all went so wrong. Sitting there, alone at the bar, I realized that I was the perfect regular.

CHAPTER TWELVE:

I went to a place known for muscles and fries trying to get a clue. The Pearl wasn't my haunt but maybe it was his. John Doe/Adonis might have fit right in.

The restaurant was next to the ad agency I despised. World famous for its work, its employees considered themselves Van Gogh and Fitzgerald. What they did was art, was once explained, "but with a further reach." I have to admit, some of their commercials were funny but this place didn't amuse me in the least. It was filled with agency types and those that worked for the shoe company. Pretension was their favorite sport. Needless to say, it was a crowd I disliked. Then again, most were.

The bartender in black seemed annoyed at my presence. My questions were bringing people down. I told him that if I worked at it, I could help his cause. I could depress them enough to drink more. He didn't find me humorous and asked if I could be discrete. I nodded and discretely showed people pictures of a corpse.

I came up empty and was just about to leave. A girl approached me, a woman, more accurately. She said she had a thought. She wasn't that pretty but made the most of her looks.

Italian shoes and French purse, designer labels all the way. The effort didn't go unnoticed.

"Excuse me." "Yes?" "Can I ask where else you've been looking?" I wasn't sure how to take her question. I named a few places, a haphazard list. She understood the theme but wanted to check. "So, you're looking for places the gay, rich and stylish go?" "Gay, rich and young, more likely" I said, hoping the conversation didn't cause me any trouble. She got quiet for a second as she thought it through. I surveyed her more carefully as I waited. Upon reflection, she wasn't such a bad looking girl for her age. I even started to imagine her without her Prada.

"Did you try Metronome?" she asked. I'd never heard of the place and told her so. "It's in Old Town above "Wear." It was like an alien tongue but I'd figure it out. That's what computers were for. "Go on a Sunday night, after ten." I wrote down the name and took down the address, it was as good a lead as any.

"If you want, I could go with you." I had to admire her aggressive style. I guess she had nothing to lose. Having a date on the job wouldn't have worked very well. So, I declined her offer. Her disappointment evident, I added that I'd love to see her some other evening. She complied as expected and we made plans for Tuesday. It turned out to be a good move.

We had dinner together at some place on Hawthorne. I felt guilty for even being there. I should have been working but a man's got to eat. The food was great but her conversation was trying. It was all about the latest fashions.

We went back to her place and kept the talk to a minimum. I sat on the bed and watched her undress. Her attraction declined with every layer removed. But as she understood and I came to believe, a little style goes a long way. I even asked her to keep her shoes on.

It was good but disappointing the way bad sex always is. It got me off and got me by which is all I really needed. The same was true for her. Our mutual letdown was covered with kind words but we both knew the story. It was mixed reviews all around.

Her other favors proved far superior. I went to Metronome above the store. A group of wealthy men displayed their young purchases. Three-Star and below, need not apply.

The mood was festive and it was all just fine. But then they started to notice me. It was too loud to talk because the music was blaring. I asked the DJ to stop, stepped up to the mic and explained why I was there. The reaction was far from expected.

As the music restarted they come to me by the dozens. A few were irritated but most were concerned. The case needed to be solved. I told them the background and asked for any leads. I could tell they wanted to help. They questioned each other and threw out some names but it seemed of little value. As much as they tried they had nothing to offer. None knew a thing about it.

I left none the wiser but was praised for my efforts. It was nice to finally find some support. As I stood on the street, I dialed Miss Prada. I left a message thanking her.

CHAPTER THIRTEEN:

He walked into The Cube with purpose and poise. A man in his fifties who projected quiet power. His clothes were understated and costly, a study in grey. I saw the admin shake her head as the visitor asked a question. More questions were asked and demands softly made. The admin pointed him in my direction.

He started right towards me. The familiar pallor of the lights made him look like a zombie. Probably not much of a stretch. As he got closer, I became self-conscious. I stank of sweat and stale coffee. In spite of hoping for this very moment, all I wanted right then was to disappear.

I guessed who he was. The eyes were the same even if the hair was not. In spite of his poise, or maybe because of it, I kept thinking of history. He was about to offer his unconditional surrender.

The etiquette and formality only served to heighten his despair. However, rules were to be adhered to. He shook my hand with firm authority. "I'm here about your case."

His name was Richard Thurman of Thurman Steel and the Thurman Music Hall. A fourth generation Oregonian. It was not uncommon for the mayor to seek his advice. We exchanged pleasantries although it was all far from pleasant. I introduced myself to him as the lead detective on the case. He explained that he had been in Shenzen or maybe it was Wuhan. I don't remember exactly but know it was one of those places in China. The sort of Asian city you only hear about when American factories had to close. He had been there for five weeks discussing "manufacturing channels."

I decided that we needed more private surroundings. Although alone in The Cube most of the day, you never knew when people might come back. I could have taken him to an interrogation room but that seemed a little too harsh. Instead I opted for the break room.

It was a small carpeted room with a microwave and fridge. There was also a coffee maker burning the last layer of coffee in a dirty pot. A soda machine leaned crookedly against the back wall. It clanked loudly for no reason. Maybe someone had tried to rob it and it had been wounded in the assault. As I took all this in, I reconsidered. Maybe this wasn't the best place for this. But it was too late. My visitor was already standing by a small table waiting for my permission to sit.

I gestured for him to take a seat in one of the plastic chairs. He rested his arm on the table and it tilted towards him. It's base was fine but the floor was uneven. I kept telling myself that none of this mattered. We could be in a king's palace and it would be none the easier.

He told me he had been catching up on all the local news that he had missed. It was difficult to find the time to read old news but he felt it needed to be done. Information was his stock and trade. The steel mill was long gone and now it was far more about "allocation of capital." Things needed to be bought and things needed to be sold. Timing was key.

It was in one of these old newspapers he had seen the story. "Unidentified Man Found Dead." A photo was included, a portrait of John Doe/Adonis. He believed that he might be able to identify him.

There had been times when people had assumed the worse and gotten it wrong. Such things were not uncommon. There was that moment of truth when they saw a clear photo. Cries of grief turned to tears of joy when they realized that it was somebody else's child that had been beaten to death.

I took the folder from my arm neatly marked "John Doe." It was the color of rust. I held it facing me, hiding my cards as I flipped through the contents. My visitor's eyes fell upon me as I looked quickly through a dozen photos. Most were far too lurid to use for this purpose. I finally found the most clinical close up and pulled it from the deck. I set it down before realizing that the table was covered in crumbs. It was already too late to brush them away.

I thought I saw acknowledgement in his eyes but he didn't say a word. I prompted him with another photo. A more flattering angle, if you wanted to call it that. It was hard to look glamorous as your body decayed over a bed of rotten fruit and garbage.

My visitor studied the photos, one after the other, searching for the answer he feared. His expression changed but there were no tears. If anything, he grew more rigid.

"That's my son."

CHAPTER FOURTEEN:

When I think of it now, it was just a fucked-up dream. I saw myself in that Atget cathedral, blurry and aged. I stood before your tomb of stone and recited the words unspoken. I said your name and set you free.

"Arise Eric Thurman. Arise from the dead." At first there was nothing but the scratches on the film. The "Vampyr" imagery coloring my twisted fantasy. And then the heavy cover of the tomb began to move.

Your thin hand grabbed it and pushed it aside. Too much beer or too much Bauhaus, Bela Legosi had nothing on you. You rose from your tomb, naked and perfect. Adam in the Garden of Eden. More likely, you were the snake. Either way you had been transformed. No longer were you just an unidentified man. You had history. A path of events in which you were directly involved. There were people that missed you and people that hated you. You were certainly a well known figure.

Anonymity was curse enough in death, let alone in life. However, you wouldn't have known that. You were one of those people that stood out from the crowd. You had no understanding of what it was to be common.

Motion stopped and the picture froze. Another Atget still. This time through the grain all your features were defined. "A Portrait of Eric Thurman Standing in the Ambulatory." Circa sometime long ago. It was the other figure that became faded into dark silhouette. The one facing you and looking for answers.

I snapped out of my daze in need of a toilet. I said my usual refrain to the figure in the mirror. My quote from the Saint of Piss. "Pre-paid minutes." The joke had already gotten old.

I'd been out of work and out of my mind. I'd been waiting for things to set right. I didn't follow procedure. Now the price would be paid. My hearing was set. It was only a few weeks out. I'd probably get off but it was my judgment that I was more concerned with.

I sat in the chair and it creaked beneath me. I soon imagined another scene that never was. Why I did this, I wasn't even sure. I guess I liked the entertainment.

We were in the car on the 205. Your father was with me, stony and silent. His rigid ways made me yearn for crying and weeping. At least then I could play my role and offer solace. I could say kind words and offer a tissue. But your father would have none of it. He would rather break quietly inside.

And in the backseat of the car, there you sat. You were just along for the ride. You weren't sad but quite the contrary. You kept laughing at the joke of it all.

You walked behind us through the corridors with an idiot's grin. The strip mall setting amused you with its function and decay. It was a place you liked and you wouldn't mind staying but you knew another task awaited. The plans had been made. The hour was approaching. You were ready for the big debut.

We entered the morgue, a grotesque threesome, and prepared for the process to begin. You stood and watched as you were pulled out from a drawer. You might as well have been clean socks. But you were much too clever to care and were just waiting for a reaction. Your moment would soon arrive.

The shroud was removed and your body was revealed. You studied the face of your father. He closed his eyes to shut in his grief. He was swallowed by an abyss of sorrow. And all the time you just smiled.

CHAPTER FIFTEEN:

And then the words began to pour from his lips. A father's grief over a son now gone.

"We were in China five weeks. Business has been difficult and this was a major step in getting things headed back in the right direction. We left him and Allison, his sister, alone. They're twins, both seventeen. If they can't be trusted to clothe and feed themselves at this point, it would be a rather sad state of affairs. She's in private school, Sacred Heart, he's at one of the charter schools, Adams Arts and Science."

"Yes, he was smart, whip smart but not a great student. He did very well in chemistry and history and less so in the subjects he found less interesting. He seemed to have lots of friends. There was one boy he spent a great deal of time with, David. They have been friends ever since they went to junior high together. I never liked him very much. I wonder if he lead Eric astray somehow."

"Eric had lots of girlfriends. No one serious from what I could tell. There seemed to be a different one on his arm every time I saw him. I suppose a few of them could have just been friends but I don't think so. Just the way they acted seemed more romantic. Things are very different between boys and girls these days. So, I could be mistaken."

"What are you implying? No, he did not like men. My son is not gay."

"Yes, Detective, I am quite sure. My son is not gay. Why? Do you have information telling you otherwise? Someone saying that he is? Well, I assure you that they are mistaken or just going about spreading malicious rumors. My son is not gay."

"No, sadly, we have not been close the last few years. You know how teenagers are. Frankly, I would have been a little worried about him if he never rebelled. Those children that say their parents are their best friends concern me. Parents shouldn't be "best friends" they should be parents."

"We had drifted apart but it wasn't always like that. Up until he was about twelve we used to spend a lot of time together. He used to love sports. Played on his school teams. Football, soccer, track...He was quite a gifted athlete. Then he seemed to just lose interest in it all."

"Up until that point we went to some sporting event or another at least once a week. We had season tickets to the Trailblazers, Ducks and Timbers. One year we made it to every single Timbers home game. He was a good kid. I really miss those days."

"No, the changes weren't that sudden. They felt like it at the time, of course. However, in hindsight, it was more a drifting away. He didn't seem to enjoy being around me anymore and started to ask if he could do other things with his time besides go to games with me. I was hurt, of course but understood...At least I told myself I understood. Maybe I never understood anything."

"It got worse when he went to that new school of his. I never understood the point of charter schools other than to get around the teacher's union. But he had his heart set on going there. I offered to pay for any private school he could get into but he insisted. As long as he was out of the horrible public school in our neighborhood, I was happy. They say Adams is a good school."

"I'm not really sure what he was interested in these days. His mother would know more about that than I would. They had a different type of relationship. Like I said, the last few years things have been a little strained between Eric and I. Maybe I put too much pressure on him. I just hated to see someone so popular and smart squander all that potential."

"Drugs? No, neither one of our children has had any experience with drugs. The more I hear how safe marijuana is the more angry I become that this city has gone off the rails. We have a large enough productivity issue in the country. The last thing we need is a work force on drugs. Nothing good can come of it which is why my wife and I have a firm and united stance on the issue. There will be no drug use among the members of our household. If either of my children were ever misguided enough to disregard that policy they would soon find themselves without the rather generous allowances I give them and any talk of going to an out of state college would be immediately put to an end."

"Allison seems content with the idea of going to U of O with her friends. Eric approached me about going to school in New York. I quickly put an end to the idea. I'm not about to set a seventeen-year-old child lose in New York City. As safe as it may be compared to the old days, it is still New York. He got into U of O and Lewis and Clark. He was also waitlisted for the University of Washington. That's where he wanted to go but it was far from certain if he would be accepted. He had the test scores but not the grades."

"No, the last time I had spoken to him was about a week earlier from Hong Kong. Everything seemed fine."

"Who would do something like this to him? I don't understand. He was a good son. He got along with everybody. Was it some sort of sex crime? That's not why you were asking me if he was gay, was it detective? Did somebody do something to my boy before...?"

"Yes, I understand. I'll tell Vivian she should expect you sometime this afternoon. I would appreciate it if you were as gentle as possible. Vivian is easily upset."

"Allison? If you really feel that's necessary."

"Please find whoever did this to him. We might not have been that close lately but I tried. I tried to be a good father."

CHAPTER SIXTEEN:

The Radovich case was sputtering and the squad was looking tired. Too many nights out in the damp with nothing to show for the effort. There were plenty of people claiming they had information. Mistakes, lies and half-truths tailored for reward, none of which helped a bit. The detectives were drowning in a flood of misinformation. What they needed was a bigger staff. Instead, their ranks were culled. There were other priorities now.

One of the detectives reassigned was none other than Gillian. Much to his chagrin, he was to ignore all things Radovich and absorb all things Thurman. I could tell he wasn't pleased. The words "quit" "retire" and "bullshit" were uttered in various combinations on a regular basis.

His anger had merit. Gillian had spent days delving and searching. He unearthed a moment by moment history of the Radovich clan. He knew where they lived. Where they stayed. Where they ate. What they ate. Where they shopped. Where they pissed. What they bought. Where they sat. Where they parked. Etc. etc. Gillian was a living, breathing history of the Life O' Radovich. And now nobody cared. He particularly didn't understand why they left the divison rookie on the case, Hersh, and not him.

He handed over the file and was told to just move on. Gilliam fumed, pouted and cursed that he should have known all along. Working hard didn't get you anywhere quicker than just killing time. He was a fool to have even tried.

Between his mood and the stench of The Cube, I was feeling ill. I convinced Gillian to get out for a while. It was only eleven but we went to a bar. An old school kind of place that opened at six. The kids all thought it was hip. They had cheap PBR and super-hot wings both of which made me nauseous. But it was still a bar and bars were better than coffee and the attitude that came with it. I wasn't in the mood for a lecture on the virtues of burr grinders.

The problem, of course, was what to eat in a bar when you really just wanted breakfast. I settled the issue with a thin BLT and coffee that tasted like oil. Gillian got a soda. Something that looked flat with a zero in its name.

"I can't believe you dragged me to this shithole" Gillian complained. "I didn't bring you here for the food." He sipped his soda as he checked out a tattooed customer. She sported a biker gang look but was probably a student. I don't think he liked her but he was just feeling bored. He still didn't understand why he was there.

"I'm sorry you got fucked but I'm glad you're on this. Lord knows I could use the help." His gaze remained tired and he didn't want to hear it but I kept talking anyway. "Look, as big as the Radovich thing is, this is no picnic. Not only do we need to find the killer, we've got to keep the illusion alive." "What illusion? That Portland considers law enforcement worthy of spending money on?" I let his tirade slide and launched into one of my own. "No, that Eric was a good kid who did no wrong and that the Thurman name remains up there with the saints."

Gillian slurped at his straw and shook his head slowly after I'd voiced my concerns. "You're fucked, aren't you?" he said. I couldn't disagree except for one small thing. I was no longer in this alone. "Not just me anymore, partner" I said. And Gillian got the point. I told him where I was and what I was thinking. He agreed that it was a weak start. We discussed playing as a team or going for glory. We decided on the latter choice. I'd go my way and he on his but we would always keep the other informed. Divide and conquer or defeated from the start. At this point neither of us knew.

There were laughs and jokes and smiles all around. I hoped that it was a new beginning. All the same, I couldn't shake the feeling that I had been teamed with a fake. A man there in name only. He promised to go through the files and come up with fresh angles. More likely he was thinking of his next brew.

CHAPTER SEVENTEEN:

A quick drive to Old Town and I was soon there. The homeless lined up for a hot meal and chatted with each other about the menu. Today was an all vegetarian ticket and more than a few were upset.

Among the faces burnt red by the sun and wind was one that I knew. It had been a long time but I would never forget his eyes. It was Reggie, aged a thousand years. The last time I saw him was at a funeral. He was crying and cursing the skies. I think he had been drunk or maybe on drugs but I don't know if that even mattered. The girl in the casket was the love of his life, Tiffany, age fifteen.

The memories hit hard of that kid dying alone. And of Reggie, back then, wearing his ripped leather jacket. He had painted "The Clash" on its worn back. He had also owned some runt of a dog that he took wherever he went. It always kept pawing and barking at me whenever I got too close.

I remembered when he came to me, not sure if I could be trusted. Tiffany was really sick but "she was a stubborn little bitch," as Reggie had put it to me that night. By the time we got to the dank smelling SRO, it was too late to do any good. Her lungs had rotted and she had stopped breathing. So much for her "bad little cold." She just laid there dead on the stained mattress as the dog kept yapping away.

Reggie smiled and said "hello" with a wave. He even gave up his place in line. "Hey, Dudek" he said and gave me a hug. It felt a little weird. "Where's your dog?" I asked. As the words left my lips I prepared for the answer. It probably wasn't going to be good. Hit by a car. Maybe even stolen. I wondered if it had even survived. "Dorothy? You remember Dorothy?" he asked. "Yeah, of course. That dog was even uglier than you." He laughed at my response and, as it happens, it was alright. Dorothy was alive and well. "The bitch even had puppies" he added.

Small talk aside, I asked how he was doing and if he still saw the rest of the gang. Some of the other kids hadn't done as well as the dog but most were hanging on just fine. One even had a good job at the bakery.

We said our good-byes and I slipped him a twenty. He wasn't about to decline. He might spend it on booze or maybe drugs but it wasn't my place to say. I waved one more time and walked away. I had an appointment to keep.

The building in Old Town had been nicely refurbished. The details had all been restored. Smooth marble floors and grand wooden staircases lead to the floor I needed. It was the offices of The Thurman Trust.

I walked into the waiting room and was immediately let down by how bland it was inside. Beige and off-white, it didn't match the lobby. It was all function and economy above all. I told the guy at the desk who I was and mentioned that I was expected. I took a seat and stared at the walls. They were all covered in posters for causes. "Save the Sea Lions." "Save the Children" "Save the Trees." The point couldn't have been made clearer. Give now or all will be lost. And it will be your fault for just standing by.

I couldn't shake the feeling that I was waiting for the dentist and started to get annoyed. I wasn't there for the cause. If she couldn't be bothered because of her schedule than that was just too bad. My anger subsided as I remembered what she had been through. My presence probably just reminded her of the pain. Starving kids in far away places were just statistics but I made her face the truth. Her son was dead and gone. As comforting as saving hundreds might be, no charity could erase that fact.

I was finally lead down a narrow passage to a corner office with no view. Behind it sat a woman, slightly older than me, who stood as I walked in. A firm handshake and apologies for keeping me waiting, I told her it was perfectly fine. As she sat, I saw the family resemblance. She had Eric's long, thin limbs.

She was the president of the trust which was a very big job, she explained. It was easy to find a good cause. The hard part was the allocation of funds to achieve the highest returns. "Bang for the buck, if you will."

I asked her some minor questions. Nothing that was too upsetting. The way she talked about Eric at first, it was as if she was skating. Move fast or the ice will give way. It was superficial nonsense about his academics, hobbies and friends. All generic and none too compelling, it felt like a bad facebook profile. I had enough of being patient and decided to press harder.

"Was Eric spending time with anybody new, lately?" I asked. "Not that I know of." "Did he have any girlfriends or boyfriends?" "Boyfriends? Eric was about as heterosexual as they came. I worried that he was going to get someone pregnant he seemed to be with so many different girls." "No serious girlfriend though?" "No. I think his last relationship with any girl that lasted over a year was back in seventh grade."

"Did he do a lot of drugs?" "No. He told me experimented once with marijuana but decided he didn't like it. He said it made him feel stupid."

"What about friends?" "What about them?" "Who were they. What were they like?" "The only one I know much about is David. They've been friends for a long time." "And what's David like?" "He's kind of shy and introverted. He really idolizes Eric. Sometimes I think too much so." "Meaning what?" "Just that Eric was very charismatic and very smart and sometimes I worried if he took advantage of David." "Took advantage how?" "Nothing too sinister. Just treating him more like a sidekick than an equal."

"Did he talk much about plans for the future?" "Oh, yes. Eric got into the University of Washington. He was quite excited about it." "I heard from his father that he really wanted to go to NYU." "Doesn't every teen-ager? New York is such an exciting place. Richard was dead set against it, though." "Why do you think that was?" "What do you mean?" "Why was he so worried about Eric going to school in New York?" "You don't have children, do you detective?" "No." "I think Eric would have been just fine but Richard and I both grew up here in Portland. Picturing ourselves at seventeen or eighteen in a place like New York seemed unfathomable. I can understand the desire, of course." "So, you backed Mr. Thurman in that decision?" "It was more like I abstained."

"Detective, what is it you would really like to know? I can't help the feeling that you're after something and I'm not helping you much with it." "I'm just trying to understand Eric as best as I can. I'm looking for any recent changes."

"Changes?" "In his behavior, his group of friends, romantic relationships..." "If there were any changes in Eric's life in the last few months they were all for the positive. He seemed excited about life in a way I hadn't seen him in some time. I think maybe it was knowing that he was finally heading off to college. He was really looking forward to it."

CHAPTER EIGHTEEN:

Predators and serial killers. It made for good TV. Some brilliant psychopath who played cat and mouse with the police. A clever game of bodies and clues. The rugged detective and his stunning female partner would be on the case. They would be assisted by the awkward genius psychologist who would get inside the mind of the killer. The genius would actually see and feel the way the murderer did and would be haunted by the mindmeld. And it would all hinge on a piece of forensic evidence discovered by the well-built lab specialist. She would use her cutting-edge gear to convict the killer with a singed eyelash and discarded Coke can.

Gillian had once been on a real serial killer case. It was a clusterfuck. Every agency and department in the country wanted to protect its turf. The joint task-force was about as efficient as the Iraqi government. A lot of talk and a lot of yelling but nothing ever got done.

And then there was the FBI. It would be hard to out prick those pricks. They were blue suited wonders who believed that they were the elite. The big guns brought in to solve crimes when those locals were in over their heads. Before 9/11, serial killers mattered more. Gillian thinks the FBI loved them even more than the media.

I'm not sure I believe that last one to be true. Serial killers were good for the ratings. The local news often ran night by night updates of the latest developments in the case. Even if there weren't any. True Crime books were published and films rushed into production. The public just couldn't get enough.

A mess of confusing and contradictory information standing in for facts. Gillian cursed as he recalled the charade. The joint task-force couldn't even agree on who the victims were. Maybe he escalated? Maybe there was a copycat? Maybe it was just coincidence the victims were the same age?

Pig Fuck.

Gillian got angry just talking about it. It was twelve years ago. One of his first cases as a Detective. The body of a young woman was found under the Cathedral Bridge. It was immediately connected to a series of killings down in San Francisco. Gillian tried and tried to convince people it was an unrelated case but nobody wanted to hear it. It was much more exciting to think of her as another victim of a serial killer on the loose.

"Sometimes we see what we want to see instead of looking at things for what they are" he had said. I couldn't agree more. Which is why it surprised me so much when I returned to The Cube and heard Gillian's new theory.

There were eleven bodies found over the last seven years that had some distinct similarities. They were the bodies of young males found bound and in the trash. A few had been stripped, but most had not. They had been found all over the country. Only six of the eleven were Caucasian. I pointed out to Gillian that if he looked it up he could probably find about a hundred more bodies like that in Mexico. Tied, killed and dumped in the trash. Sadly not uncommon. But Gillian wasn't to be deterred.

"Are you just fucking with me?" I asked. He denied it. He said it was just a very preliminary thing but he thought he might be onto something. I thought he might have been joking.

It was only later when I got a soda from the break room that I put it together. This was Gillian's revenge. He was still feeling abused for being pulled from the Radovich case and decided to fuck them back. He could claim that he was working on a new theory and sit on his ass all day. It wouldn't surprise me if he tried to get a free trip out of it. A little vacation to talk to people about the case.

The passive-aggressive prick didn't care if he took me down with the rest. So much for watching my back. He'd just tell the boss he was hard at work and leave me to sink on my own.

CHAPTER NINETEEN:

Hiss. Crackle. Pop. We're back among the trash. The streets reflected flashing lights. Johanson wagged his tail. And there you were. Naked and bound. Aren't you cold? We both knew the answer to that, you little fucker.

Crackle. Crackle. Hiss. I saw the body bag zipped. Soundgarden soundtrack played as I fell on Black Days. Chris Cornell spoke the truth but I wasn't really listening. My mind was too distracted. I looked through the light and squinted through the glare. The rain wasn't going to end.

The crime scene faded as a talk show began in my brain. You sat at a desk but you weren't on just yet. The sidekick carried the weight. He made a few cracks which weren't even funny but the crowd applauded all the same.

The set disappeared as the guitars ripped me apart. It was a feeling I knew all too well. But no matter how blaring it got I couldn't seem to hear it. The voices were just too loud. "Tell me about Eric" I asked. "What about him?" Dave answered. "When did you see him last?" "About a week before." "Did he say anything about going anywhere or hanging out with anyone?" "No."

My interview continued with my uncooperative guest. "I thought you guys were close. Wouldn't he tell you if he had something big planned?" "It wasn't like that. He would do that. He'd just go off by himself for a while and not tell anybody where." "But you guys were tight" I said. "That doesn't mean he told me everything. I have no idea where he was." Liar.

"Did Eric sell drugs?" I asked. "No." "Did Eric do drugs?" "I don't want to really answer that." "You just did. Where did he get them?" Dave looked down at his hands. He finally mumbled an answer. "It's not hard. Eric knew people." "Which people? Give me some names." "I don't know. People. Eric knew everyone. Every time we went out people always came up to him and said "hi." Like he was a rockstar or some shit." Dave slumped a bit more into his chair. "Did it bother you that he was so popular?" I asked. "No. Why would it?" "I don't know, jealousy?"

"I heard Eric got into the University of Washington. Were you upset that he was going to go to school so far away?" "Seattle isn't very far. It would have been cool to go visit him there." "Where are you planning on going?" "I don't know. Maybe nowhere."

Hiss. Crackle. Pop. An answer suddenly appeared. I was back at the scene of the crime. Not the trash heap but the moment. I saw you on the floor bound up pretty but still very much alive. I saw him sitting, watching and waiting, the bag held tightly in his hand. He did it out of jealousy. He did it out of love. He just couldn't bear to let you go.

"You say you were close to Eric. Everybody I've talked to says the same." "Yeah. So? We were friends" Dave responded. ""Friends" can mean people you had a few words with and never saw again. You guys were more than that. You really cared about each other." "Yeah, I guess." "And I know you want to do anything you can to honor that friendship and help me find Eric's killer." "Yeah. Sure" Dave said. "So, I'm going to ask you a question that might seem embarrassing but it's important. Did you and Eric ever experiment with each other sexually?" His face contorted in disgust. "What? Like we were fags? No!" "It's OK if you did. There's nothing wrong with that and nobody needs to know if you were." He sat there in disbelief.

"It's OK if you tell me. No judgments." "But we weren't. Neither one of us was into that." "With each other or in general?" "Either. What the fuck is wrong with you?" "Did you kill him?" "No!" "Maybe you got jealous. Maybe you got sick of being treated like a joke and it pissed you off. Making sure he was found like that would have really embarrassed him. Is that why you dumped him in the garbage like that?"

"No!" "So you did dump him in the trash?" "I never said that. Why are you doing this?" "Just tell me the truth. Why did you kill him?" "I didn't kill him. He was my friend."

I kept hammering away. "Just tell me why." "I want a lawyer" "Why because you're guilty? Only guilty people need lawyers." "No." "You loved him and he broke your heart. I'd be angry too. Maybe even angry enough to kill him." "No." "He used you."

I let those last words sink into him. He then repeated his earlier question. The one still echoing in my head. "What the fuck is wrong with you?"

CHAPTER TWENTY:

The drive up the hills was quite pleasant. For a change there was sun in the sky. The car weaved through the narrow roads and onto the main road. The view from the Skyline Bridge was spectacular. Below you could see the brief cluster of skyscrapers that defined downtown. Among them was Richard Thurman's office. Beyond that, the river curled under the bridges like a beautiful snake. You could even see the mountains in the distance. Snowcapped and hazy, I still marveled at Mt. Saint Helen's. It had been decapitated by a volcano.

I was almost disappointed as the bridge came to an end. I no longer had a view. I saw only houses and nicely kept lawns as I continued along my way.

The Thurman house was behind a wall but you could still see it quite clearly. It was a nineteen-twenties mansion on a hill. It reminded me of the Great Gatsby.

I parked my car and was let in by a maid. She was white, not brown or yellow, which surprised me. I thought maybe she was Eastern European and enjoying Capitalism but it turned out she was just from Gresham.

Mrs. Thurman had called and said she was late. The maid was told to give me access. I was lead through the house, all marble and wood, and pointed to the Grand Staircase. Eric's room was the last door on the left.

I glanced in the bedroom of Mr. and Mrs. and saw stacks of clothes. I guess the maid was doing the laundry before she had gotten disturbed. There were several more rooms before I reached the end of the hall. One was a bedroom done up in pink and white. The bed wasn't yet made. Another was strictly for games. There were arcade machines, a pool table and the latest in video entertainment.

Eric's door eased open and I stood in his room, trying to take it all in. It had its own balcony with a view of the city. His king-sized bed was tidy and neat. In fact the whole room was perfect. There wasn't a speck of dust in it or a thing out of place. It was so clean it was depressing.

I looked at his books and was impressed by the titles. Histories of empires fallen and text books from school. A few looked pretty daunting. There was very little fiction among them. Just an untouched copy of "The Scarlet Letter" slouching against Salinger.

There were trophies on the top shelf in various poses. Football players and hockey sticks in shiny gold. As I looked more closely at them I noticed they didn't go past two-thousand and eight. His athletic achievements seem to have ended when he was in the ninth grade. At least the official ones.

There was a nicely framed photograph on the wall of New York City. A black and white image from the nineteen-fifties of the Queen Elizabeth against the skyline. It was a rather impressive photo. There were two smaller ones of New York, as well. One was of the Empire State Building and the other of The Chrysler.

There was a desk with pens in a black mug and catalogues from various schools but very little else. There was a stereo that must have cost thousands. However, I didn't see any albums or CDs. I assumed he preferred to download.

There was something wrong but I wasn't sure what. I just sat quietly on the bed. The maid had been in and over-tidied but there was more to it than that.

And then I looked around and realized there wasn't anything there. The room might as well have been a set. It was furnished with all the required amenities and just a touch of art. But nothing was being expressed. At least not in the normal way. There were no posters of bands or photographs of friends. No souvenirs of recent trips. Not one sign of anything personal. In fact, it felt like a nice hotel.

Hotel room thoughts were sidetracked by the sound of footsteps below. I assumed it was Mrs. Thurman. As I got up and left Eric's room, I heard her voice for the first time. Soft, young and sweet. It was Allison.

I heard her thank the maid and send her off as I walked down the stairs. I stepped into the kitchen. She had her back to me as she got something to drink out of the fridge. Tall and lean, she was wearing jeans and a sweater. Not the Catholic School Girl outfit I might have imagined. She turned to me as she sipped from a tiny bottle of water. It was imported from somewhere in Italy. She smiled and seemed kind of embarrassed. I'm still not sure quite why. She was beautiful to be sure. A heartbreaker already. But all I could keep thinking about was how she looked so very young.

"Hello" she said, as she pulled the bottle from her mouth. "Hello. I'm Detective Dudek." "I heard" she said. "My mother should be here any minute. I'm sorry she's kept you waiting." "Actually, it's worked out well. I'd like to talk to you for a few minutes about your brother, if I could." "Don't you think we should wait for my mother to get home for that?" "No, actually, it's probably better if she's not." She wanted to ask why but then put it together. Some things grieving parents don't need to hear.

She offered me a beverage and then we sat at the table. She seemed a little nervous. "I'm sorry about your loss." She nodded and waited. Formalities seemed pointless. "Did your brother have a computer?" "Yes, he just got a new Macbook Pro a few months ago." "Do you know where it is? I didn't see it anywhere in his room." "Sorry" she said. "Maybe it's at Dave's. He often left his stuff over there." "I keep hearing about Dave but haven't talked to him yet. Was he a good friend of your brother's?" "He might be the only friend of my brother's, in some ways." "What do you mean? Your parents thought Eric was very popular" I said. "He was, I think, depending on what you mean. But Dave was the only person that was always there. They've known each other forever. At least since junior high."

"Were you and your brother close?" I asked. "I guess. Kind of." "You don't seem so sure." She took another sip from her water. "No. We were. For sure. There really is something about being a twin that normal people don't get. But then when we got a little older, we went more our own ways." I waited as she thought about it more. "I think we both really wanted to establish our own identities instead of always being thought about as some sort of pre-packaged set."

"Listen. I'm really going to trust you on something" I told her. "I haven't told your parents this and I'm hoping I won't have to." She looked at me with concern. "We found a lot of drugs in Eric's body. Not just weed but prescriptions and some more hardcore stuff." She stared down at the table. "I'm not surprised." "Why do you say that? Did Eric have a drug problem that you knew about?" "I suspected. He always hid it well around my parents. Not that they would have a clue anyway. But I knew something was up." "When did it start?" "Probably about a year ago."

I wasn't sure if I should get into the next subject but I decided to go ahead. I was really confused and needed straightening out. Allison was just the one. "Did you know much about Eric's personal life? Do you know what sort of people he liked to go out with?" "You mean hang out with or like a date thing?" "Both." "Like I said, we weren't that close anymore. Hang out with was Dave and all sorts of random people I didn't even know. A lot of them were already in college. Date? I couldn't tell you."

"Do you know if your brother was gay?" She was amused by the question. "Why would you even ask that?" "It came up in the investigation and it might have relevance in terms of pursuing leads." She looked me in the eyes and tried to stifle a laugh. "No, my brother was definitely not gay." "Are you sure? Maybe he was ashamed of it and tried to hide it from people." "In Portland? Why would anyone have a problem being openly gay in Portland? "OK. Do you think he was straight but possibly experimented with homosexuality?" The look she gave me made me feel stupid.

"Look. Sex for us isn't like it probably was back when you were young. Trying new things is pretty normal. Some people do it because they want to and some people do it because everyone else is. There's a lot of pressure. But straight guys wanting to do other guys? That's not "experimenting" that's just gross. Nobody is into that."

She wanted to ask a question. I decided to let her. "Why are you so convinced my brother was gay?" she asked. "I'm not. And, honestly, I'm not sure how much it matters anyway. It was just one more piece of information that might have helped us understand him and what happened to him."

We heard a car outside. Mrs. Thurman had finally arrived. In those moments before she walked in, the conversation shifted. "Do you think my mother would think it's appropriate you were asking her teenage daughter all this? Asking her if her twin brother took it up the ass for kicks?" The threat didn't phase me as much as her need to say it. "If you want to tell her, go ahead. I'm just doing my job." "Of course you are." And then I saw the blood ties clearly. She was Eric's twin, alright. She had the same smile.

CHAPTER TWENTY-ONE:

I got off the elevator on the thirteenth floor. The high-efficiency heater had gone haywire. The Cube felt like a swamp in Savannah. An unpleasant return to the plantation as we toiled for our masters.

Sweat stained my shirt by the time I got to my desk. Hersh, the rookie, said "hello." Gillian didn't bother to turn around from his desk. He smelled like a dead rat. I quickly tried to come up with another excuse to leave. Sitting and sweating were just a bad combination.

I brought him up to speed on my conversation with Allison. I also mentioned the missing computer. He told me we had to find it, no matter what it took. There was a good chance the emails might lead us to the killer.

Before I could question his statement, he took me to another aisle. On the floor sat a giant white board with arrows and some names. Also on it was a photo exhibit. Dead Boys, Found Naked and Bound.

There were seven photos total. Grainy digital crap. Printed badly but clear enough. The naked bodies all looked the same. The victims were all young, ages between fifteen and twenty. They had all met the same fate as Eric. They had also been tied up and stripped before being dumped.

The poses were slightly different. Most were bound in front. But one was even hogtied. A similarity that was hard to dismiss.

I kicked myself for thinking that Gillian was just being an ass. He believed in a serial killer and wasn't just jerking my chain. From what he had to show me, it was clear that he had spent some time on this. This wasn't some angry payback. This was a valid theory of why Eric had been killed.

He explained the similarities. I had to admit there were a bunch. The men were all openly looking for some fun. The internet was their favorite method. They met their date and met their demise pretty much the same way. Stripped, bound and strangled. The idea was probably sold to them as erotic. It's hard to say what people will do when sex is ruling their brains.

"Look at this." He pointed to the names and dates. It actually didn't make much sense. The murders had taken place over eight years in five different states: Oregon, California, Illinois, Florida and New Hampshire. That wasn't a natural dispersion. Usually bodies were found in groupings that had some logic to them. All in the same region or along the same highway. There was always some sort of pattern. This grouping seemed to have none.

And then there were the different poses. Hogtied seemed special and of some sort of significance to the killer.

With one exception, only one of these other victims had been found in that pose.

Finally, there was the rope. The brands were inconsistent. Two of the victims weren't even bound with rope. Wire was the preferred method of their killers.

But Gillian was convinced and he found my objections weak. "Maybe he uses whatever's around to tie them up and doesn't stick to the same kind. As for the hogtied pose, tied up and naked is tied up and naked. I'm not sure I see such a difference." The one thing he agreed on was the lack of obvious pattern. But there was one. He was sure of it. We just hadn't seen it yet. If we could find his computer, it would all become obvious. Eric was killed by a serial killer. It was a theory I couldn't really swallow.

Gillian was pissed and I couldn't blame him. I was giving him a really hard time. "Look, maybe I shouldn't have showed you this so early. It's a theory. You want to just throw stones at it all day, go ahead but it's more than you've come up with so far." It was hard to argue his point.

He was waiting for information to come in from all the other cases. I offered to help him go through it. He told me he had it covered and I should keep pursuing my own leads. It was code for fuck off and die.

I asked him if he showed the C of Ds yet. He said he already had. The boss wasn't pleased but for the opposite reason. He thought the theory might be sound. As much pressure and hype as there was now, nothing would compare to this. We were in for a fun time ahead.

"Detective Dudek. Could I see you in my office?" It wasn't a request. I walked through the oppressive heat of The Cube and took a seat in the chief of detective's office. The leather chair squeaked as I sat. There were condensation drips forming on the ceiling. At least if I sweat, it wouldn't be from the grilling I knew was coming.

"Detective Dudek, I just received a very interesting phone call." I waited. And waited. I knew I was really in for it. When the C of D's was really pissed he played this little game with his target. He would make them actively take part in their verbal torture. "And who might that be from, sir?" "Mrs. Vivian Thurman. And do you know what that phone call was about?" "No, sir." "Would you like to guess, detective?" "No, sir." "Come on, you're a detective. Put a theory forward." "I'd rather not."

"Mrs. Thurman was very upset. Irate, I think is the word some people might use to describe her." He waited. And waited. Bastard. "Why was that, sir?" "Drop the sir bit, Detective. You're just making it worse on yourself." "Yes." I just caught myself in time. "So, you were telling me about why Mrs. Thurman was upset."

"Detective, her daughter complained that you made her very uncomfortable. That you kept leering at her and making her feel awkward." "Leering? No. There was no leering." "Are you sure?" "Yes. I am." "She, the daughter, also claims that no matter what the two of you were talking about you always steered the conversation back to sex. Is that true, Detective Dudek?" "Not exactly." "Not exactly does not provide me with a lot of comfort. Would you care to explain what you mean by that...exactly?"

And so, I did. Or tried. I told him how I had wanted to question Allison without her parents around so I we could talk about things more openly. By "things" I had to make it clear to the boss that I meant Eric's drug use and sexual habits not hers. I did so to spare the parents the embarrassment and discomfort of hearing things they might not want to know. I also did so because I was hoping Allison might be more inclined to open up to me without her mother listening to every word she said. The more I talked, the more I felt like that guy who confessed to me. My answers made about as much sense as killing somebody with a wheelbarrow for looking at your girlfriend making waffles.

"Is she pretty?" he asked. "Who? Allison Thurman?" He nodded. "She's a kid." "Is she a pretty kid?" "Yeah, sure. I guess." "You guess." "Yes, she is a very pretty teenage girl." "And it didn't occur to you that speaking with her, alone, about various sexual variations might make her uncomfortable?" "No. I mean, it might have but it wasn't a major concern. I was more worried about getting honest answers."

The C of D's leaned back in his chair. I was screwed. He let out a heavy sigh. "On the day God gave out common sense, did you stay home with a cold or something? To call this an error in judgment would be an understatement." "I was just trying to gather information on the case, sir." That set him off good. Not the sir. My statement. His voice got very soft and quiet. I had to almost lean in to hear him.

"You've been a detective how long? Nine years?" "Yes." "And in all that time you haven't realized that solving cases is the least of our concerns? Of course, that's part of it but only part. Please be a little more aware of those other aspects of your job."

I thought that was the end of it. I was wrong. The C of D's had just begun. "I happened to walk by you and Detective Gillian discussing his serial killer theory. It didn't sound like you were being very supportive." "It's too early to say. There are some holes in the angle at the moment." "Are you sure there's nothing personal going on between the two of you?" That one caught me by surprise. "No. I mean, yes I'm sure. We get along fine. I've even been to his house and met his family." "Interesting. If I might make a suggestion, Detective. Working on your interpersonal skills might not be a bad idea. You're a good detective when it comes to closing cases, one of the best I've ever seen." "Thanks." "But that won't matter if you alienate everyone around you in the process."

I nodded and started to leave. "And one last thing." "Yes?" "If you need to talk to Allison Thurman again, make sure an adult is present."

CHAPTER TWENTY-TWO:

Everything was green. Intense. Vibrant. The sun reflected off the wet grass as the kids walked across it. They still separated by the rules of old. Jocks among jocks. Burn-outs among burn-outs. Nerd among nerds. But this was no "Breakfast Club." One of their own had been found dead.

The rumors were flying fast. He had died of a drug overdose. They found him with a dildo up his ass. He was kidnapped and held for three weeks before being killed. He was a drug dealer and shot when a deal went bad. He got in a fight with a gang member. He was a gang member himself. He was found with a gang member up his ass. Young imaginations are capable of great creation.

I glided across the walkway as the eyes turned upon me. A few smiled. Most just stared. And then they whispered to each other as I walked past.

The building was at least two stories, maybe even more. Flat roofed. Concrete façade. Lots of glass. A modernist pavilion executed on a budget. John Adams Charter School. I got to the door but I couldn't see in because of the reflection. I think that's when it started hailing. Portland weather is so unpredictable.

I walked down the crowded hallway. I had forgotten what schools sounded like. That constant rumble of voices. The clang of metal lockers slamming. The sneakers squeaking on the linoleum floors. And then the bell rang. Like packs of scurrying rats. They rushed by and then disappeared out of sight. Learn well, my children. The taxpayers expect results.

I entered into the office. The principal was expecting me. I stood for a moment waiting. I saw a kid about Eric's age run in. He was trying to explain why he was late again. Something about his father.

I was led into a tiny, over-stuffed office. Its windows faced a leafy courtyard. The hail had already stopped. "Strange weather we're having" he said. It was the principal of the school, Todd Williams. A man in his late-thirties. Educated at Oregon, he was a local, born and raised. It was his idea to create this charter school. It was one of several that had risen from the ashes of the Portland Public School System. Adams was about "Progressive techniques built upon classic methods of education." The more he tried to explain what that meant to me, the less I seemed to care. All I knew was that parents seemed proud when their children passed the admissions exam to attend. "My child is at Adams" seemed to have some meaning to them.

After talking about the weather, Mr. Williams voiced his "deep concern" for his students and how they would react to the tragedy. Eventually, we discussed Eric. Mr. Williams took pride in knowing each and every one of his students. Or so he declared. From the way he talked about Eric, he was probably briefed. Prepped for the interview by other teachers in order to have something properly authoritative to say.

"Eric was no angel" he explained. "But overall, he was a good kid." I asked about the discrepancies that had cost him his wings. Eric had gotten detention a couple of times in the last year. He'd got caught skipping class and going to the iHop instead.

He'd always been one of those students that frustrated teachers. He was extremely bright and possibly even gifted. But good luck teaching him anything he didn't want to learn. His grades in some subjects had been exceptional. Most notably, History and Chemistry. In all else he was distinctly average. In the last semester his grades had taken a plunge across the board. "Do you have any idea why?" I asked. "No, but it's not uncommon for seniors. Most of them are already accepted at college and they, mistakenly, think they can slack off." The college reference rings true. After Eric had been told NYU was a no-go, he probably didn't see much of a point.

I got the names of his teachers and wrote them all down. I was particularly interested in talking to his history teacher. Maybe she had some insight into his brain that a manila folder with grades and tests scores couldn't capture. What was more important to me was his friends. Eric had many, or so I was told. They might actually be able to tell me something about him.

I should have known such a request wouldn't go down easy. Williams produced a litany of reasons why he thought that it was a bad idea. "I'm afraid we have to respect the privacy of our students." "I wouldn't want them any more upset than they already are." "We've brought in grief counselors. Maybe after some time has passed in which they were allowed to heal." They should have awarded him a PHD in Bullshit. "This is a murder investigation. Your co-operation isn't optional."

Calls were made and lawyers were consulted about my questioning the kids. I told Williams I'd start with Eric's locker and the teachers first while he took care of the details. I'd have to pull some out of class but I figured the kids could use the quiet time. Their formal interviews would come soon enough.

Not surprisingly, Williams even gave me grief over getting into Eric's locker. I explained that the dead had no expectation of privacy. He was swayed. He got the maintenance guy to go with me down to Eric's locker.

It was a red metal closet at the very end of the hall. The janitor cut the lock off. It was that same hotel feeling. There were text books and school supplies but little else. No photos taped to the inside of the door. No "Clash" decals or personal taste in anything indicated. In spite of knowing the odds were against it, I had hoped to find that missing laptop in there. It wasn't.

The first teacher I interviewed was Mrs. Clayborn. She proved rather interesting. Unfortunately, it had nothing to do with Eric. In her mid-forties and looking quite suburban, she had spoken French since age nine. Eric had been in her class for a year to meet his requirements. He had barely gotten by. She had little to say about him and barely knew him. She was far more interested in me. She had a ring on her finger and hair that was brittle because she couldn't just leave it alone. Over-dyed and over-processed, it was a look I didn't care for. None of this stopped her from making her play. She was looking for some excitement. I guess I was it but it wasn't working for me. So, I just walked away. I'd love to say I didn't even think about it but that would be a lie. I could have used the company.

Next on the list was Mr. Gerber, a man who seemed quite perplexed. Eric had done extremely well in his Chemistry class but almost failed biology. What frustrated Gerber was he knew how smart and engaged Eric could be. However, if it didn't interest him, he didn't bother. "It wasn't like he didn't try" he explained. "It was more like he just couldn't. His head might know he needed to do well but if his heart wasn't truly in it, it was hopeless." I have to say, it sounded odd. Eric seemed like a pretty strange kid. I thought back to my own days and marveled at my consistency in comparison. Since age five I'd failed to meet expectations.

Gerber continued and advanced his theories on why Eric's grades had suffered. "I think there may have been something going on at home. He never said anything but I know these kids." A rather funny statement given what he said next. "At least Eric wasn't on drugs all the time like some of the other ones. It really is an epidemic."

He launched into a speech, both inaccurate and irrelevant, about the evils of drug-taking youths. It would have been amusing to light up a joint as he continued to rant. Maybe I would have gotten a sermon on gateway drugs and jumping off of buildings. Gerber was just the type. Straight-laced and moralistic. I could guess which way he voted. Not exactly the

Mayor's base. I thanked him for his time, feigning concern over the future of the next generation.

I was already bored and wanting to move on. I needed to talk to the kids. I kept to my word and continued the motions and, in hindsight, I'm glad that I did. Teacher number three was one of my favorites and not for what she said. She was young and perky with no ring on her finger, just the way I liked. She had been Eric's English teacher and was filled with hope and faith.

As I stared at her legs, I felt like an ass. I remembered that night in the rain. Eric was dead and I was his advocate, this wasn't the time to get laid. I remained all professional as she smiled. I listened as she spelled out her name. "Elizabeth Kamden with a K, not like New Jersey."

The chatter ceased and we got down to business. "Eric was an angry kid." I asked her what she meant. She had prepared for the question. She pulled out an essay he had written. It rambled on and on how the Baby Boomers had fucked him and how hippies deserved to die. It wasn't well written and seemed incoherent but the point had been made well enough. Eric felt screwed and didn't see the point of trying too hard. The country was already fucked.

"It's not unusual for adolescents to be angry. I know I was at his age. What's unusual about it is the way it's written.

Like he just sat down, vented and turned it in." She explained to me that Eric was usually good with words. She showed me an earlier assignment he had done and I could see her point. It's topic, "Themes in Of Mice and Men." It was well thought out and polished. It followed all the rules. It was also mind-numbingly dull.

I looked at the date on the first essay, the one about the hippies. I expected it to be around the time his parents laid down the law about NYU. It was. The date on the other one was about a month earlier. "Eric was having a hard time with his Dad about then" I said. "Really? I never heard." I told her about it. She said it all made sense. "Sometimes, people just need an escape valve." I wasn't sure if she was talking about the ranting essay or Eric's plan to go to New York. I didn't bother asking. None of this was helping my cause.

I made my way back to the principal's office for another scolding. Like it or not, the time was now. I was going to talk to the kids. And then the bell rang as I walked through the halls. I was caught up in the flood. They were all so young and intrigued by it all. So filled with gossip and cruelty. Sometimes I still hear the whispers.

CHAPTER TWENTY-THREE:

When I first met Dave he reminded me of the abominable snowman in the old cartoon series. A minor character who sometimes got the best of Bugs Bunny. His black hair fell over his eyes. His whole appearance was big, doughy and uncoordinated. He wore ripped jeans and a light blue t-shirt. At first I thought it was designed to look old. Then I saw the pit stains and realized it wasn't a fake. Well-worn and comfortable, it had seen better days. I saw the word on the chest of the t-shirt and smiled. I could see why it was his favorite. Written big and bold in seventies style was the name of a mythical company. "Soylent Corporation."

"It's people. Oh, my God. It's people." I said, misquoting the film. I thought he would be amused. Instead he looked at me like I was a moron. "I love that movie, Soylent Green. Charlton Heston, right?" He nods. If I was hoping to win him over, I was mistaken. For all I know, he was horrified that I got the reference. He might've promptly gone home and burned his beloved t-shirt. I should have known better.

I decided to abandon my ill-fated attempt to connect and move on. "I'm Detective Dudek. I understand you and Eric were friends." He didn't say anything. I hit him with all the usual questions.

"When did you see Eric last? Did he tell you where he was going? Can you think of anyone that might want to hurt him? Where were you that night? No, you're not a suspect. Just routine. Did Eric have a girlfriend? But nobody special? Other than you, who were some of his other friends? We know Eric did some drugs. Any idea where he got them from? How would you describe Eric's mood the last time you saw him? Agitated? It means on edge. Sorry. Of course, you know what it means. I'm used to dealing with some pretty uneducated people. So, his mood? Can you tell me some of the places Eric liked to go hang out? Anywhere over by the East Bank? I know there are some bars over there toward Stark. Yeah, yeah. And fake IDs don't exist. I really don't care if he was drinking or doing drugs or whatever. He's dead and I want to find out why. You can understand that, can't you Dave? Is it Dave or David? I'm really not trying to bust your balls. I'm just looking for some answers. You don't happen to know where his laptop is, do you?"

Every question was met with a shrug or the shortest answer possible. "Yes. No. I don't know. I'm not stupid. We're underage. Dave. Whatever. No." His disaffected attitude was getting on my nerves. I thought about laying into the kid, right then and there. But that was not the time or place. I'd get him down to The Cube and do it right.

And then there was Janelle. She'd been to bed with Eric a few times. Remembering my folly with Allison Thurman, I asked for a teacher to be present in the room. The only one available was Mr. Just Say No which would have put a real damper on any hopes of Janelle giving me straight answers. I decided to take the chance and go it alone.

"I heard you and Eric used to date." I asked. "Date. I hate that term. But yeah, we hung out sometimes." "A lot or just once or twice?" "I don't know. A lot I guess. For a while. Then, not so much." "What happened?" "I don't know. We just got tired of it, I guess." "Did he break up with you?" "We weren't really going out so I don't know if you could call it that. He just stopped calling me for a while. His loss." "Do you know why?" "What do you mean?" "Did he give you any reason for moving on?" "He's a guy. You're all like that." "We know Eric did some drugs. Do you know who he got them from?" "No." "Janelle, it could be important. It might help us find out what happened to Eric that night." "Is it true they found him naked? Did some perv molest him or something?" "I can't talk about the details of the case." "But you expected me to tell you all about my private life?" "It's a murder investigation."

Janelle eventually gave me a name. Carl Kraft. He was a former Adams student now in his first year at PSU. Portland

State isn't a great school, as you can tell from its very name. But it was cheap and right there in town so it had its share of fans. According to Janelle, Carl and Eric hung out quite a bit. Carl had a fondness for coke and sex. Or, when he couldn't afford the coke, which was most of the time, Meth and sex. I almost went ahead and asked Janelle what kind of sex but caught myself just in time. I wasn't in the mood for another lecture.

On my way out, I ran into Miss Jersey. "Miss Kamden with a K." We made eye contact, so, I walked over to her. "More questions?" she asked. "Yeah, but not about the case. I was wondering if I could take you to dinner, sometime." She smiled. "I'm flattered but..." I don't remember the rest. I think I had stopped listening.

CHAPTER TWENTY-FOUR:

I was fucked up by design. I sat in my chair, headphones on, enjoying my well-earned buzz. I was feeling nostalgic and wanted to go back in time. The Sex Pistols were doing the trick. Like a clichéd teenager, I enjoyed the rage and subversion. A submarine with other intentions. All good fun for Johnny and company.

Nine percent beer was rotting my guts. But man, it sure tasted sweet at the time. A Belgian Strong with a sure-fire kick. Too bad it was served by a guy. He talked too much about the hops and bored me to tears. I wasn't in the mood for the lesson. The beer was hearty but it hadn't come cheap. I would pay the price the next day when I woke up still feeling sick.

My mind went to Carl and my interview long ago in a land not far enough fucking away. He was so smug in his rented Victorian. A business major into minor drug deals, I wanted to bring him in. But it would have made little sense. He was too happy to tell the tale. He gloated about his deeds and bragged about his indiscretions. Maybe he was trying to get me jealous.

Eric had been over quite a few times. The nights were about drugs and sex. Carl might have embellished, but I'm sure there was some truth to his story. Sodom and Gomorrah, he knew the right people and was well known for throwing a good bash. The girls were willing. At least a few. Experimentation was the main theme. Boy on girl. Girl on Girl. Whatever combination suited. It was all so decadent, at least to Carl. He was a Caligula in his own mind.

At the time I didn't care. I was all business. But now I could indulge in the scene. I focused hard and traveled to that ancient world. I was soon there in his living room, by the bay window. I thought I could even smell the weed.

The Stooges ranted. Iggy was looking for some danger. Naked young bodies were everywhere. It should have been the stuff of cheap thrills. A scene from Kubrick. But I couldn't seem to control the channel. A flip of the switch. The song was over. Guantanamo images invaded.

Stripped and stacked upon each other, bodies assembled for cruel amusement. Laughing witnesses photographed the crime. Piles of human flesh squirmed like worms. And there he was, the man of the hour, writhing among the throng. Eric. John Doe. Adonis. Just having a really good time.

I didn't like where my mind was going and decided to try a different tune. There was nothing new about it. It's Zeppelin from Seventy-Three. I skipped "Stairway to Heaven" but enjoyed the rest. Some things never seemed to get old. But then a thought hit that I found quite disturbing. It irritated me to no end. Were they still using "Rock n' Roll" to sell Cadillacs?

I started to get tired but knew I would never be able to sleep. I lay there in the dark and tried to think of Miss Kamden. It didn't seem to work very well. Too drunk to fuck, even with oneself. It doesn't get much more pathetic than that. I gave up the ghost and turned on the TV. If I'm lucky there will be a good movie.

CHAPTER TWENTY-FIVE:

"Quit your fuming" Gillian said. "Fuck you" I replied succinctly. We were in a car on the 5 in Washington. "I didn't ask for you to come along. In fact I even told him maybe I should go alone but you know how he is. He insisted I drag your sorry ass along."

We were headed to Longview. A bland little town of strip malls and flimsy houses off the 5 between Portland and Seattle. Gillian had determined that an ex-con kiddie diddler up here matched his profile. He was still hanging tough to his serial killer/predator theory and the C of Ds was letting him run with it. Why I had to get sucked into it was a whole different issue. According to the boss, interviews held up better when two Detectives were present if things went to trial. True enough but I wasn't seeing this as leading to anything more than a wasted day out.

"You ever eat at that British place?" Gillian asked. "What British place?" "The one on the other side of the highway. I was thinking of stopping there for lunch before we talk to this prick." "I'm not sure I know what place you're talking about." "You know, the British place. There's a big, huge sign painted on it's roof. I always wanted to try it. Maybe gets some of those sausages." "That shit will kill you. Besides,

I think it's further up. By Aberdeen." "No, it's not. It's closer. I know it is."

If it was closer, we missed it. We ended up at a burger joint right off the highway. When I asked for my burger medium/rare they made me sign the order ticket. A waiver for the botulism that might ensue.

I patiently listened to Gillian recite the reasons we needed to talk to this guy. His name was Percy Kindle. He'd been arrested twelve years ago for kidnapping a fifteen-year old kid, molesting him, then dumping him on the side of the road. I agreed that he might be the type to escalate but I still wasn't seeing it. There's a big stretch between fifteen and almost eighteen in terms of preference. If this guy's thing was raping children than I wasn't sure Eric fit the bill.

My biggest issue was that Eric had gone along with things voluntarily up until the very end. There was no bruising or signs that he struggled against the ropes. Gillian, however, disagreed. "They found enough downers in that kid's blood he might not have even known what was happening. Of course, he didn't resist." He also had uppers, alcohol and just about everything else in his system but Gillian didn't want to hear about that. "You're just pissed because you were on this before me and couldn't put it together. It happens to the best of us. Don't sweat it." His cocky attitude wasn't helping his cause.

"You ever find that computer?" he asked. "No. I searched his room. I searched his locker. I asked his best friend. Nothing." "Too bad. I have a feeling it would break this thing wide open" he said. "I thought it already was thanks to your brilliant Detective work." I was kidding. Gillian didn't think it was funny.

We finished eating and arrived for our courtesy call about a half-an-hour later. The Longview PD had no problem with us poking around on their turf as long as one of their own could be present. We introduced ourselves to the kid in uniform at the front desk. He reminded me of Johanson. I wondered if I should tell Gage to end that idiot's torture. He'd paid and then some for fucking me with the press.

The kid introduced us to the C.O., a fat guy named Halloway. He offered us some coffee and his condolences after we told him where we had eaten.

The three of us drove out in two separate cars to a house not five minutes away. It was tacky and modern and looked pretty flimsy but I'm sure it beat living in a cell.

Halloway knocked on the door and made the intros. Our host was none too pleased. He reluctantly agreed to answer our questions and showed us through the door. We sat on a sofa that was covered in cheap leather. I recognized it from IKEA. The rest of the house was neat and tidy. It wasn't at all what I expected. If I hadn't seen his record, I never would have known Kindle wasn't just an average guy.

I sat back in the chair and listened to Gillian hammer away. Kindle answered carefully and didn't seem to get rattled no matter how rude the questions were. I didn't join in. I wasn't expected to. I had just come along for the ride. I sat there and watched, Halloway too, as Gillian kept questioning our host.

As the interview turned interrogation I got over my anger and could see Gillian's reasons. This guy wasn't just a pervert, he knew Portland well. In fact, he liked to meet with young men there on a regular basis. How young was the question. But it was clear from his answers that Kindle was the right sort of creep. Maybe he'd go for older if he had to. In some minds, fifteen to eighteen is all the same thing.

Gillian put out the idea that maybe Eric had been one of his acquaintances but had changed his mind half-way through. There was a struggle and a panic. Kindle grabbed the bag and suffocated Eric, so frenzied that he didn't even know what he was doing. As plausible as it sounded, Gillian didn't believe it himself. To him, it was murder all along. But if Kindle bought it then that would be the end. It would lead him down a path of lies he could never escape from.

He didn't. In fact, Kindle had an alibi. He hadn't even been in Portland that week. Or the week before. He was in the Olympic Peninsula fishing. He had stayed there alone but had plenty of witnesses. He bought worms for bait every day. Gillian didn't like the answer and hammered away. He pointed out it wasn't all that far. If you had the will, it wasn't that long a drive to Portland and back. Maybe Kindle killed Eric there, in some remote cabin, and dumped the body later. But even as Gillian said it, he knew it didn't make any sense. Why not just get rid of the corpse on site? Remote lakes and dark forests are a fun-filled vacationland for dumping bodies.

Gillian kept at it but the battle was lost. I did my part and hit Kindle on my way out. "You know we can't get you. You're too good. But you can tell me. Did you do it?" Kindle let out a snort. "Why would I tell you that, if I had?" I waited for him to continue. I could tell that he wanted to say more but he never did.

CHAPTER TWENTY-SIX:

"What's wrong with you?" she asked. "They call it the Pig and Porter for a reason. Why would you order the chicken?" Emily was just giving me a hard time. "Why? Is the chicken really bad or something?" "No, it's just not as good as the braised pork I think you should get." "Maybe I'm doing it to show you I'm an independent thinker. A man not afraid to go it alone and face the challenges of standing up to the crowd." "By ordering the chicken?"

This was all before. In the days when my biggest complaints were about the rainy weather and foul smells of The Cube. The beer was good. The company terrific. Even the sixties rock soundtrack in the background seemed right. Zombies, Stones and Small Faces. How couldn't that be good for the soul?

Emily's co-worker, Angie, was hanging out after her shift. Angie was the type my mother would have described as "Bubbly." She was filled with energy. She danced as she served. The guys just couldn't get enough.

Just twenty-two, she was a tattooed wonder. Every mark was a work of art. Some were cartoon characters. Some abstract designs. Some were words she had found to quote. "I will show you fear in a handful of dust." It was scrawled in beautiful cursive across her back. I had the privilege of seeing it once or twice. It depended on what she wore.

When I had asked her about it she said she just loved the way it sounded. And that was all there was to it. I like to think she was lying and trying to protect her real reasons. Something close to the heart. But when it came to Angie, that was reason enough. Some things really were that simple.

I chatted with her for a while as Emily took orders. Angie was all excited about her latest beau. Some guy from art school who did installations. He sounded like quite a catch. It was her next news that thrilled her far more than the guy. She had finally made the team. She had gone from Fresh Meat to a Blocker with The Heartless Heathers. She had made the senior roller derby team.

I congratulated her and told her I was a fan of the Raquel Welch movie. I wasn't sure she'd get the reference but it turned out she knew it well. It had been shot at the Expo in Portland and a bar in Kenton. A bit of local history.

The Detective within me knew where this was headed. Sure enough, I soon promised to go. There was some big bout at the Coliseum. Angie promised it would be a good game. Her team was headlining in a match against The High Rollers for a shot at the top of the league.

I promised again I would be there and then my dinner was served. I got an earful from Emily for my side. "You better go if you promised her you would or she'll spit in your food next time." "Are you going?" "I wasn't. It's my first night off in forever." "Please." After more pleading, Emily reluctantly agreed. She said she was doing it more for Angie than for me.

CHAPTER TWENTY-SEVEN:

We were headed South at a pretty good pace. There was less traffic than usual. Gillian didn't talk much but he rarely did unless he had something to say. An hour in, he finally broke the silence. "Do they have a butler?" he asked. "Who? The Thurmans?" "Yeah, if they do, let's pin it on him." "At least we ruled Kindle out" I said." "Great. What do you call that again?" "What?" "When you prove something didn't happen?" "Proving a negative." "Yeah, that's it. Another dollar earned proving something didn't happen. Great."

These weren't exactly happy days. But at least Gillian had a theory. It went like this. Some perv hooked up with gay men around age eighteen. He got them drunk, gave them drugs. Then he took them somewhere with the promise of sex. The men complied. They even let themselves be tied up. Just a bit of kink for a thrill. Then our perv watches them struggle. He fondles them a bit but doesn't bother to rape. He's after much more of a high. He puts something over their heads and watches them gasp. The struggle is part of the fun. He gets himself off somewhere along the line. Murder as aphrodisiac.

Four victims fit his hypothesis. At least according to Gillian. The victims were all between seventeen and twenty-two. All had willingly let someone tie them up with their clothes off. All had been found asphyxiated.

"The vics even look kind of alike" he added. The victims found in Oregon, Florida, Illinois and Michigan seemed the most alike. The last one was his latest find. Some twenty-year old was found dead in Ferndale, a suburb of Detroit. It was back in 2004. He had been found in a trash bin and had been tied in a similar way. It was even the same type of rope as the victim in Illinois. Gillian had eliminated some of the earlier cases he had thrown into the pool. They didn't match up quite as well. At least for now, four dead was enough. Patterns could be found. Glory could be claimed. It still spelled serial killer.

"If you're right, our guy could be on a cross-country tour. What makes you think he would stick around Portland?" I asked. "He probably didn't. I just want to get my case developed. That way when I give it to the Bureau they can't fuck me out of the credit." He was already imagining the Sixty-Minutes piece. The journalist's authoritative voice. "The case broke when Detective Chris Gillian of the Portland Police Department noticed an eerie similarity between his victim and the others..."

"I didn't realize it was your case. I guess I can just spend the rest of the day drinking." It was a dumb thing to say but I said it all the same. His case. My case. Our case. Upper case. All just meaningless labels. It didn't matter who claimed ownership. Gillian had baited me and I had grabbed it without thinking. I felt like an ass before he even responded.

"Yeah, well tell me then. If it's your case too, what's your angle on things? As far as I can tell you've just been dicking around and hitting on high-school cheerleaders." Anger enveloped me. I wasn't used to being accused by my partners of being lazy or incompetent. I buried the fury and covered my tracks. It was not the right moment for a fight.

"Actually, I think you nailed it" I said. "Yeah, you think my multi-state murderer thing might have some weight after all?" "No, the other thing you put forward. The butler did it." He didn't like the humor but it still did the trick.

He held my hand through the obvious. He made the case for his cause. Three of the victims had matching characteristics. The type of victim. The method of death. The way their bodies had been disposed of. It was still a stretch but there was an argument to be made. Three out of four could well be a match. My problem was the one that still seemed the exception. One Eric Thurman, found dead in Portland, Oregon.

CHAPTER TWENTY-EIGHT:

The night came quickly. The bout was a blast. Much more exciting than I had figured. Emily tried to explain the rules. Something about Blockers and Pivots but I was too distracted to listen.

One of the girls on the track looked very familiar. It took me a while to place her. It was Allison Thurman, age seventeen, dressed as a Catholic Schoolgirl. Fishnets and plaid skirt, she was hitting all the right buttons for anyone with that particular fetish. Her jersey was tight and the lettering small but I could make out the name on her back. "Sister Mercy" it said in black type.

"How old do you have to be?" I asked. "To play? I'm not sure." Emily looked at me oddly and then she explained. What we were watching was the junior team. They called themselves The Rosebuds.

Emily tried again to let me know what was happening. It was becoming a little clearer. "Sister Mercy" was a Jammer not a Blocker and her only purpose was to score. Pass the other girls, leave them in the dust. Points would be awarded accordingly. From what I saw, she was a star in the making.

The main event started later. It was actually a bit of a letdown. Angie was there but barely got to play. When she did, she messed with the crowd, blowing kisses and shaking her tail. The audience ate it up and a romance began. She was destined to become a favorite. In the meantime though, she needed some help with her skating. She was spending too much time on her ass.

The night passed quickly. The main event became far more fun. There was a girl on the track that I thoroughly enjoyed. I couldn't take my eyes off her even though she wasn't my usual type. Emily's age, maybe a few years younger, she was straight from the nineteen-forties. Average in height but amazingly curvy, Lana Turner had nothing on her. He name was "Dom," simple and short but with a directness I had to admire. Green jersey aside, it was pure leather and aggression.

"Somebody's got a new favorite. Somebody's got a new favorite." It was said as a mocking chant. I wasn't embarrassed, so much as surprised. Emily was playing with me because she could. "We should go to the after party so you can talk to her." "What after party?"

I kept thinking of Dom and what sort of girl she might be. I enjoyed every one of her moves. The speed and the violence. It was clear she played to win. I was jarred from my thoughts by a nearby distraction. A girl sitting in the next section of the stands. "Sister Mercy" had changed her clothes.

She was back as she was. The way I had first met her. Allison, Eric's sister.

CHAPTER TWENTY-NINE:

Fast forward through time. Sky on fire. A rare afternoon sunset in a city that's always grey. I submitted to the demons and indulged myself. Rollergirl fantasies became Technicolor dreams. It was shaping up to be quite a day.

I stood before her and waited to be judged. Naked and exposed, she saw every flaw. Even though I was fully clothed. It was a beautiful moment but soon turned to terror as I slipped deeper into the abyss.

"Get on your knees" I was instructed. But it wasn't the voice of my seductress. It was a haunting echo. A voice I had never heard. White light. Skeletal vampire. John Doe/Adonis emerged from the fog. Your words made me fear all there was. "I think it's a little late for that" you said. I hadn't realized I had been doing it but my hands had become clasped in prayer. I remained there frozen and silent. There was nothing I could say.

Visions flooded to me of Mercy. Little Sister of the Lies. She skated to her song and sang her corrosion. The crowd was on their feet.

I closed my eyes and closed my brain. I just wanted it to go away. I was pulled up by Emily. She kissed me softly. She tasted of stale beer but it was a moment I still savor. I was the one who was far too sober. Emily and I, that night in the rain. Her making fun of my name.

"Sir Kills A Lot is lame. How about Cop-Sucker?" she taunted. "Nice. Whatever, Em-A-Lay." "I want to be a mean name. Killer Softly." "How about Tit-Tania?" I suggested. "I think one of the rollergirls already took that one. You can do better than that, Cop-Sucker." I looked at her and grinned. "Anybody ever tell you, you're kind of a surely drunk?" "I am not. I'm nice." And nice she was. She kissed me then. It was a moment I hadn't expected. I'd been waiting so long and now it was there. All I could think about was how it was wrong.

But her body felt warm and it was cold outside. So I followed her into her place. It was far less shabby than I had imagined. She was a neat girl in many ways.

I pulled down her zipper and yanked down her jeans. I kissed my way up and down her thighs. It could have been. It should have been. But it ended with the drunken kiss. The one that tasted of stale PBR. She took my hand but I refused to follow. I said goodnight, right there, outside.

She said she was sorry and thanked me profoundly the next day and day after that. I had won her over and proven my worth. I was officially a really good friend. I never told and probably never will. Nobility was not involved. I wasn't too drunk. Either was she. It would have been a memorable time.

But I was stupid and misguided and played the game all wrong. I was betting that one day we might have that night together and quite a few more. It was an idiot's decision and I was a fool. I should have just gone with what was on offer.

And then I heard a voice. Not Emily's but Allison's. Sister Mercy had come to play. "Wake up, Sunshine." The voice awakened me and I rose from near death. I'd been asleep on the living room floor. She wasn't there, of course. Just me alone with my vomit. The mental sort, not the physical. I hadn't puked on the floor but my mind was feeling a little dicey. I really was a fucking mess.

CHAPTER THIRTY:

My crocodile brain struggled to wake up from its ancient slumber. Every memory had to be forced from a muddy grave. The images and words must connect. Organize. Structure. The logic of recall. I remember.

We didn't skip the light fandango. The only thing a whiter shade of pale was the rollergirl emerging from the ladies room. They drank even harder than they skated. Marines after battle. Comrades trading war stories. Penalties should have been given. It wasn't a clean hit. The exchanges were heated. Another round for all.

Loud and annoying. It wasn't my scene. But Emily had insisted. The after party. Two blocks off Grand. Twelve blocks from a trashy crime scene.

"Do you see her?" Emily asked. "Who?" "Your new obsession. Dom." I enjoyed the harassment the way I should have enjoyed the rest of her later. Would have. Could have. Will next time. The regret still burns inside. "Well? Do you see her?" she asked again. I didn't. Dom was nowhere to be found.

The music was loud and the crowd irritating. I just wanted to go home. I barely recognized the girls without their gear. On the track they were "other." Here, they were just girls. At least if you weren't paying attention. On closer inspection you could smell the attitude. It far exceeded their looks. If confidence breeds desire, then this was a stalker's delight.

Most girls talked among themselves. A closed shop to all but those that were worthy. A familiar high-school classic. Curious onlookers, male and female alike, were forced to watch the exotic creatures from afar. A few commoners dared to break into conversations with compliments. "You were great tonight. Can I buy you a drink?" In their day jobs as teachers, accountants and non-profit types, the girls would be distinctly average. Here. For now. They were something special.

"What am I buying you?" I asked Emily. "Whatever. Mirror Pond, I guess." I stood in line at the bar between Smash Her and Wet. A Betty and Heartless Heather, respectively. They were talking about Aphrodite's injury. Tendons torn. Ligament damage. Might as well have been talking about the weather.

I finally got the beer and sought out my companion. Emily was deep in conversation. I recognized the other face. One of the GnR blockers. Big and nasty. A crowd favorite. I think she was hitting on Emily. "She's trying to convince me I should give it a try" she said. I wondered if Emily meant just the skating. "I don't know. From the conversation I just overheard, it's pretty brutal. Something about a girl being on crutches for five months after having surgery." The blocker smiled, proud of her courage and valor. "Oh, yeah, we get hurt all the time." She went into a litany of her injuries.

I was tired and yearning for bed. Alone under the sheets in a sound slumber. This was my old man fantasy. The preference for sleep, over sex, a sure-fire sign I had my priorities askew. If there was someone young and willing who had other ideas, I could have probably been swayed. But it would have been up to them to make it easy. I really wasn't up for the effort.

The blocker was an all-star and not just in derby. Her focused play had left me the odd man out. I couldn't get a word in with Emily. I decided to walk away.

I stepped out to the back. The patio was covered and heated. Then it all went slow motion. That first real encounter. I walked across the cement and beyond the senseless banter. There was someone I needed to talk to.

"Hello" I said. She turned my way. "Hello." And so our conversation began. Me and Julie, otherwise known as Dom. We started the well-worn Tango. Few words were spoken. Neither of us over-investing. It was the first game of many to come.

I told her I admired her skills. A derby queen rock star, on the track and off. She just said "thanks" but she drank in the compliment. Being the center of attention suited her well. It was something you could deduce from her attire. Whereas the other girls all dressed in street clothes and almost became mere mortals, Dom embraced her role fully. Form fitting black dress and spiky, high-heels to match, she looked every bit the part. A costume and persona. An expression of deviant fetish and unseemly fantasy. It was all part of the marketing.

She was one of the old school before derby was just a sport. An athlete who channeled Betty Page. Bigger than life. Part of the spectacle. It had all been researched and tested. Fans didn't want girls in uniforms who ignored their audience. They wanted to be whipped into a frenzy. The branding consultant that worked with the league had said so.

The conversation was short but I walked away impressed. I wouldn't mind getting to know Dom a little better. I glanced across the patio and saw a smile. It was actually more of a grin. Emily had been watching and observing the encounter. She seemed pretty amused. "So, did you ask her out?" she said. "No." "Why not?" "It just didn't feel right." She continued with the harassment and taunts. I replied in kind. I asked if she was turning dyke after the conversation with her fan. "Not my thing" she said. And that ended the fun, assuming there was any to be had. We left about an hour later.

Dom made me wonder where the act stopped. One thing's for sure, it would be an interesting way to get beaten and blue. Far better than what lied in store with Emily.

Already drunk and feeling mischievous, it could have been a great night. Instead it was invites inside and an awkward exit. A night of remembrance and regret.

CHAPTER THIRTY-ONE:

"The murders are connected." Gillian's diagrams had a new shape. The gallery of the dead was now connected with lines. It all appeared perfectly linear. Five murders, one after the other. And so on, and so forth, until the end. Murder one was outside of Detroit back in '03. A twenty-two year old man named Rick Detrich found naked, bound and dumped by an old factory. Number five was Eric Thurman. Found naked, bound and dumped in the trash by a converted warehouse nine years later. "Maybe the killer just had a fondness for industrial architecture." My joke didn't go over well. "I don't know why you can't take this seriously. There really are such things as serial killers in the world." "Yeah, and there really are such things as white Goldfish, that doesn't make it real likely we'll come across one." "Goldfish? What the fuck are you talking about?"

He went back to his staring and imagining. A grand hypothesis was in the works. Eric Thurman would herein be referred to as "Victim Number Five." At least in Gillian's mind. "If you're so sure it's a serial killer, don't you think you should contact the Bureau?" Gillian gave me the best fuck you look I had seen in some time. I wasn't about to drop it. "You clearly think you're onto some sort of pattern. Why don't you share it with our comrades from Quantico?" I expected him to react with anger. What he did was worse. Sheer stubbornness and determination. "No, it's mine until I can't get any further with it. That's all there is to it."

I walked away and left him to ponder. It wasn't that complicated. Gillian was reaching for the exotic. That one in one hundred. The stuff of feature films and talk shows. Most murders were far more mundane. An insult from a stranger. A vengeful lover. A drug deal gone very bad. These were the phrases that appeared on crime reports in files marked "Case Closed." But Gillian would not be swayed. I believed him when he said he saw patterns. Humans make connections. Even when there are none there to be made. We look for reason in chaos. Create myths to solve mysteries. There is a basic rejection of the inexplicable because it is too unsettling to contemplate a world of "just because."

The same battle was being fought and lost by those hoping for a quick resolution to the Radovich case. The theory that had gained the most traction was put forward by the rookie, Hersh. He surmised that the Radovich family had been targeted because they were not the nice family that they first appeared. Mr. was into some sort of serious shit. Exactly what shit, involving who, was still the matter of some debate. But they were trying. Every tree was shaken. Every skeleton rattled out of the closet. Radovich was targeted for a reason.

"Our guest has arrived" Gillian said. He gestures across The Cube to two figures. One was a woman around my age, maybe a few years older. The other I knew as much by his slouch as by his face. It was Dave. I'm sure he was none too pleased to be asked back for another interview. I had insisted. Gillian wanted to find Eric's computer to prove his link to the serial killer. I wanted to find out what else Dave was hiding.

Gillian was all polish and profession, the nice cop sorry to have to inconvenience them. It went without saying that I was the asshole, the bad cop in more ways then one. In fact, I wouldn't even be in on the interview. I would just be watching it through the glass. Fish in the aquarium. Sharks in the tank. I was hoping Gillian would come through for both of us.

He showed them to their seats and dimmed the lights. No need for high-stress tactics. The woman Dave brought along wasn't his lawyer but his mother. I would have much preferred the suit. Somehow teen-age boys weren't very open to talking about sex and drugs with their mothers' present.

Gillian started the proceedings. The first lines from the play. "Hey Dave, thanks for coming down again. We really appreciate it. Is it David or Dave?" "Dave is good." "Great.

Thanks, Dave. So, we brought you down here because honestly, we're a little stuck. We've had a really hard time putting together a couple of things regarding Eric. We were hoping you could clear them up for us. Do you think you could do that?" "Sure. I guess." "Eric's sister, Amy..." "Allison" "What?" "Her name is Allison." "Right, sorry. Eric's sister Allison says that he had a laptop computer that he took everywhere with him. We can't seem to find it. Do you have any idea where it is?" "No." "Well, just think for a second. Where did he like to use it?" "I don't know. Home." "He never took it with him anywhere?" "Sure. I guess. I don't know." "Did he ever take it over to your place?" "Just once or twice to play games on." "But it's not there right now?" "No." "Are you sure?" "Yes, I'm sure."

"Maybe it's at school." "We checked in his locker. Is there anywhere else at school he might have stored it?" "No. I don't know." "Please just take a second and think about it. It would really help us out with our case if we could find that laptop." "No. Sorry. I can't think of anywhere."

"Alright, we'll leave that for now. Aside from you, who were some of Eric's other friends?" "I told that other detective all that." "Well, I wasn't there for that. Would you mind telling me again? I would really appreciate it." "I don't know. He had lots of friends. Bill, Tyler, Worm,

Derek…" "Slow down, I write pretty slowly. Sorry. Do you have last names for these guys?" "Bill Newman, Tyler Aranasky, Worm is Denis, we just call him Worm, Denis Holcroft, I think…" "Thanks."

How about anybody older?" "No. He has some other people he liked to hang with but that was his thing. They really weren't my crowd." "What kind of crowd were they?" "College kids. They were just totally into themselves just because they had their own places and went to that crappy school." "Which school?" "PSU." "Was one of them named Carl Kraft?" "I don't know. Sounds right. But. Maybe." "Did you ever meet him with Eric?" "Maybe just once when Eric and I ran into him at Kontrol. I really don't remember." "So, you never spent any time with Carl?" "No."

Lying sack of shit.

CHAPTER THIRTY-TWO:

She sat alone in Stumptown. I wasn't impressed. I had insisted she bring an adult. If things weren't tricky enough already, Gillian had bailed. It looked like I was in this alone. It was just going to be Allison and I.

"I thought I asked you to have an adult with you" I said. "I will. She's just late." I offered to get her a coffee. She declined and told me she was set. As I stood in line trying to ignore the lecture on free-trade, I thought back to Sister Mercy. It was hard to put the girl at the table, so young and bland, together with the rollergirl I had once seen. No fishnets in sight. Not even a skirt. Sweater and jeans was the course of the day. I guess she liked True Religion.

I painfully endured a discussion on Marion Berry afternotes and finally got a large iced tea. I returned to the table. Allison already looked bored. "Thanks for coming but unless your..." I was cut off mid-sentence by the shock of her escort. Maybe it's what I had hoped for all along. Her third-party request. The adult walking in was a girl named Julie, otherwise known as Dom.

She strode into Stumptown and owned the place with her presence. She just had that natural charisma. The curvy body helped, as did the black leather boots, but her aura went far beyond. Gillian should have been there. This was going to get me nailed. All the same, the opportunity had to be taken. I certainly had a good motive. A cause that was worthy. I decided to play it as it lay.

Julie held out a bag from Buffalo Exchange and handed it to Allison. She looked inside and was evidently pleased. She pulled out a white t-shirt. Its design was familiar. Pulsar lines of white over black. Conversational gambits regarding t-shirts had failed miserably before. All the same I said my bit. "Peter Saville" I said, bathing myself in pretension. "What? No, Joy Division" Allison corrected. "I meant the guy that designed the album cover. Allison didn't say anything. "Somehow I didn't have you pegged as the Joy Division type" I added. "Thanks for the superficial judgment."

I took my slap and watched as they hugged in that odd way that girls often do. Julie got up to give her order, leaving Allison and I alone, once again. "Do you know why they called themselves Joy Division?" I asked, digging myself in deeper. Her reply was succinct and right on point. "Yes." There was no further elaboration or expansion of her answer. I guess none was required.

Julie returned and we began in earnest. Allison's attitude hadn't helped her cause. I hit her with the full court press. My questions rolled off, one after the other. Her responses were so useless they didn't even register. Wear her down and wear her out. It was the only way left for me to go.

"When's the last time you saw your brother before he died?" "We still haven't found his laptop, are you sure you don't know where it is?" "We heard Eric liked to hang out with a PSU student named Carl Kraft. Do you know anything about him?" "We believe it involved sex and drugs. Did Eric ever mention anything to you?" "Eric went out a lot. Where were some of his favorite places to go?" "His teachers seem to think his behavior changed over the last few months. What can you tell me about that?" "Did Eric deal drugs?" "I'm assuming Eric had a fake ID, do you know where he would have gotten it?" "Tell me more about Dave?" "Was Dave resentful of Eric? Jealous that he was so popular?" "Do you think Dave might know where that computer is?" "When's the last time you went out somewhere with your brother?" "I know kids drink and I don't really care. This is a homicide investigation. But what sort of bar do you think Eric would have gone to?" "When did he start to lose interest in things?" "Didn't your parents ever suspect something was wrong?"

It was only her last answer which remotely interesting. "Only after he was dead." It was deadpan but sincere. The rest of her answers were of the "yes," "no," "whatever," variety. It was hard to determine how much was ignorance and how much was willful deception. I had no doubts that Allison was hiding things. She was a teenager and that's what teenagers did.

"Allison, I'm not asking you all these questions for fun. I'm really trying to figure out what happened to your brother and why. Don't you want us to find out what happened to him?" She looked at me with a determined gaze. A study in disaffection. "He's dead." My anger became real. I didn't need to fake it. I'd had it with her lack of cooperation. "Maybe we should do this more formally, down at the station." I looked over at Julie. She had nothing to add. This had all been a waste of life.

As I got up to leave, her veneer cracked. Then again, it could have just been part of the act. "What do you want from me?!" Allison said. I studied her as I contemplated my answer. This pretty girl that held the key. "Besides, that" she said.

Dom was smiling. She found the whole thing amusing. A flustered old man detective. Or so I thought before she spoke up. Maybe I was just feeling insecure. "She really is trying to help you as best that she can. She just can't give you the answers you want to hear." "It's not so much answers I want to hear as answers of any kind. Something a bit more than "whatever."" I got up to leave. "I'll expect you and your mother down at the station before the end of the week."

"Maybe I should get a lawyer" Allison said. "Why? Feeling guilty?" "No, are you?" She was a smart ass kid who deserved a good spanking but even the thought could get me suspended.

I left them both at the table. Allison still laughing. Julie didn't think it was funny anymore. She got up from her seat and followed me out to my car. She assessed the damage from my expression. "She didn't mean anything" she said. "Whether she did or didn't is irrelevant. She knows more about her brother than she is letting on. I don't understand why she wouldn't want to do everything she could to help us. It was her brother. Doesn't she give a damn?"

Julie looked off to the distance and made some decision. Something deep inside her brain. "I'll talk to her. I'm sure I can get her to cooperate." I thanked Julie for her efforts. As I got into my car I reminded her that I had meant it about a proper interrogation. Someone had to teach Allison that this wasn't all a game.

CHAPTER THIRTY-THREE:

"This is where we found him" he said. It was the voice of Homicide Detective Roy Bennett. Seattle Homicide. I was still a little shell-shocked from being dragged up there. Gillian got a call that there was a murder with a similar M.O. to the Portland case. The boss gave him the go ahead to make the run up the 5. I was just the sidekick.

We were standing in the room of a cheap motel near Boeing Field. "Sorry we couldn't hold the body for you but we had to get things moving" Bennett said. "No, I understand. I'm just grateful for the heads up." Gillian explored the first of two double beds in the room. One was unmade and stained with piss and shit. The final gesture of the dead.

The room was well worn. The carpets were fraying. There were marks on the lampshade that become more visible when it was turned on. The motel had been part of a reputable chain up until about eleven years ago. Then it lost its franchise.

I was still far from convinced that this new case had anything to do with Eric. But I was outvoted. Given the weakness of my leads, the chief told me I better get on board. I was to give Gillian some support and try to build the case. It wasn't as difficult as I imagined.

The victim was identified as Ronaldo Thomas. He had paid for the room himself. He was nineteen-years-old and in good physical shape except for the small fact that he was dead. Tied up and asphyxiated. He was found with the plastic bag still over his head.

Bennett and Gillian continued talking as several small aircraft passed above. A neighborhood dog started to bark. I could only make out fragments of the conversation. The rest was engine noise from planes. "Visa. Paid in full." "Alone." "No CCTV. Broken." "The maid found him." "Obviously not auto-erotic given his hands...rope" "No." The plane noise was deafening. I wondered how anybody got any sleep in a motel like this. I suppose it wasn't that sort of place.

My attention was drawn to a small round table. It was covered in cheap wood veneer that had chipped at the edges. There were two chairs around it. One was parallel to the wall and facing an old-style television. The other chair was at more of an angle. Askew and out of place. It was probably nothing but it made me think. It lead me down a path that was highly improbable.

"Could I see another room?. One that isn't occupied?" I asked. "Why, these accommodations don't meet your exacting standards?" Gillian joked, venom in every word. "The manager is right around the corner" Bennett said.

I found the manager in the office. A Salvadorian woman in her fifties. If she was upset about a body being found in her motel, she didn't show it. Just another night at the inn. After an awkward exchange in broken English, she led me to the room next door. It was an identical layout to the one before. Two queen beds, a dresser, crap TV, a suitcase rack, a small round table, two chairs. What else did anyone need?

I walked over to the table. The chairs were straight and parallel to the wall. I pulled one out and sat on it. I adjusted it a little so that I faced the bed. It's one of those cop things that sometimes you just know. You feel things without understanding them. Someone sat just like I was, upright and comfortable, facing the bed. They sat back and watched Ronaldo flop around gasping for breath. A fish out of water choking on air. They enjoyed every bit of his frenzied struggle.

I returned to the scene of the crime. Gillian and Bennett were still talking. "Nice trip? Why don't you get us some coffee if you can't find anything better to do." "Fuck you, Gillian." Bennett looked at us trying to judge if we were kidding around or really at each other's throats. "Was the bag that suffocated him held down by someone or tied somehow?" I asked "Oh, God. I know where this is going. You still can't see the connection. What's it going to take?" Bennett answered my question. "It was sealed tight with electrical tape. Why?" "I was just trying to figure out if there was one killer or two."

I told them my theory about the table. How someone had sat in the chair facing the bed. A view of Ronaldo's last seconds. It was probably the killer but what if it wasn't? What if that chair was for the members of the audience? Two killers, not one. A tag-team murder. A death for show. Partners in every way. It made no sense but I said it anyway. I put my thoughts into words. "Holy shit, maybe you're a detective after all. I'm stunned and amazed. Too bad your theory is shit." "Shut it, Gillian." "You two always go at it like this?" Bennett asked. Gillian grinned. "Only on good days."

We followed Bennett from the motel into downtown. Their HQ was over on Fifth toward the Needle. It wasn't as flashy as The Cube. There were no awards in sight. However, it had the advantages of working plumbing, climate control, and ventilation. You could even breathe inside.

Bennett lead us into his office. It had a view of the Sound. He handed Gillian a file. Crime scene photos. Digital memories before the room was cleaned and rented to the next happy customer. "You're going to tell me that doesn't remind you of our guy on the East Bank?" Gillian handed me the photos. It was hard to deny there weren't similarities between Ronaldo's corpse and Eric's.

"Did you search his home yet?" Gillian asked. "Yeah, there's a couple of my guys over there right now. I'd take you over myself but I need to do some things." "No problem. Do you happen to know if they found a computer?" I asked. "Couldn't tell you. You want to go over yourself, or you can just wait for my guys to get back. I think they're already done over there." Gillian looked at me to see if I had a preference. I was surprised he gave a damn. "Let's see what they found. We'll wait."

Gillian and I went out and got some food, if you could call it that. A fast food place filled with a mix of homeless and tourists. The locals must have known better. Tensions eased and moods softened. It felt like we might actually get to be Detectives. "So, are you convinced yet?" Gillian prodded. "That this guy was murdered. Sure. It fits well with a few of your other vics." "You know what I mean." "Yeah, I know what you mean. No, I'm not sure yet. I still think ours was different." Gillian shook his head. "How many people you think are out there tying up guys naked and strangling them to death?" he asked. "I don't know. Seems to me, you have a personal fondness for the first part already. Maybe you escalated." Gillian actually laughed.

CHAPTER THIRTY-FOUR:

I saw the ring, shiny and cruel. An evil time travel device from ancient lands. It had transported me to a here and now I wanted to escape from. Emily was getting married.

"Why didn't you tell me?" I asked. "He just asked me last night." She looked at me. Gauged the response. Tallies the damage done. "Congratulations." "Thank you. Not just for that but for, you know. Not letting me get all freaked out about Billy." I nodded. Words wouldn't do the trick. Finally, I said a few anyway. "You guys are great together. Some things are just right." I wanted to leave. I wanted to be somewhere away from her. Her sympathetic eyes cut me like razors and I didn't feel like putting on a show.

Details were discussed. Dates and plans. I flew on autopilot, not listening to the words pouring from my mouth. I saw us sitting there, having this very discussion. A food cart court. Coffee and pie the excuse for the meeting. I was distant. Away. This wasn't happening. It wasn't supposed to be this way.

I could already picture her at the altar in white. The groom as pretty as can be. They are the perfect set. A match beyond just looks. It was hard to avoid the self-pity. I told her again, I thought it was the right move. "But too many EEEs" I mumbled, trying to make a joke. I could tell she was still thinking about that night. Drunken kisses after the bout. I silently prayed that she would let it go. But her intentions were heartfelt and pure. She couldn't help herself from talking about it again. Her gratitude was malicious. Her words of thanks only reminders of mistakes.

CHAPTER THIRTY-FIVE:

Julie climbed into my car. Stumptown was far too crowded. "Are you sure you don't want to go inside?" I asked. "No, this is private." I watched her adjust her legs and try to get comfortable. A cop car wasn't the most luxurious.

"I'm really going out on a limb here" she said. "How's that?" "Because I'm pretty sure what I did was illegal." "Then we probably shouldn't have this conversation until you've had the chance to talk with a lawyer, first." She ignored my advice but made one request. She asked that we go somewhere else to talk. She thought the car would be fine but it made her feel awkward. Instead, we just went for a walk.

I was starting to worry that I was being played. That she really had nothing to say. I shouldn't have worried. What she hit me with was worth the wait. Something I probably never would have guessed. "Eric and I were going out."

She gave me all the details about how they had met through the derby. Eric was there to watch his little sister. Born eight minutes later, she was still the pretty baby. He had gone to cheer her on. When Dom had met him, she assumed he was older. He had been sitting with a college crowd. He even got into the bar for the after-party.

She was twenty-eight. He was seventeen. But she didn't realize that until much later. They kept things a secret at Eric's request. He claimed that it would upset his sister. It turned out his prediction was right. When Allison discovered the relationship, she was furious. However, it wasn't for the reasons Julie feared.

"Her concern wasn't for Eric. It was for me" She said. Allison thought that Eric was a bastard. He had a history of ripping people to shreds. Friends were used. Women were broken. It's just the way he was. Dom took the warning to heart but thought she had it under control. She wasn't the type to let her boyfriends step out of line.

I pictured the scene in a general sort of way. In spite of myself, I thought Eric was one lucky kid. A teenage guy with a woman like Julie. It hardly seemed like a crime. More pressing than that was that other little detail. Eric had been murdered. His assailant yet to be found. I turned to Julie and pressed for more. Her words continued as I looked into those dark eyes. Julie, Dom, lover and coach might just be full of lies.

"When was the last time you saw, Eric?" I asked. "The night before he was killed. He spent the night." "And the night he was killed? Where were you?" I asked. "Practice, then out with the team. Then home. Why?" "I'll need the names of people that can verify that." She looked at me in disbelief.

"You think I did it?" "No. But you didn't do yourself any favors by waiting so long to come forward." She looked down at the ground. The next thing she said was to herself more than me. "I didn't think it would be like this. Maybe this was a mistake."

I tried to imagine what she had expected. Just a casual walk through the park? I was irritated and annoyed. She should have come forward. This was all far too after the fact. I needed the truth and I needed it now. I wasn't in the mood to play.

"Look, I'm going to give you a choice here. You can get a lawyer and we can do this formally, down at the station" "Or?" "Or you can be honest with me and just tell me all of it. I'm really not interested in how old Eric was or wasn't when you slept together. He was killed and I want to find out who did it. If you had anything to do with that, then get a lawyer." "I didn't!" "Good. Then tell me everything, OK? It doesn't matter how awkward, embarrassing, or how bad it makes you look. I need to hear all the details."

She told me the specifics about the last night she was with him. Eric had seemed both anxious and excited. When she asked him to explain, he said it was nothing. They argued about his failure to share. He was keeping it in and shutting her out. It pissed her off to no end.

They didn't talk at all that next day. The day he met his demise. She assumed it was payback for the argument and the way she had called him an ass. She had no idea who he met or where he planned to go. She knew even less about his final moments. All she knew she had learned from TV. Eric was dead. Her lover was gone. She couldn't say a word about it. After all, her relationship wasn't legal.

"So, why are you telling me now?" I asked. "Because I trust you." It was a good line but harmed her cause. Trust wasn't the word of the moment. Her actions were more likely the result of my speaking with Allison. Better to get ahead of the lies and make good while you can. Try to deal with the sordid past. Embrace your role. Embrace your mission. Play the tortured and guilty confessor.

CHAPTER THIRTY-SIX:

"So you're nowhere?!" the boss said, nailing it on the head. "I wouldn't go that far." "How far would you go, detective?" I knew it wasn't a question that warranted a response. I was losing ground at a precipitous rate. Gillian stood by his cubicle as he watched it all. He enjoyed seeing me get my priorities straightened.

The call had just come in from Seattle PD. The murder of some guy named Ronaldo. Gillian had gotten permission to go but I was lagging behind. I kept claiming I had my own angle. "And what exactly is that, Detective? Explain this angle you have to me" The C of Ds said. I tried to explain it as best as I could. As the words came out, I dug the grave deeper. It all sounded like a bunch of shit. Kraft had said a lot but nothing too damning. At least not about the murder of Eric.

The C of Ds was losing his patience. He was hearing it from all sides. People were wondering why there was no progress. This serial killer thing, as far fetched as it sounded, at least gave him something to say. I was told to drop everything, at least for now. No Julie, Allison, Carl or Worm. If Gillian didn't need me, I could always drive back down. Or leave the car and just take the train.

"Well maybe there are some things in life you just do because it's your responsibility."

Weissbaum also introduced me to the concept of "back-up." Virtually every household and grocery item in his house had a back-up. The guy would never run out of paper towels or ketchup. And he treated his back-up stash with the same urgency most people have for first-string items. In a pinch, all of us will run out to pick up a quart of milk, a dozen eggs. But he once asked me to run out to a 24-hour market at midnight to pick up a half-gallon of Breyer's coffee ice cream; I figured it was an emergency. When I brought it back, I discovered he already had a full, unopened container of Breyer's coffee ice cream in the freezer; he just couldn't open it until the back-up was safely in place. He even insisted on having a second child soon after the first in order to have a back-up kid, just in case.

Okay, you get the picture—the type of man we're dealing with. I'm not even going into his collection of ointments, creams and lotions; suffice it to say, if you have a rash or a pimple, Weissbaum will take care of you. You forgot what he looks like? I told you, Dennis the Menace's father—a skinny, geeky guy with a narrow face and pointy nose and glasses way too big and black and mature for him.

But say what you want about all his quirks—his rubber spatula collection, the kitchen drawer just for graters and peelers—Weissbaum was a damned good cameraman. You want your son Sheldon's bar mitzvah reception on video? Call Weissbaum. Your daughter Suzie's shower? Weissbaum is your man. Yankela's bris? Arnie again. A knack for capturing the important details at any function: your Aunt Rosie slapping Uncle Nat's hand when, with his heart-condition, he reaches for a ladle of sour cream to put on his potato pancake. Your pimply cousin Hershel high-fiving the clarinet player, because he too plays the clarinet. ("What we pay in music lessons," his mother says, "between Hershel's clarinet and Yankel's accordion.") The groom dancing with the maid of honor off to one side, his hand just a little low on her back. The bride's father pinching the behind of the young

Hispanic bartender with the muscular forearms. Weissbaum got it all, missed nothing.

When he finished a job, Weissbaum would edit the original footage, adding music and cute credits—"The Bat Mitzvah, starring Sylvia Hertzberg"—that sort of thing. Not astoundingly clever, but adequate for family audiences.

The problem was that he began to stick copies of his finished jobs on his personal viewing stack. It could be boys night out at Weissbaum's place—Goldberg, Greenblatt and me sitting on Arnie's bed to watch a movie—and we could wind up, four grown men, watching "The Fischman Bris." An hour of strangers eating sponge cake. It was torturous, and Weissbaum made us sit through it, kept saying we were just about to get to the good part.

"Arnie, what's the good part? Does that homely woman with the mustache wipe the chopped liver off her chin at some point?"

"Shhh," he says, like we're going to miss something important, like I'm interrupting—Ira Fischman's Uncle Saul is loosening his belt.

Of course nobody is a hundred percent balanced in my circle of friends, but there's still another problem with this Arnie Weissbaum. He started videotaping his daily life. Not just special occasions—birthday dinners yes, we all do that with our camcorders. But no, he taped ordinary, everyday comings and goings, and added them to his stack. So now he, and often the rest of us, also watch reruns of his life:

"Oh yeah, this is good, this is the day I called for information about plane fares out West."

Sure enough, there's Weissbaum on the screen, talking on the phone to United Airlines. Once, I wandered into his room and his neighbor's baby was asleep on the bed. Weissbaum—presumably baby-sitting—was sitting next to it, eyes glued to the tube. And what was he watching? A video of the baby, asleep, with himself sitting next to it.

"Arnie," I began, instantly exasperated.

"No, no, I know what you're thinking, but this was about five months ago—she's really changed...shhh."

Shush? This is a sleeping baby. There is no sound. The latest development in what I feel is a growing disturbance in his character occurs one day when we are all gathered on his bed, watching a video of Weissbaum doing his laundry. I hear a whirring sound and I gradually realize we are being filmed—that he has his camera set up on a tripod in the corner, and that it won't be long—a matter of months, maybe—before we'd all be watching a video of ourselves on his bed, watching a video of ourselves on his bed.

Weissbaum, caught in his own hall of barbershop mirrors, desperately trying to freeze a moment in time, trying to double his life span via simulcast.

"This is what artists do," he says. "These moments are beautiful—unique, essential, complete—time-capsule material, I think, for future generations."

***

I once tried to beat Weissbaum at his own game, his own stick-to-the- rules thing, and I almost nailed him, but the guy was truly invincible in his own way. He was staying at my place, and I told him I wanted to see if my answering machine was working properly. I asked that he stay in the apartment while I went down to a phone booth and called in. "Don't pick up the phone, no matter what," I told him, and left. A minute or two later I call in and say over the monitor on the machine to a gleeful Weissbaum, "Weissbaum, pick up the phone...I'm serious, forget what I said about not picking up, I'm begging you man, this is an emergency, please pick up!" He told me later I'd almost had him, but his sense of playing by the rules was too strong: The game was, "don't pick up no matter what." Weissbaum won the game. We later try the same gag on Greenblatt's sister. She picks up instantly:

"What's wrong?" she asks, terrified.

"What are you doing?" I scream at her, "I told you not to pick up no matter what!"

"But you said it was an emergency."

That's why we're not married.

But stories about Weissbaum I could tell all day, and I just might...why, you're in such a hurry? You have someplace to go? You're a big shot like Finkelstein? So go, I'll talk to myself.

For all his oddities, I'll admit Weissbaum knew me, could call my shots from a distance. For example, he knew how I was with women. The guilt. He knew that if I had coffee with a woman, I somehow considered it a major commitment; and if I had tea with someone else a few days later, I would feel intensely guilty, as if I had cheated on the first woman. He knew that I wanted out of my relationship with Greenblatt's sister after about two weeks, but it took me three years to get up the courage to end it. If Weissbaum observed me having the most casual of conversations with a woman—a checkout girl in the supermarket, a nice-day-isn't-it kind of exchange—he would sidle up to me and whisper, with contained ecstasy,

"Four years," meaning that according to his assessment of the situation, it would take me at least four years to extricate myself from my relationship with the checkout girl. And the amazing part was that I sort of believed him, and would hang my head and walk away with the burden of my newest entanglement, muttering to myself:

"I never should have opened my mouth with her. I could have asked the produce man about the grapes, there was no need to ask her about the damned grapes. Now I'm in over my head and Weissbaum predicts four years. Damn. You can't be too careful. And fucking Weissbaum is never, ever wrong. Ever. Christ."

Weissbaum, of course, was generally wrong about practically everything, nearly all of the time. Except in those matters that concerned Juan Marichal's lifetime won-loss record. About Juan Marichal and Willie Mays, Weissbaum was hardly ever wrong. (Though not infallible. His major claim to fame in the 60s was being a regular caller to the Bill Mazer Sports radio talk show, identified as "The Mays-Marichal Fan" on the air. Mazer often made mincemeat of him.)

In the early days of the Human Potential Movement, Weissbaum and I used to go to countless seminars where we were forced to acquire

a taste for "long and meaningful hugs." People would hug us as if we were their oldest and dearest friends, and we had to stand there wondering how long their meaningful experience was likely to last, not wanting to interrupt.

The above scenario was the ideal arena for some major competitions. Weissbaum's game was this: The person who hugged the fewest people that he didn't really want to be hugging was the winner. Like golf—lowest score. But the game was subtle. Because we would watch each other like hawks, passing judgment on each other's hugs, placing them in one of two categories: authentic or torture. But we tried to fake it.

The way to cheat would be to enter into an embrace with feigned enthusiasm, and claim that you really wanted to hug that particular person. But Weissbaum wasn't born yesterday. Weissbaum had a sixth sense for this sort of thing, an uncanny knack for seeing the truth. I'd be enveloped in the all-encompassing arms of some total stranger, trying to look comfortable, and Weissbaum would be standing right there, behind the person, grinning madly, shaking his head in mock disgust, tallying a point for me on his little score pad. I'd be helpless to protest. It was just no use. Weissbaum knew. You couldn't beat the man with this kind of thing.

"Look…" I imagined saying to Weissbaum's imaginary fans at some imaginary Hundred-Dollar-A-Plate Testimonial Dinner at the end of his imaginary illustrious career as an imaginary professional athlete, "…in matters such as these, Mr. Weissbaum was King, okay? Do you understand my meaning? The man was God when it came to these sorts of things."

It was also in vogue at that time for all workshop participants to kiss each other on the lips when saying hello and good-bye: men and women, men and men, women and women, friends and neighbors, in-laws and wives, etc., all the combinations. Naturally, to anyone as homophobic as Weissbaum and I, the idea of kissing men on the lips was repulsive. But it seemed to us that if we declined or appeared to resist the kiss, people would probably assume that we were gay. For only men strongly rooted in their heterosexual

identity could risk kissing other men on the lips publicly without feeling threatened. So the two of us would brace ourselves, walk around the room, and cheerfully kiss men on the lips to prove that we were straight. Real men rope in wild horses on the plains, and kiss on the lips, or so that was my reading of it.

Weissbaum, the genius, would go on to develop some very elaborate theories concerning sexual preferences:

At one time, he reasoned, if a man was involved with a woman, or was married and had children, it was a pretty safe bet that he was heterosexual. And so each time a woman showed interest in him, he felt relieved; he assumed that the woman's interest automatically cleared him of any homosexual possibilities. But more and more, much to both of our consternation, we kept running into guys who had been married, had children, and "came out" and declared themselves to be gay at the age of thirty-five, or forty, or later. Again and again we uncovered such cases. Eventually Weissbaum concluded that the sure-fire way to determine whether or not a man was gay or straight was by his marital status: If a man was married, chances are he was gay; if he was married *and* had children, he was most certainly gay. Since at the time Weissbaum and I were single, and generally preferred the company of men, we were in the clear.

I had a theory of my own, which I explained to Weissbaum:

"Look, Weissbaum, if a man resists homosexual experiences— fears them, is repulsed by the very idea—there is a good chance it is because he is secretly gay and doesn't want to admit it to himself. You with me?"

"I think so," he replied, getting nervous.

"Okay. Now it follows, then, that in order to affirm one's heterosexuality, one has to stop resisting homosexuality. In other words, buddy, when you are truly able to let go and fully enjoy sex with a man, you will then know that you are straight."

The simplicity of it baffled Weissbaum. "So if I have a lousy experience with a man, if it turns me off, if the whole idea turns my stomach, it doesn't prove I'm straight?"

"*Au contraire, mi amigo.* You won't let yourself enjoy it because you're secretly afraid of the consequences if you had a good time. So in fact, your lousy time is a sure sign that you're a full-fledged homosexual."

"But what about the fact," Weissbaum replied, breaking into a sweat, "that I'm having the best sex with women that I've ever had. It's exciting, erotic, lusty, fulfilling..."

"Sorry. You're trying to use those experiences to prove that you're straight. What kind of person do you suppose would need to do that?"

The answer was plain.

"So what's the solution?"

"Elementary, Weissbaum, elementary. First, you need to stop using your experiences with women to prove your masculinity. And then you need to stop resisting men—let yourself go with a man, dive in totally, really enjoy it."

"And that will prove I'm straight?"

"Without a shadow of a doubt. Straight as an arrow. John Wayne straight."

"Well, I have to admit, I was impotent with this girl last week, and I am occasionally turned on by the young boys I work with..."

"Congratulations, you're on your way...and there's one other thing."

"There is?" Weissbaum didn't want there to be one other thing.

"Yeah. My therapist told me that there are certain homosexual men who actually prefer having sex with women."

"What the fuck does that mean?" Weissbaum was getting upset.

"It means that it's just possible, 'ol chum, that you are a one hundred percent, out-of-the-closet, big-time homosexual, and, it just so happens that your sexual preference is for women."

Poor Weissbaum. For the first time in his life, the guy finally had started to have some successful sexual relations with women, and I convinced him that from every possible angle, it simply reinforced his primary identity as a homosexual. The fact that he

eventually got married—three or four times, in fact—made it even worse; when he and Sally have kids, it will nail the lid on the coffin. Okay, bottom line, only my opinion: This Arnie Weissbaum's a real crackpot. But you didn't hear it from me.

***

Crazy Arnie Weissbaum, they called him. "Where are you going?" Wilner's mother might ask. "Going over Crazy Arnie Weissbaum's." Eventually even all the parents fell into calling him Crazy Arnie Weissbaum. And Weissbaum was delighted. Basked in pleasure at the title. Would stand up at parties and say, "I'm Cwazy Arnie Weissbaum, and you know what? I'm weally weally weally cwazy...watch this!" (At which point he would jump up and down making funny faces and noises, putting his fingers in his ears and nose.)

From the beginning he was like an idiot savant with numbers, a precursor to his passion later on for baseball stats. See him there in first grade, gazing dreamily out the window while Ms. Dunlop drones on teaching arithmetic: "Class, if you take two red balls from this pile, add them to these three green balls over here, how many balls do you have altogether?" The other kids start counting it out on their fingers, Crazy Arnie's still staring out the window, starting to bug the teacher. "Crazy Arnie? I hate to interrupt your reverie young man, but whatever is so terribly interesting outside will have to wait until later. Please pay attention!"

"I was paying attention," Arnie protests.

"In that case, maybe you'd like to step right up here and tell the whole class the answer."

"No problemo." He virtually leaps to the front of the room.

"Listen kids," he says, even then a coach. "The color of the balls is irrelevant, it's a diversion. Let's get straight to the facts: hold up one of your hands everyone. Good, now how many fingers do you see?"

In unison, thirty-one kids say five. One kid, poor Allie Lembeck whose pinky got too close to her father's chain saw, says four. Crazy Arnie turns to the flustered Ms. Dunlop and says,

` *"There, now everyone knows the answer, except Allie. You're on your own with that one. Meanwhile, I've got a window to get back to."*

Okay, there it is: The kid played hardball. He had strict standards, a real no-nonsense guy, a parameters man, always playing by the numbers. Later, in his teen years, a cop pulled Crazy Arnie over.

"Have you been drinking young man?"

"Why yes Officer, yes I have. In fact I had a shot of 80 proof tequila followed by 12 ounces of beer. I weigh exactly 134 pounds; if you figure a shot to be 1.25 ounces at 40% and let's even assume it wasn't a lite beer, which it was, if you do the arithmetic you'll see that still puts me in at well under the .08 legal blood alcohol level...now where's a breathalyzer, gimme a breathalyzer."

Weissbaum's father taught him everything he knew, and eventually Weissbaum would pass the lineage on to his son. Generation after generation of lunatics. His father played poker every Friday night with his three friends, and they referred to themselves as "Dick, Doc, Duke, and the Deacon." His father was Doc, and nicknamed Arnie Doc as well, who would in turn one day call his own son Doc. Crazy Arnie sat by his father's side, caring for his chips, computing the odds, giving over the percentages and probabilities:

"Hit me," his father would say, then looking to Arnie for his next move, "Doc?"

"Sixty-three percent chance of drawing a six or lower, Doc."

His father had him doing the family books by third grade, keeping a ledger, paying all the bills. Giving his own mother an allowance:

"This is just some petty cash I'm giving to you for spending money—a little bonus. Don't spend it all in one place."

See him there, in the supermarket with his mother pushing a cart. She reaches for a half gallon of milk and Crazy Arnie Weissbaum grabs her wrist in mid-air:

"Whoa, lady, slow down. That will put us over budget for the week. I only wrote us in for a quart of two percent, plus a jar of Bosco."

"But Arnie dear, your little baby brother needs milk."

"Sorry sweetheart, the kid has to learn to make do. I wish I could help you out, but I'm afraid I can't budge on this one."

He certainly didn't get the numbers thing from his mother's side. She was an immigrant, and like Finkelstein's parents, had survived a year and a half in Auschwitz and lost both her parents there. She was the opposite of Weissbaum. She was terrible with numbers. Couldn't remember her own phone number. There was only one number she could ever get straight: 183452. That one she never forgot, because it was burned in blue across her forearm and in black across her heart. Whenever she tried to do the arithmetic—any arithmetic—it always added up to 183452.

But you'd never know Crazy Arnie was the son of a survivor. No signs of the syndrome whatsoever. Wilner, yes, you could see it a mile away, how he lived his life like a prisoner pressed up against a wall waiting for the searchlight to pass overhead so he could make a break for it. Wilner, yes, looking over both shoulders all his life, steering clear of Volkswagens. But Weissbaum somehow got out from under, learned everything he knew about the war from one episode of Hogan's Heroes. Other kids went trick or treating dressed as hobos, maybe as Superman; only Crazy Arnie went as Goebbels. He just didn't get it, and never would.

As for the political events taking shape on the East Lake Playground, Weissbaum was utterly oblivious, and absent. He was the only one who didn't think tribally, didn't divide the world into Jews and Gentiles. No, for him it was all one team, *with Grisatti the ace shortstop and Taylor the clean-up batter. In Weissbaum's post-Jackie Robinson, level playing field, sports trumped the racial divide.*

So it should have been no surprise that Weissbaum was nowhere to be seen during the war years at East Lake. Wilner does the arithmetic one day, the way a Jew can't help but do when meeting a German— "And where were you in '39?" Weissbaum would have had to have been in the picture, yet Wilner has no recollections of Weissbaum during those critical times. At a certain point, it was if Weissbaum just disappeared and they somehow had separate childhoods, albeit in the same town, the same school. Just where was Weissbaum when I was standing alone, Wilner thinks, when I needed him? Where was he with his video camera when it might have counted for something? We could have gotten the events on record like a black and white newsreel.

Nobody remembers Weissbaum being around at that time. Yet he has evidence, he has proof: "I was there the day Holler knocked the crap out of Grisatti, sure I was. I was there the day Philip showed up from Brooklyn, the new kid, I saw it all. Sure I did."

Even then, Weissbaum was a cameraman, of a sort, the newsman's knack for invisibility, for being in the center of the fracas and getting it all down, getting the good shots, the scoop, without calling attention to himself. Weissbaum, cub reporter, a press-pass-flashing entree to meetings behind closed doors, a gift for being right up front, in the dugout, in the locker room. He got the stories, he took it all in and nobody noticed him; a gift for disappearing, the "who was that masked man?" approach, a hit and run guy.

They saw pictures of their sixth grade graduating class: there's Goldberg, rotund and proud; there's skinny Wilner, looking scared. See Finkelstein in his three-piece suit with the vest; Bernstein holding Lipschitz in a headlock; Moscowitz standing like a girl, hands on hips. No Greenblatt or Breshman, the Lower East Side kids. But strike them all dead if it isn't Weissbaum himself, standing there in the third row, just left of center, skinny and smiling. They suspect foul play, tampering—a doctored photo. No one remembered growing up with Weissbaum past the age of seven or eight.

But he remembered them, remembered their childhoods better than they did, knew everything about them: "Norbert, the do-over kid, used to infuriate Philip."

"How do you know that?"

"If you have eyes to see..."

"Seriously, where were you back then?"

"Veni, vidi, vici."

"Who'd you have in Hebrew School? For Aleph class?"

"Mr. Lovich."

"Beit?"

"Mr. Kirsch."

"Gimel?"

"Freed."

"Daled?"

"Schnitzer."

He was eerily accurate, a This Is Your Life *surprise guest who the featured person can't quite place. But there was no questioning it anymore: Weissbaum knew things, Weissbaum had been there. (Knew Lovich, knew Kirsch, Freed and Schnitzer.)*

Now, let us watch Weissbaum: turn the tables, do a double reverse, put a tail on him *and see what we can find out. Hire a private eye; inform the house dick, "Dig up whatever you can on this guy." See him there in McQuicksand's, in the back row. Listen to her take attendance on the first day —all the "Wilner?"/"Here"s and "Goldberg?"/"Here"s and always the "Finkelstein?"/"Present," Finkelstein's great roll-call ad-lib, rivaling only Grisatti's paradoxical "Not here." But listen: there is no "Weissbaum?" coming from Quick; like the asterisk by Maris's name the year he hit 61 homers, Weissbaum's the asterisk on McQuicksand's class list, the "anybody's name I didn't call come see me after class" guy. Weissbaum, the addendum, the administrative add-on, the bureaucratic slip-up.*

And in gym? Always "I got Taylor" first, then "I got Grisatti"— Christians before Jews the agreed-upon etiquette for all sports—then "I got Goldberg" and "We'll take Bernstein." Everyone dreading being the last one to be picked, having to stand there unaffiliated while new teammates are slapping each other five, saying, "All right, all right, we got Bernstein," greeting each other like old army buddies, instantly bonding. Only one poor shlepper is still standing around, sneaker laces untied, born to bat ninth, to play short right—an extra position created for extra baggage. Born to block, all the other kids told to go long, go short, buttonhook, hand-off, circle round —the last kid, never privy to the action, never even gets to touch the ball! Just stands there waiting to be picked, filled with shame, self-contempt for being so pitifully unskilled, unwanted, unnecessary, ought to be playing dodge ball with the girls.

And whose fate was it, this picked-last miserable orphan of the playground? Obviously, it was Moscowitz. Always Moscowitz. Without fail, Moscowitz. So where was Weissbaum? That's the beauty of it, the irony. Weissbaum was in a league by himself; went the last person

picked even one better: He wasn't picked at all! Nobody ever said, "I got Weissbaum." He was never even in the running. Because everyone considered him a manager, even then, as if he had long since retired from active play. You'd no sooner think of putting Weissbaum in the field then the 1960 Yankees would have played Casey Stengel. He just stood on the side and watched the games, recording every detail, in the days before camcorders. Knew which bat Wilner used—"The Louisville #30, Nellie Fox." Knew when Goldberg changed his stance—"You started putting your right foot way back in the box, and choking up." Had a laser sharp mind for early elementary school stats—Bernstein's won-loss record, Finkelstein's number of at bats, Moscowitz's dubious record for consecutive strikeouts.

Crazy Arnie Weissbaum, the archiver, the sports nut, even then, before VHS, before Beta. Weissbaum, the man behind the scenes, missing in action. Crazy Arnie, the coach who wasn't there.

CHAPTER TWELVE

Wilner

To say that Norbert Wilner was afraid would be a gross understatement. When Joyce Milk passes him the little note under the table at 2:15, he receives it as a message from death itself. He begins to perspire profusely. His heart begins to beat rapidly and he feels his stomach contract and twist into a hard and twisted knot. With trembling hands he unfolds the paper and reads:

"I challenge you to a fight on the corner of Oak Lawn Avenue and 30th St, behind B'nai Shalom, today at 3. Be there."

It is unsigned, and that makes it worse. It reveals that Grisatti is so confident of his position with regard to Wilner that he knows that Wilner would know who the note was from. And Wilner does know; oh, how he knows; he knows all too well.

He looks at the clock: 2:16. In but one minute, he has experienced a major, life-smashing crisis. He feels the helpless panic of a fish already hooked. Kicking and splashing about, wriggling frantically, desperately, Wilner is nevertheless being reeled in by the calm, steady hand of a professional angler who has done this a thousand times.

For Wilner, survival is now officially at stake. All his body's alarm systems go off at once: inner sirens and bells clang, red lights flash, the emergency sign blinks URGENT on and off, announcements are made

for all hands to come on deck. The interior of Wilner's psyche is not unlike the Alamo—Grisatti is an army of a hundred thousand ruthless Mexicans to Wilner's tiny little fortress of a few hundred good men.

The clock: 2:18. He thinks quickly: The dismissal bell rings at 2:50. McQuicksand's class is on the first floor. Grisatti's is on the third floor. Wilner will get out first. There are perhaps two minutes to play with—the time it will take Grisatti to get down the two flights of stairs. But Grisatti will take his time. Grisatti has no need to hurry. He will walk slowly, proudly, cockily trading cracks with his boys about the feast he is about to make of one Norbert Wilner, sissy-cum-laude.

Philip, I must get word to Philip. He's my only chance. But what is Grisatti doing? Why hasn't he told Philip that he saw me dealing with Taylor? What's he waiting for? Oh my God, oh God I think I see. He knew I would turn to Philip. He wants Philip there. He'll spring his little tidbit of information on Philip just as I am about to be pulverized to death, to smithereens. Just as Philip is about to step in on my behalf, Grisatti'll smile and open his big mouth.

Grisatti's plan, the way Wilner perceived it in his delirium, is foolproof, is brilliant and perfect. He actually forgets his condition for just a moment and admires Grisatti's craftiness. And he feels that his next action is as inevitable as the fisherman's next turn of the reel: Part of the perfection of Grisatti's plan is that Wilner will consciously do exactly what he knows Grisatti wants and expects him to do—he feels powerless to do anything else—and that is, quite simply, to send word to Philip. An SOS through the school corridors. He has no choice. It isn't even himself sending word; it is his panic, his terror, reaching out to his only true ally, an ally whom he has already betrayed to save his own neck.

Norbert's skinny arm is in the air, holding up the number one finger, which indicates to McQuicksand that he needs to urinate. (Why she needs to know exactly what it is that each student intends to do in the bathroom is a question that never occurred to anyone.) He is dismissed to the bathroom and he tries to saunter out of the classroom casually, but no sooner is he out the door than he bolts down the hall, takes the stairs three at a time, turns onto the second floor,

abruptly stops running as a teacher passes—Wilner coughs to obscure his panting breath—the teacher out of sight, Wilner silently dashes to Philip's classroom and stands outside the door and waves frantically through the window on the door until he gets the attention of fat Celia in the third row.

Celia is fat but she is no dummy. She can tell by Wilner's wild gesticulations that he is looking for Philip. The pair's friendship is no secret. In another moment, Philip is in the hall, looking at a perspiring, out-of-breath, haggard Wilner. He grabs him by the shoulders and shakes him:

"What's wrong, Norbert? What is it?" Wilner can't speak and simply hands Philip the note.

"What's this? Who's it from?" Philip asks.

"Grisatti," Norbert half gasps, half cries.

"Grisatti!" Philip exclaims, as if he is suddenly understanding the surprise twist at the end of a whodunnit. In the excitement of the moment, it never occurs to Philip to wonder how Norbert knows who authored the note. And it's a good thing for Wilner that he doesn't wonder, because Wilner had not anticipated such a line of questioning and would most certainly have spilled everything: "I know it's from Grisatti because he's been threatening me because he saw me with Taylor" and so forth; and that would have been the end of it.

Or would it? Perhaps Philip, old softy that he is, might have listened to the story in silence, shaking his head, digesting its ramifications, and then forgiven Wilner his trespasses, and pledged his continued support. It's just possible that that might have happened, and the shape of Wilner's life from that day on would have taken a dramatically different turn than the one that it would in fact take, because Philip doesn't ask, and Wilner doesn't tell, and Grisatti would be laughing all the way to B'nai Shalom.

Meanwhile, Philip wastes no time. He acts quickly, with the style, precision and grace that led him to be in the position of leadership that he is in. He is not without resources; his constituents number eight or nine. He has Bernstein on his side, and little Freddy Lipschitz. Bernstein is a bulldog: a respected ballplayer, and no pushover in a

wrestling match. Popular with the ladies. All the fourth and fifth grad-
ers look up to him. A good man for Philip to have working with him.
Lipschitz is tiny and scrappy, but is renowned for his speed and agility.
He has publicly outrun Grisatti himself on any number of occasions.
He will serve as "runner" for Philip in the plan that he is spontane-
ously creating in the face of the Grisatti threat.

To Wilner he says but one thing:

"Don't worry. I will not let you get hurt. That's a promise. Meet
me in the basement boy's room right at dismissal. Bring Finkelstein
and Moscowitz. Now move it, go back to your class. Don't worry about
a thing. Let me handle it. Trust me."

Wilner nods, dazed, and turns toward the stairwell. You'd think
he'd be relieved. But it is actually worse, much worse. His heart has
dropped even further down into his stomach as the sheer gravity and
precarious nature of his situation starts to sink in: He has turned to
Philip instinctively, just as Grisatti knew he would. And now he is all
alone with his secret, truly alone. Now he must make his own plan.
And as he stumbles blindly down the stairs like a little drunken sailor,
he sees exactly what he will do.

CHAPTER THIRTEEN

Gelberman

Bernstein was pissed. We bailed him out. Purely selfish, on our parts. We all kicked in fifty bucks and got the sucker back on the streets. Why? Who wants to deliver deli to a prisoner for six months? One time it's funny; twice maybe. Three times and you feel like it's worth fifty big ones just to get Bernstein to buy his own damn cold cuts. Plus to see Bernstein with the red dot between his eyes kibitzing with the old Jewish waiters at the Carnegie Deli again—every one of them with a *shtick* of his own—was definitely worth it:

"Someone put LSD in my matzah balls..." Marvin, the head-waiter says to Bernstein, "I took a trip to Israel."

"Yeah, you know where I can get some?" asks Bernstein, dead serious, the "Matzah-Ball Drug Czar" forming as a fantasy headline in his mind, his dreams of Outlaw Greatness not yet fulfilled by his mere six-month jail terms.

"Think of it fellers," he continues, turning to us. "Picture it: scary-looking dealers in sunglasses, midnight in Harlem, mumbling under their breath as you walk by, 'Coke? Jamaican sens? Bernstein Matzah Balls?' I love it. Come on ladies, whattaya say?"

"Please don't call us ladies," says Greenblatt, "I'm gender-sensitive."

Greenblatt had been gender-sensitive ever since he took a job delivering singing telegrams and often had to enter busy Wall Street offices wearing a girdle and a nurse's uniform. I used to sit in the car and help him on with his nylons, and then watch as he grimly got out and headed into New York's financial district looking like Charlie Manson in drag, with a helpless look on his face, as if to say, "How did I wind up wearing a bra on Wall Street?" But the sheer absurdity of the question was even beyond his capacity to comprehend, let alone formulate in words. Just this baffled, astonished look, as if he had suddenly awakened and discovered himself in a very strange dream and couldn't remember how he got there. ("Am I a man dreaming I'm a nurse," Greenblatt would reflect, quoting Chuang-Tsu, "or a nurse dreaming I'm a man?")

"No Bernstein," I pipe up, "we are not going to back your matzah-ball empire. Don't even think about it…it was a silly joke from Marvin, not a divine message about your mission in life."

"Who's talking mission?" Bernstein says, "This is Karmic-Kosher Theater, the Electric Jewish Acid Test, the coming together of spirit and flour, come on girls, you're either in the soup or you're out of the soup, now who's in?"

"I have a better idea," says Goldberg. "How about we *eat*?"

"Please don't call us girls, " says Greenblatt, "I'm gender-sensitive."

"You're clinically depressed," says Bernstein. "Now hear me out: Raise your hand if you've ever come to my mother's for *Shabbes* dinner."

All of us—me, Greenblatt, Goldberg, and Marvin, the waiter—raise our hands reluctantly.

"Okay, now raise your hand high if it was the best home-cooked, old-country, Eastern-European Jewish cuisine you've ever had."

Tentatively at first, looking at each other sheepishly to see if anybody else would raise their hand, we all raise our hands. Because it was true: Mrs. Bernstein, apart from being a notorious drug fiend, was the Jewish mother of Jewish mothers in the kitchen. Her

rugelachs were out of this world. *Kichel* to kill for. Little *shneckens* like for a king maybe. I was beginning to guess Bernstein's idea.

"So?" he says, as if he expects us to get it by now. "So we market them as Mrs. Bernstein's Matzah Balls, and we don't even need the LSD. My mother becomes to matzah balls what Paul Newman is to salad dressing. And the rest of us just sit back and rake in the dough. Now who's in?"

(To make a long story short, as ridiculous as this sounds, this really did happen, and the Bernsteins really did turn over a new leaf from that moment on: They got out of the drug business, made a killing in matzah balls, and eventually retired in Miami. All this from a one-liner, a little quip from Marvin, the waiter, and lives are changed forever. How do you figure? You just never know when one of those catalytic moments is at hand, because it could very well be disguised in the most mundane form. Yet if we keep our ears and minds open, God descends even in the Carnegie Deli with the next message.)

"Listen," I say, "there's someone I want you guys to meet. I met this guy, a rabbi of sorts..." and I try to explain Miltie to them.

"Is he Jewish?" Bernstein asks.

"Yes, but he's not suffering."

"Impossible."

"Really."

There's a silence at the table, as everyone ponders this marvel, a Jew who's not suffering almost a sacrilege. They all agree to accompany me to Miltie's the following night.

"But in the meantime," Goldberg says, "how about we *eat*?"

So we eat. I get the "Buddy Hackett," Greenblatt gets the "Shecky Greene" on rye, Goldberg orders the "Myron Cohen." All the menu items are given celebrity names, and I can see Bernstein's mind working: He's picturing his mother's name right there on the menu alongside the great ones, his own Ethel Bernstein joining the ranks of Sid Ceasar, the prince of blintz, and Molly Picon, the czarina of farina. Right alongside the Jerry Lewis Beef Flanken and the Joey Bishop Boiled Chicken. It was, for a man like Bernstein,

a dream worth living for, a noble and mighty purpose. To get his family name on the Carnegie Deli menu would be to reach the very highest station in life.

He spent his life pursuing such possibilities; clearly, his priorities were unusual. Never striving for ordinary comforts or common success, he would latch onto a most unlikely notion and devote himself the way others might go through med school. Already we had watched Bernstein spend three years trying to get on *Candid Camera*, until he was finally served with a court injunction to stay away from Alan Funt's residence. We watched him jump through hoops and shell out a couple hundred dollars in bribes to get his nephew on some Saturday morning *Wonderama*-type show. ("Because when I was a kid," he tried to explain, "I never got to be in the fucking peanut-gallery, and I lived to regret it. I'm not about to make the same mistake with this kid.")

Okay, sure, some people think Bernstein smoked just a little bit too much mara-ga-hoochie in the 60s and scrambled his brain to the point where his was a trivial TV-universe. He out Warhol'd Warhol by actually hanging a real bowl of Campbell's Soup on the wall. Not the can—a bowl of soup.

"This is the real statement," he said. "You can eat mine."

Ordinary fame did not interest Bernstein. "Making it" for him meant the Carnegie menu, *Candid Camera*. It meant Ann Landers responding to a letter of his in her nationally syndicated column:

"Dear Stoned-with-Mom," she had publicly answered Bernstein, "I highly recommend you and your mother procure treatment from one of the many substance-abuse clinics located in all our major cities."

These were the triumphs in Bernstein's distorted world. Marvin brings our food over. Moscowitz comes a few minutes later. Then Breshman. Eventually Weissbaum shows, and Finkelstein. With Marvin, the waiter, and Jorge, the Puerto Rican busboy, we have a *minyan*.

"Before I order, I'll start with water," Moscowitz says to Marvin.

"Would you stop with the poetry? What is with this guy?" asks Marvin.

"I'll take a Jackie Vernon with a side of Henny Youngman," says Breshman.

"Give me a Billy Crystal, hold the Woody Allen," says Goldberg.

"Sophie Tucker, rare," says Weissbaum.

"Here's the scoop, I'll take chicken soup," from guess who?

"This is how I earn a living," mutters Marvin, leaving with the order, "waiting hand and foot on a bunch of comedians."

"What about us, Marvin?" I respond, "You think it's a pleasure to sit here and eat? We come here because we *have* to, because we're genetically pre-disposed to eat this stuff, compelled by forces beyond the scope of our own lifetimes, driven by the primordial Hebrew appetite of the Patriarchs. You have a problem with it, don't complain to us; talk to Abraham, raid Sarah's kitchen and find out what she put in her *kneidlach*, what Old Testament ingredients she sanctified in the land of Canaan, we're talking the very theology of *tzimmes*, the veritable sacred history of *flaumkuchen*, the verily-I-say-unto-you of Scriptural recipe..."

"Okay Reb Wilner, I think he got the point," says Moscowitz.

"You should talk?"

"How about we get down to the business at hand," suggests Weissbaum.

"*Eating* is the business at hand," says Goldberg, "what is *with* you guys? We *have* no business at hand. We're a group of guys meeting for *lunch*. What is the big *deal*?"

And so it goes. The *kibitzers kibitzing*. Or, as Goldberg liked to say, "It takes a big *zetz to zetz* the *zetzer*." What's a *zetz*? A verbal jab. A sub-division of *kibitzing*. Put together a bunch of *zetzes* with a few *shticks* and you got a *kibitz*. Extend the kibitz over an evening and you got yourself a *shmooze*. *Shmooze* your life away and you end up with *bupkis*—nothing.

"Which brings me to the reason I called you all here," I announce. "You didn't call us here," points out Weissbaum, the stickler for accuracy.

"Nevertheless, had I called you here, this would be why: to tell you shlubs that we must, each of us, devote ourselves to a high and mighty purpose greater than ourselves, something bigger than our own lousy little delicatessen lives, a commitment to something noble..."

"Send the pickles this way, if you get a chance," says Goldberg, the King of Nosh.

"I promise you my brothers, my *landsmen*, there is more to this life than indigestion and belching on 57th Street; there are greater meanings that go way beyond seltzers and egg creams, your ryes and your pumpernickels, your platters and side dishes. I'm telling you, our heritage is bigger than the merely culinary. Our God was a jealous God, not a chef. Something is alive in me, what can it be?"

"Well whatever it is," Weissbaum responds, "do us all a favor and kill it, because you're starting to bug the shit out of me."

"Who had the Rodney Dangerfield?" Marvin comes with the rest of the orders, puts down our food, and pulls up a chair. Finally, with the holy offerings before us, we all shut up and eat.

***

Early the next evening we all meet at my place for a snack—I give the boys some nice borscht with sour cream and boiled potatoes—and we head over to Miltie's. Even Marvin, the waiter, comes along. Something about ten or more Jewish men together and you start feeling slightly nervous, as if God might pop in for a surprise visit at any moment. I knock on Miltie's door, the others behind me like a Jewish Boy Scout troop, like Semitic trick-or-treaters, Sephardic Christmas carolers, Ashkenazic Avon ladies, standing there in the hallway.

"Marvin!" Milton exclaims upon opening the door.

"Miltie!" Marvin responds, and the two men embrace and begin dancing a mini-*hora* right there in the entryway, holding hands and dancing in a circle, singing "Hava Negila." The rest of

us clap in rhythm. Instant wedding music. Goldberg should have brought his accordion. (In our younger days we had played in a band together. But not like ordinary kids growing up in the 60s with their Fender Stratocasters and Farfisa Mini-Compacts, playing "Midnight Hour" and "Mustang Sally." No. With Goldberg on the accordion, Weissbaum on trumpet, and me on guitar, we played foxtrots and merengues, the alley-cat and bunny-hop. Other kids were smoking pot in the high school boy's room and jamming with their fuzz boxes; we were playing the Dineson Lodge Purim Banquet, original medleys of "Tzena Tzena," "Belz Mein Schtetle Belz," and "Chosen Kalle Mazel Tov."

Picture this: a Junior High School "Battle of the Bands" in the gymnasium. First, Ramsey Gallagher and the Fireballs play "House Of The Rising Sun," by the Animals. Then Tony Richards and the Cavalcades do "A Well-Respected Man" by the Kinks. Then Bruce Vogosian and the Huns do "Satisfaction" by the Stones. Finally, Phil Goldberg and the Melodious Players do "I Left My Heart In San Francisco" by Tony Bennett. We were the laughing stock of East Lake Junior High School. 'Course little did anyone know that Goldberg actually played a mean accordion and would wind up knowing more about music than any of those big shots with their rock and roll and their fancy electric guitars—Gibsons, Guilds—and their Fender Super-Reverb amps, Ampeg Gemini IIs, their expensive Shure microphones. But us? We did medleys: "Who Can I Turn To?" right into "As Long As He Needs Me." In short, we were musical sissies.)

"How do you two know each other?" I ask in astonishment.

"What, I shouldn't know Marvin?" asks Miltie.

"What, I shouldn't know Miltie?" asks Marvin.

"What, I never eat at the Carnegie Deli?" asks Miltie. "It hasn't been my home away from home for thirty-seven years? Marvin's not like a brother to me? What? Come in, come in everyone, you think the whole apartment building wants to listen to us make a racket in the hallway? I'm going to make you stand in the doorway forever with your coats on? Come in already, for God's sake."

We go in. There's barely room for all of us. We sit and stand, squeezed into the small space like sardines.

"So nu? You are all friends of my friend, so I welcome you to my home, for it has been said, 'when your friend brings a *minyan* to your door, your studio apartment becomes a Holy Temple'—Samuel, verse 15. Okay, so it was Sammy Schneit, my brother-in-law, he should rest in peace, but a more pious man I never met—okay, maybe a bit of a *shnorer*. So let's not waste our time. In the next world God won't make small talk with us, why should we use up words here? Who knows how many words the Holy One gives each of us? We may all be on the last paragraph, the last sentence, we should make it count.

"Now," he continues, "what's the problem? I'll tell you the problem: insufficient joy. Period. Not enough laughter of the heart. Shortage of Divine belly laughs. Agreed? Agreed."

Who would disagree? Greenblatt with his anxiety, Moscowitz with his torment? Who could argue with sorrow? No man couldn't stand a substantial increase in his daily joy quotient. Even Bernstein with his Hindu bliss states, Finkelstein at the height of his St. John of the Cross office-supply raptures—we could all use more. Even Breshman with his tennis endorphin highs could always play another set. Miltie had crossed the barriers of individual differences and touched on something common to us all: the desire for greater joy, a relief from misery, suffering, anxiety, neurosis, fear and despair. ("So big deal," Greenblatt's sister would say later, "it takes a genius to know this? I told you you were miserable the day I met you, but you never brought your *meshugeneh* friends over to meet *me*.")

"Therefore," Miltie chants in the traditional Talmudic singsong that every Bar-Mitzvah boy learns and every Yeshiva student uses daily, "whenever the Almighty looks down and sees not so much joy in the hearts of his children, it is time for them to receive a *tikkun*, a fixing, from a Holy Rebbe, and failing that, a good poke in the ribs from a Rebbe Without a Cause, yours truly. So how do you like that, you bunch of *mamzer goniffs*"—Yiddish for

"bastard thieves"—"you *shaineh kinderlech*"—"beautiful children." "But first, how about a nice cup tea?" We all nod.

"Not so fast," Miltie counters, "you think an old man keeps a dozen teacups in his kitchen? You think I stock styrofoam like I'm expecting a bunch of Jewish hoodlums for lunch? You want tea, you get it "to go" around the corner at Louie's Diner. And while you're there, pick me up a nice danish they keep under the glass contraption on the counter. Who's going?"

Bernstein raises a hand, heads for the door.

"There's no house on fire, sit down a minute...you have money? Good, I won't insult you by forcing you to take money from me. Make it two danish...what do the rest of you want?"

Bernstein's got a pad out, taking orders:

"Cheeseburger, well-done, hold the cheese."

"Tuna-melt on toasted English."

"Side of onion rings, large Coke."

"Such *chazzerai* you want to bring into my house?" Miltie comments.

We all tell Bernstein we'll pay him back. We won't. The guy owes us, after all: fifty bucks each to spring him from the slammer. The least he could do is buy us a little snack from Louie's Diner. He stands in the doorway awhile, stalling, fidgeting, waiting for us to kick in some money. We don't. Finally, he gets it, and goes.

While Bernstein's away we sit and chat a bit, kibitz awhile, *schmooze* for a spell, tell Miltie about Bernstein and his mother.

"Not Ethel Bernstein?" Miltie asks.

"The same," I say.

"A woman after my own heart. And cooks a meal that's out of this world. And some of the best Columbian bud you can imagine...so that's her boy, what's his name?"

"Bernstein."

"Of course, Bernstein. I like him. Very generous. I should have hit him up for a dozen bagels while he's buying."

Before long, Bernstein returns and we eat, most of us standing like we're at Nedicks or Orange Julius.

"Now, my friends, I will tell you what you need, each and every one of you, to be happier...who knows the answer?"

"Death?" Greenblatt asks.

"Nitrous oxide?" from Bernstein.

"Wrong," Miltie says to each.

"Hot corned beef on rye with Gulden's Golden Brown, side of slaw?" Marvin peeps shyly.

"No, but you're a lot closer than these high falootin' spiritual no-goodniks...what each and every one of you need, my good friends, is a woman, a nice, Jewish wife, a *balhabosteh.*"

"I'm already married," says Finkelstein.

"Me too," says Weissbaum.

"So maybe the two of you should get divorced," says Miltie, "How should I know all the answers?"

A woman? A wife? A Jewish woman-wife? What a concept. Truly staggering. All of us become silent, all of us stop chewing. A woman? Never in our wildest dreams did any of us consider this option as a solution to our fundamental existential loneliness. All of the teachings, across the board, from every tradition, had instilled in us the absolute conviction that relationships are not only *not* the answer to anything, but may even be the problem itself! Ninety-nine percent of the books on the self-help shelves begin with some variation of "You have to love yourself before you can love anyone else. You must be committed to your own well-being before you are capable of committing to another." Since none of us were committed to our own well-being, we just naturally assumed relationships were out of the question.

I'm generalizing. Goldberg had his lady who didn't like him. Weissbaum had Sally who we all assumed was a living saint, and Finkelstein had his Lilah with the charge cards and weekly facials. But as for the rest of us...I for one tried to take the injunction to love myself to heart, and I really devoted myself, but I found I needed to keep my relationship with myself open so that if things didn't work out I was free to see other people. Certainly, my three years with Greenblatt's sister were nothing less than a harsh prison

sentence and I had decided to avoid Jewish women forever after. But when I last tried to be with a non-Jew, I eventually realized it could never work—I needed more pain around me in order to feel at home.

("The Gentiles don't feel things the way we do," my mother trained me to believe. "Right," I would respond inwardly, "they're *happier*.")

So, damned if you do, damned if you don't. I gave up. And now this, from Miltie. A woman! Who would have thought?

"I don't mean to pry, Reb Miltie," Goldberg pries, "but aren't you a single man?"

"Where is it written," he adds, "that's what's good for the goose is good for the gander? Did I say everyone should have a wife? No. I said that you and you and you should have a wife. And you and you. And you too. This is specific information. Particular. Personal advice. Coincidentally, it happens to be the same for all of you. And off the record, I wouldn't exactly object to a roll in the hay with Ethel Bernstein, I wouldn't kick her out of bed. Okay, *genug*, now let's sing."

We were all in a mild state of shock. We had come expecting a fancy metaphysical discussion of the Absolute, an inter-religious dialogue on the Divine Reality, some catalytic teachings. Instead, we got the same spiel we got from our mothers when we went home: Find a nice, Jewish girl, get married, settle down, God forbid you should get a job and be a normal person. But somehow to hear this from Reb Miltie carried with it a different impact. With our mothers, we had a built-in screening mechanism, an anti-*hocking* device that allowed most motherly advice to go in one ear and out the other. This is not disrespect. This is survival. We learned it in those crucial, formative, pubescent years. While Gentile boys were out hunting with their dads and going through those father-son rites of passage, camping out in the woods, building fires, we were all home in our pajamas, pleading with our mothers to let us stay up a little later.

But coming from Reb Miltie, this was different. To this we paid attention. We were open, and he nailed us when we were

vulnerable. So we sang. "Di di, de de de, de di, di di, de de de, de di." We sang a *niggun* with Reb Milton Gelberman, and we all left dreaming of romance and misery. (Okay, not all. Not Breshman.)

***

Okay, so I've screamed out in terror, the primordial mortal fear, naked and raw, standing alone and incomprehensibly small in a vast, infinity of indifference, surrounded on all sides by dangerous and threatening forces, cruel possibilities, unbearable tragedies, mocking laughter. It's a good opening. Two words—"I'M SCARED"— roughly capsulizing not only my entire life to date, but perhaps, the history of the world, the world that is heart-broken.

So I begin from my place of brokenness. I am the shattered vessel of the Kabbalah incarnate, one of the very vessels that, from the beginning of time, could not contain the brilliance of the Divine Light and so smashed apart into a million fragments, the putting back together of which is the only sacred task, the lives-long job of soul-making: the *tikkun*, the fixing of the shattered vessels, the raising up again of the scattered sparks of light, to be able to once again contain the Divine. Making whole. Cheering up.

I cross to downstage right and slowly transform myself. Quietly chanting a deep bass tone from the depths of an invisible well, I slowly don the black caftan of the Chasid, methodically wrap myself in *tefillin* and *tallis*, the furry *streimel* on my head, I put on some rouge, and a long beard. I tell a story:

"Late one night, on a night of the full moon, it came to the great Baal Shem Tov's inner sight that a great danger was facing his people. He asked his disciple, Reb Dov Baer, to come with him deep into the forest, guided by the moonlight, to a secret place. There, the Holy Rebbe created a fire by simply touching a branch with his hands, and as the fire blazed before them, Dov Baer saw that the bush within the white flames was not being consumed.

"The Master sat in silent meditation before the conflagration, then stood up and began praying with a great fierceness. It was a prayer Dov

Baer had never heard before, and though he was never to hear it again, every word remained etched in his memory forever. At last his teacher stopped his prayers and smiled, saying, 'The danger will be averted. Come, we can go back now.'

"Many years later, Dov Baer himself was a revered teacher and Rebbe. Once again, a grave danger faced the Jewish people. He knew what he had to do. He asked his follower, Reb Moshe Leib, to join him, and together they went back to that sacred, hidden place of the Baal Shem Tov, deep in the forest. But only a soul like that of his beloved teacher had the ability to create a burning bush with the touch of a hand. So Dov Baer turned to Reb Moshe and said, 'It may be that we cannot light the fire, but let us meditate and pray, for I still remember the exact prayers of the Master.' And for the first time since hearing them, Dov Baer uttered aloud the prayers he had heard from his teacher's lips so many years before, in that same place. And when they returned to the city, they learned that the danger had passed.

"Still another generation later, Reb Moshe Leib himself was looked upon as the beloved Rebbe and leader of many, many Hasidim. And again, a situation of great peril threatened the people of Israel. He had nobody at hand to accompany him, and so he returned to the secret forest sanctuary alone. He knew he could not light the fire; he also could not remember any of the prayer. But at least he knew the place. And that proved to be enough.

"And then finally, many years later, a certain Reb Israel of Rizhin was called upon to perform the same task, and he declared to his followers: 'We cannot light the fire, we cannot recite the holy prayer, we do not even know where the place in the forest is. All we can do is tell the story of what happened.' And he did. And it was enough."

Telling the story is enough. Even *my* story.

***

I do some research on this Mordecai character, and come up empty-handed. No mention of him in any of the Rumi literature or the historical documents of Persia, circa 1200. Nothing in the

Britannica. Dead-end Internet searches. It is almost as if Reb Miltie made him up. Then it hits me: he *did*. Make him up. Mordecai is a fictitious character, a mouthpiece for Miltie himself. Miltie is Mordecai, Mordecai is Miltie. In hindsight, it is suddenly obvious. It doesn't take anything away from the simplicity and power of the poems—it actually makes them even more of a living transmission, and I realize they are subtly working on me, chipping away at something. Something old, hard and stuck. Something cellular. I pick up the book and flip it open:

> *Stop the pilgrimage and unpack for good.*
> *The Holy Land is where you already live.*
> *Only there will the Tender One*
> *remove Her sarong*
> *and swim in the clear blue water*
> *of the soul who has stopped looking.*

> *Mordecai has some news:*
> *The God that lives somewhere else*
> *is an imposter.*

CHAPTER FOURTEEN

Moscowitz

Moscowitz was a baby, there was no getting around it. Having him on your side was useless. He was filler, the last guy to be picked. He threw like a girl. He was the only person who was actually afraid to fight Finkelstein, and when he did he would flail his arms around aimlessly and harmlessly, with his head facing the other way. His only real break was hormonal—he was one of those kids who shot up about five inches during summer vacation between fifth and sixth grade, and so in his "senior" year at East Lake his new height suddenly brought him a slight measure of respect where none had existed before.

Hormones or not, Moscowitz was no real force to be reckoned with, and most everybody knew it. He certainly didn't instill any fear in the hearts of men like Taylor or Grisatti. On the contrary, he inspired, if anything, outright laughter and scorn. How did this chubby little Philip character, Taylor and his cronies would muse, expect to overthrow the playground when his following consisted of wimps like Moscowitz, and Finkelstein with his false bravado, and Wilner who bargained his way through the day like a shopkeeper on Orchard Street? It was as if Philip was the champion of the losers, the rejected; he commandeered an army of misfits.

Wilner befriended Moscowitz in private only. That is to say, when Moscowitz became, as he often would, the brunt of the group's derision, Wilner would be right there, taunting him along with the rest:

"Don't be such a baby, Moscowitz. Better go home, your mother's calling you, baby! Go eat your milk and cookies."

But in private, Wilner, a baby himself, would become a different person and, with only the slightest tinge of guilt, would play with Moscowitz for hours, like a close friend, even a best buddy. It was almost as if he expected Moscowitz to understand that, given Moscowitz's pitiful reputation, Wilner couldn't possibly acknowledge their friendship publicly, for he would then be risking his own reputation by association. And in fact, Moscowitz, on some level, did recognize this, and forgave Wilner, and was grateful for the private friendship at least. Moscowitz, in his self-contempt, didn't really feel he deserved any better.

There was no way that little Moscowitz could possibly have known that the humiliation and shame he experienced with his friends was in fact a manifestation of the group's own fear—each individual shuddering to see such a vulnerable part of themselves so painfully obvious and externalized in the form of poor Moscowitz, the baby, the chicken, the girl for Pete's sake! Only girls were afraid; only girls threw and fought the way Moscowitz threw and fought. Moscowitz was the very prototype for sissy. His mother kissed him on the cheek in front of all the other boys, and Moscowitz didn't even wince or make any faces to indicate that he minded. And he allowed his mother to bundle him up in winter so that he came out to play looking like a moving pile of winter clothing with a red nose sticking out.

In summer, if a ball bounced right in front of him—"short-hopped him"—and smashed him in the eye or teeth, he would cry, right there on the ball field; in front of all of us, he would cry like a little kid. Wilner couldn't believe his eyes and ears the first time he saw it happen. If Wilner's little mind had had the vocabulary at the time, he might have thought to himself, "There but for the Grace of God go I."

And now, with Grisatti's note crumpled and clutched in his sweaty hand, with McQuicksand droning on about Paul Revere and

the Boston Tea Party, with the clock reading 2:48, Wilner was about to face the ultimate test of his life. It was as if his world was asking him, "Are you man or Moscowitz?" and inwardly his heart was dropping because he knew he was Moscowitz. He was a baby. A chicken. A sissy. A scaredy-cat. A girl. It was all over for Wilner. The jig was up. The charade was over. The truth would be revealed. The world would know him for what he was: a no-good, sniveling coward.

Although he already knew what he would do, knew the outcome of the afternoon's major event, had already conceived his own personal plan, he nevertheless carried out Philip's orders in the meantime. He passed Moscowitz and Finkelstein notes:

"Basement boy's room immediately upon dismissal. Stop. Emergency. Stop. Philip presiding. Stop."

Poor Philip, Wilner thinks. He is so devoted to his boys he can't see us for what we are: a bunch of Jewish shlemiels, weaklings, wimps. What Philip hoped to accomplish that afternoon was beyond Wilner, but it was no longer his concern, either. For his was a solo plan that would only become known to the rest after the fact. Wilner's day of reckoning.

2:50. The bell rings. Boom. To the boy's room. The men are assembled: Finkelstein, Moscowitz, Philip, Lipschitz, Bernstein and Ivanovich, the new Russian kid who had just turned up at East Lake that week and had been swept right up by Philip—tiny Ivanovich having no idea what he was getting himself into, only glad to be befriended so rapidly in his new school.

Wilner enters. Philip is in the middle of outlining his plan and pauses just long enough to give Wilner a nod of confidence, as if to say, "Don't worry, kid, I got everything under control," and then resumes speaking, using his "captain's voice" —an adult voice of authority and control, learned from years of imitating war heroes in old movies.

"...Okay, so Lipschitz, I need you at my side the whole time, understand? Your job is to just be there, you follow me? You don't worry about Wilner, you don't listen to a word Grisatti says, your whole attention is fixed on me, riveted on me, waiting for the slightest, subtle indication from me—a quick glance, a wave of my hand behind my back,

anything—and then off you go to the shack behind B'nai Shalom. That's it, Lip, you got it? Are you sure?

"Okay, so you can leave. You get started, you run ahead to 30th and Oak—don't get too close, don't give yourself away, I don't think Grisatti quite knows you're aligned with me. Just get a fix on his position, where he has his men stationed; then you run back and meet us on our way, give us the full report. I may send you back to double check, and then back again to us. I may run you like a little son-of-a-bitch, Lipschitz, and you gotta do it. You have no feelings today, Lip; anything you feel doesn't count. You don't exist today, my friend. Today you are a pair of legs, a relayer of information, you are a machine, a mechanical convenience, you follow me? You got a team of men here counting on you. Without you we have no communication, we're stranded, we're goners, we're shipwrecked like a bunch of drowning men hanging on to a piece of rotten driftwood. Got it? Comprende Senor Lipschitz? Good, now out with you, beat it, get the hell out of here." Lipschitz turns to go. "Oh and Lip..."—Lip pauses at the door, turns his head—"...good luck."*

Boom, Lipschitz is gone before Philip takes his next breath, disappearing, a phantom, he was never there. A picture of devotion. Philip knew what he was doing. He didn't assign jobs idly. He wouldn't have put Moscowitz in Lip's position, obviously. Of course, neither would anyone else. You'd have to be a complete idiot to give Moscowitz that sort of job. Make Moscowitz your runner and he's liable to trip on his own sneaker lace, scrape his knee and go crying to his mother to put a band-aid on his boo-boo. So what use did Moscowitz have for Philip? Where did he fit in to the elaborate web Philip was masterfully weaving?

Simple: he would be a decoy. Divert everyone's attention at the right moment. "Moscowitz, you just shuffle along to B'nai Shalom like you're going home from school, holding your books with both arms like a girl, the way you usually do. Anybody taunts you, you ignore them and keep moving." (Philip was brilliant—he had created a plan that required people to be themselves. It is the mark of true leadership to know how to use that which is most readily forthcoming from one's

people—good or bad, strong or weak—to one's advantage. Philip's plan actually called for Moscowitz to be Moscowitz.)

"...but most likely nobody will say anything to you today, Moscowitz; today, Wilner's in the spotlight." Saying this, he shoots a proud glance at Norbert, who inwardly shrinks from the look, while trying to smile back. "So not much chance, my bet, that you'll even be noticed today, Moscowitz, which is perfect, because your job will be to casually circle back around and get as close to Grisatti as possible without being too conspicuous. We're talking psychic camouflage, Moscowitz, guerilla tactics. You're right next to the man and he can't see you. You think invisible. You blend into the woodwork." *(Asking Moscowitz to be invisible was like asking the Pope to be Catholic, like asking Wilner to be afraid. Philip's gift.)*

"Now, Moscowitz, baby, listen carefully. Your job is simple. I'm not asking you much. I'm not asking you, God forbid, to risk anything. All I'm asking you to do is watch me, and when I give you the nod, you drop your books right in front of Grisatti, all your papers flying about, maybe one book actually lands on Grisatti's toe—not so it hurts. It's all one big accident, and you go berserk when it happens. You start bawling like a little kid, you dash about grabbing books and papers, clutching them under your chin, picking up one book only to drop another, it's a big mess, it's a scene, it's noise. It's just a single moment I'm after, just the edge I need to have Grisatti shift his attention for just a moment off Wilner, off me. And that's when Finkelstein and I spring into action."

Finkelstein! Wilner thinks. *Philip's crazy if he thinks Finkelstein and he are going to handle Grisatti and his boys. And he hasn't even mentioned Butch Taylor who will most definitely play a part in all this.* (Even in Wilner's trembling state, he has all sorts of questions for Philip, gaps, things he doesn't understand.)

"Relax, Norbert, I'm not finished," Philip says, as if reading Wilner's mind. "I'm building slowly. We got time. Grisatti's not going anywhere. We need him to get stationed first or we're cooked anyway. We got Lip out there now, scouting. And it's all for you, my friend, so just relax. You're the one guy in all this who doesn't have to remember

anything. Nothing. You've got no job. No signals to memorize. All you do is show up. Period. Easiest thing in the world. You just show up and the rest is history. In fact, you don't even need to be in here any longer. You don't have to know the plan. Don't worry your little head about it. We'll take care of everything. You wanna go, go."

But Wilner, paralyzed, remains. *Easiest thing in the world,* he repeats to himself. *Just show up. Easiest thing in the world...*

"Now, who knows what key fact I left out?"

"I do," Bernstein responds.

"Of course you do, Bernstein." Because Bernstein remained unaccounted for in the plan. But then, so did Ivanovich, the Russian, and the precise nature of Finkelstein's mission was also unclear. But somehow everyone knew that Philip was referring to Bernstein at the moment.

"Okay, where did I leave off with Lip? Sure I told him about running back and forth, but what else did I tell him? Anybody remember?"

"The shack," Moscowitz pipes up.

"The shack!" repeats Philip. *"The shack the shack the shack. Moscowitz, you got a good head on your shoulders, no matter what anyone says. Now wake up you guys: I told Lip to watch for my signal and then off he goes to the shack. But why the shack? Who's in the shack?"*

Finally, it was self-evident. Bernstein, of course, would be stationed in the shack, awaiting Lipschitz's message that reinforcements were required. He would be the surprise cavalry coming over the hill in the nick of time, if he were needed. If he wasn't, why, then, Bernstein was free to sit back in the shack and read a comic book, relax, enjoy himself. Bernstein was Philip's trump card; he would only play it if he had to.

As far as Taylor and Grisatti knew, Bernstein was unaffiliated. He was widely known as a great ballplayer—solid number three man in the line-up, reliable left fielder. And he was respected as a fighter, based not so much on any actual fights, for Bernstein was by nature a peace-loving man, but on his stature and obvious strength. Had Bernstein been of a different bent—had he wanted power—he would long ago have become a force to be reckoned with on the playground;

he would long ago have posed a real threat to Butch Taylor himself. But everyone—Grisatti, Taylor, and Philip (or so it seemed)—simply maintained a polite, working relationship with Bernstein, grateful that he seemed content to live in the safety zone of his own strength, neither making waves nor interfering with the waves of others. In a word, he was apolitical.

So how did Philip get Bernstein on his side? Certainly not through coercion. Bernstein could not be coerced. Not blackmail; Bernstein wouldn't, and wouldn't need to, stand for that. In fact, no one there in the boy's room knew the answer to this question, and neither did anyone else at East Lake. It was some sort of secret pact between Philip and Bernstein that only the two of them knew.

And it wasn't as if Philip "had something on him." It was more like a secret vow of brotherhood, a mythical tie of some sort, grounded in ritual. Nobody knew, and apparently Philip wasn't about to disclose the reason now. (On a smaller scale, it was as well-kept a secret as Jerry Lewis' private passion for the muscular dystrophy kids.) Suffice it to say that it was a remarkable disclosure to even reveal that Bernstein was on their team, let alone why. And so Bernstein saunters out of the boy's room and slowly exits the school and makes his way to the shack behind B'nai Shalom.

"Okay, where were we," Philip continues. "I've given Moscowitz the sign, his papers are flying through the air like confetti, a ticker tape parade for Wilner's victory. Lipschitz is poised, waiting for my signal if I think we need Bernstein. And now, Ivanovich, the surprise element, the dark horse, a subversive. Who would have thought? The new kid, the Soviet boy, working for us. Nobody in a million years. I can hardly believe it myself. Nobody enlists after one week at East Lake. Ordinary people take a year just to learn who's who, just to get a sense of the political climate, to size up the situation. But Ivanovich is no ordinary man. Ivanovich is a ringer. This is kid's stuff for Ivanovich. He was in the goddamned KGB in Russia, for chrissakes. They had him on border patrol in Siberia for crying out loud. The guy has been around. He's killed people, for the love of Pete."

Ivanovich grinning from ear to ear at all the attention. He doesn't understand a word Philip is saying, but he knows he is being acknowledged and praised.

"Ivanovich, listen up: As soon as you see Moscowitz's books hit the ground, you count to yourself 'one dasferdanya, two dasferdanya, three' and right on 'three' you move. You're behind Grisatti himself, you go down on all fours, Finkelstein leaps through the air and gives Grisatti a shove and right over backwards he goes, right over our little Russian espionage agent...Grisatti doesn't know what hit him. There's chaos all over, it's a circus. Moscowitz is screaming and papers are flying, Grisatti's on his back and by now I'm sitting on the bastard's chest pinning him there while Finkelstein and Ivanovich keep his men off me, Lipschitz is still trained on me like a laser gun, Bernstein's jerking off in the shack, Wilner stands there untouched, an observer at his own fight; he blends into the crowd, nobody even remembers that he had anything to do with the whole business. I make Grisatti call his men off. I make him cry 'uncle.' I don't get off him until he says 'I give up, you win, I'm a beaten man, I gotta hand it to you Philip, you've got quite an outfit working for you.'

"And that's the long and the short of it. Child's play. The whole thing is cheesecake. It's embarrassing. Grisatti doesn't have a prayer. He's out there, right now, probably standing with his arms crossed, joking with his people about what's he's going to do to our boy Wilner, wipe the street with him, punch his face in, and so forth."

(Wilner's heart speeds up, he sees himself creamed by Grisatti, he sees Grisatti leaning over the fence with blood streaming from his nose, only it's not Grisatti this time, it's him, and he hasn't heard a word Philip has said, he has heard no plan, he heard only "punch his face in.")

"Okay, any questions?" Philip asks.

Sure I have questions, Wilner thinks. What happens when Philip is sitting on Grisatti, asking him to give up, and Grisatti plays his trump card? Oh, by the way, Philip, Norbert imagines Grisatti saying, did you know that your little friend Norbert Wilner has been hanging around with one Butch Taylor lately? I don't suppose that would

interest you, would it? I just happen to have a little more information on the matter, but naturally it's a bit uncomfortable discussing it with you perched on my lungs. Perhaps we might have a little meeting like civilized men? Or perhaps we should ask Norbert himself about this? Or, of course, there's always Mr. Taylor himself, who happens to be among us this afternoon...

Taylor! What about Taylor, Norbert thinks. Does Philip really think that Butch Taylor will just watch all this without getting involved? Well, perhaps. Taylor would want to remain neutral. He was still king. He would enjoy watching his number two man and the chief contender have it out. It would clarify matters at East Lake. The outcome would tell him if this chubby Jewish kid was actually a force to be reckoned with, or just a lot of smoke and mirrors. But would Taylor expose Wilner if it came down to the gitgo? Of course he would. He felt no loyalty to Wilner for his crummy little bubble gum pay-offs. He had been using Wilner. He didn't need him, and if the situation did arise, he would certainly feel no compunction about seeing Wilner destroyed. Still, he wouldn't bring it up on his own. Only if Grisatti initiated. If not, it was in Taylor's best interest to allow events to unfold without him putting his two cents in. Later he could deal with Philip—with "the Basketball"—one-on-one, and use the "truth about Wilner" for his own purposes, to weaken Philip's defenses at just the right moment.

All these possibilities go through Wilner's mind the way a chess master contemplates all possible outcomes from a single move. But none of it mattered to Wilner, because he had his own plan. And he was committed to it with unshakable conviction. It would be a betrayal, but as far as he could tell, his previous betrayal was about to surface anyway, so what would be the difference if he added one more betrayal to his list of offenses? Besides, as far as he can surmise, his very survival demanded this one last betrayal.

In his decision comes a certain relief. He no longer fears for his physical safety—his nose, his face, would be safe. Now he only needed to fear the consequences of his last, great betrayal. And this fear, in some strange way, was even more pronounced than his fear of Grisatti pulverizing him to death. Had he been he able to think clearly, he

would have chosen to risk getting beaten up, to go along with Philip's plan. But he wasn't thinking clearly. He had no idea that his little personal plan, his betrayal, would have the far-reaching consequences that it would indeed have. No idea whatsoever. He was responding on a much more instinctive and immediate level, the way someone might quickly pull their hand back from a flame: no thought is involved; one's avoidance of pain automatically activates the response. Wilner was on automatic. He actually had no choice. But he didn't know that. He thought he was choosing. "Okay, boys, I'm proud to be working with men of your caliber. Now let's move on out."

Philip, Wilner, Moscowitz, Finkelstein and Ivanovich file out of the boy's room in the basement of East Lake Elementary School.

"Norbert, you hang back a bit, give us a chance to station ourselves." *Wilner is white; frozen.* "Don't worry kid. You have my word, so help me God, both my parents should die in a car wreck, you won't be touched. They'll have to kill me first. You're gonna be an innocent bystander. It'll be like watching television for you. It's so incredibly simple. You just come on by, on your way home from school, you just wander over to 30th and Oak, you just show up. Got it?"

"Got it," *Wilner replies, feigning a tiny bit of confidence.*

"Good; now, are you okay on your own, or do you want an escort? No reason Finkelstein can't arrive with you..."

"NO!" *Wilner says quickly, with a sense of urgency. He had to be alone to carry out his plan. An escort would trap him. Philip mistakes his urgency for pride.*

"Okay, buddy, good. You're on your own. I'll see you in about ten minutes. In about fifteen minutes you'll see me sitting on Grisatti like I'm having a bowel movement, you'll hear him begging me to let him go. In twenty minutes it'll be all over, we'll be at Carvel having a Lollapalooza."

Philip and the others walk across the playground, towards the highway, towards 30th Street and Oak, towards Grisatti. Wilner stands alone in the doorway of East Lake, watching his friends, watching his life change forever.

Greenblatt's Sister

Women. This is a vast subject. This is not so easy. I must admit, I'm a little confused. I once read somewhere that the sexual urge is indiscriminate; that with the right conditioning and openness, one could be sexually aroused by a doorknob. Lenny Bruce said that "men will *shtup* anything, even mud." While I have never *shtupped* mud, I *did* once experiment with a carved-out, fresh pumpernickel bread, as per a reader's suggestion in *Penthouse*, lining the interior of the bread's mock vagina with butter for lubrication. I didn't actually find that this was as pleasurable an experience as being with a woman, although I'm certain the soft, cushioned embrace of a fresh loaf of bread has its advantages over the cool, brassy feel of a nice doorknob. And perhaps rye or whole wheat would have been the way to go. Maybe mayo instead of butter. Hold the lettuce.

But women, unlike either fresh bread or shiny doorknobs, make demands. They want stuff. They expect things. Especially Jewish women, when they're with Jewish men. Potentially a dangerous combination, possibly lethal. What do they expect? They expect you should suddenly stop being a two-bit prince of *shleppers* and become a real man, give them kids, a house and pay for the

whole works. A tall order for a near-40ish single Jewish man—me, Greenblatt, Bernstein, Moscowitz, the rest, none of whom has ever had even a single plant in the house, too much responsibility. To leap from plantlessness to marriage was beyond the scope of any of our wildest imaginings. We spoke of this a few days later, after Miltie's words had had a chance to sink in:

"Do you think he really meant *women*, as in adult females who have their periods?" Moscowitz asks me innocently on the phone.

"Not only that," I tell him, "but he meant the kind who have *husbands*."

"Unbelievable," says Moscowitz, "now what do we do?"

"We should start small—goldfish maybe, you only feed them once a day."

"How about fresh flowers—you stick them in water 'til they die and that's that." Moscowitz, the genius botanist.

"Well, same idea with women," I tell him, "you marry them until one of you dies and that's that." I hang up. The phone rings.

"Norb?" I hear Greenblatt's voice. "It's Jerry Greenblatt."

"I know, I used to date your miserable sister."

"Listen, remember the other night at your rabbi friend's house?" (Do I remember?)

"It really wasn't so long ago," I tell him, "I remember."

"Well he said something to us near the end and I can't for the life of me remember what it was, but I remember thinking it was important, something we should do...does any of this ring a bell?"

"He told us to find Jewish women and get married."

"AHHHHHHHHHHHHHHHHHHH!!!!! AHHHHHHH-HHHHHHHHHH!!!" I hear screams on the phone like someone was tearing off his genitals, his Sam Kineson impression.

"Jerry? You all right? Jerry?"

"AHHHHHHHHHHHHHHHHHHHH!!!" But really loud, to wake up a whole neighborhood, to make Mrs. Fleishman in 7B dial 911. Jerry hangs up. The phone rings.

"Hello, may I please speak to Mr. Norbert Wilner."

"Speaking."

"Mr. Wilner? This is Mr. Weissbaum." All my friends are crazy. Nobody just calls. Everybody's got a gimmick, their *shtick*, like a calling card. Weissbaum's was to be extremely formal. (Weissbaum's an obnoxious imbecile, but you gotta love him.)

"You might remember me from the other night," he continues.

"Yeah yeah I remember, what's up?"

"Please be patient with me Mr. Wilner, although I understand that your time is very valuable and I will certainly try not to detain you for very long."

"What's up Weissbaum?"

"Your rabbi friend told you to find a woman, right?"

"Right."

"I'll give you Sally for an undisclosed sum and a woman to be named later."

"You're a funny guy."

"Thank you for the feedback, Mr. Wilner. Well, I guess I'll be going now, gotta skiddaddle, hit the road...ta ta." He hangs up. I pick up the phone and dial Bernstein:

"Bernstein? Where are guys like us going to find women?"

"It's all handled, relax."

"Whattaya mean, all handled?"

"I'm placing personal ads for each of us in the *Jewish Press, Hadassah Monthly,* and the *Jerusalem Post.* Here's yours: 'Soulmate Wanted: Flexible hrs, gd bnfts. 37 yr old Jewish gypsy bohemian fringe artist type, sad, fearful, incapable of intimacy or commitment, no real job or future, moderate substance abuser, seeks wealthy Jewish blonde virgin who will mostly leave me alone and bear my children.' What do you think?"

"Perfect. Let me hear yours."

"That *was* mine."

"I like yours better."

"Don't you get it? We place one ad for all of us and then pool the responses."

And so it happened that about three weeks later we were all sitting around Bernstein's living room floor, pouring through photos

and letters. We divided them into categories that Weissbaum made up: "Repulsive," "Maybe," and "Unattainable." We concentrated, obviously, on the Unattainables.

"Because really, if you think about it," I explained to the fellows, "the truly unattainable wouldn't even be reading the personals, let alone answering them. The fact that they answered indicates that they are attainable, which puts them in the 'Maybe' category, which automatically shifts the 'Maybes' down a notch to 'Highly Unlikely.'" Moscowitz sat in a corner, pouring over the 'Repulsives.' We let him.

"Myra Schlamowitz," Moscowitz announces, holding up a picture of a slightly chubby and homely person wearing glasses and holding a stuffed Garfield, under which she had written the caption, "I'm a real Garfield nut!"

(The amazing and unbelievable truth about this story, though, is that Moscowitz really did ask Myra Schlamowitz to have coffee with him, and three months later they were engaged. And for two miserable people, they are basically happy together. She's a real Garfield nut. And as it turns out, unbeknownst to all of us, so is Moscowitz. A match made in the funnies.)

It scared the rest of us to conjure up images of Moscowitz and Myra in the bedroom.

"It's a very frightening concept," Greenblatt says.

"Don't dwell on it," Bernstein says.

"Every pot has a cover," I say.

So the personals worked for Moscowitz. The rest of us weren't so lucky. Bernstein saw Lucy Friedman only once. He went to her apartment, got her high and a little tipsy, told her he loved her and wanted to marry her, made love, left and never saw her again. (Again, truth is stranger than fiction: Bernstein got Lucy pregnant that night, and she gave birth to a daughter, Cookie, who, twenty years later, would sue Bernstein for half the rights to the Matzah · Ball Kingdom. Unbelievable.)

As for me, Greenblatt's sister got wind of the project, and answered the ad under a false name—Billie—and sent a photo of

a Playboy Centerfold. (Weissbaum always thought they were "cen-
terfields" and he would always gape at the lewd photos thinking,
"Jees, I wonder who they got in right?") (I, on the other hand, find
that the names of centerfolds always remind me of characters from
the old television series, *Petticoat Junction*, which featured three
daughters named Billie-Jo, Bobbie-Jo, and Something Else-Jo.
Recently Greenblatt's sister informed me that she and her husband
had considered naming their child, had it been a girl, "Fanny-Jo."
I imagined a Jewish *Petticoat Junction*, set in a Polish *shtetl*, with
three daughters named Fanny-Jo, Esther-Jo, and Ruth-Jo.)

Naturally, blinded by my own Jewish desire for the Ultimate
Gentile, I believe it really *is* the Playboy Centerfold responding to
our ad, and I go for it, like a shmuck. Greenblatt's sister has a friend
call to arrange our meeting, and I show up the next day, at the Lincoln Center fountain, to meet my sensuous soulmate—wondering
if she'll convert to Judaism—and there stands Greenblatt's sister. I
still don't get it. I'm thinking coincidence. I'm afraid that I'll have
to introduce Greenblatt's sister to Billie-Jo, that my blind date will
be destroyed by an extremely awkward beginning. *I have to get rid
of Greenblatt's sister, pronto,* is what I thought. *Get her out of here.*

"What are you doing here? I ask her.

"You want to know?"

"I don't want to know?"

"You don't want to know?"

"Yeah I want to know."

"So I'll tell you," she says, and takes out a *Playboy* centerfold
and says, "meet Billie" and sticks her hand out for me to shake. I
am basically shaken to the core of my being and acknowledge this
by lying:

"You jerk, I knew it was you the whole time."

"Yeah you knew. That's why you're wearing your special musk
oil that Bernstein brought you from Tibet that you never *once* wore
when *we* went out. That's why you're dressed like you're about to
spend the night with the Rockefellers on their yacht"—she was
exaggerating...basically, I had on new jeans. "Don't tell me you

knew—you *didn't* know, and you *don't know* from nothing, and you still think you're going to find someone better than me out there with blonde hair you asshole?"

I understood then that she knew I didn't know, and consequently, I was helpless, and just resigned myself to listening; it was the least I could do to pay for my crime, now that I had been caught red-handed. So I listened:

"You think this person is real you moron?" as she holds up the photo, raising her voice, attracting onlookers, her specialty. "This is not a real person," she says, and crumples up the picture and tosses it away. "*I* am a real person." (She was exaggerating. She was a real *zetzer*, and she gave me a *loch en kopf*.)

So my first attempt to fulfill Miltie's instructions were a disaster. But I learned something: never underestimate Greenblatt's sister. And she was right about two things: I *do* still think I'll find someone better out there with blonde hair, and, I *am* a moron.

***

Greenblatt's sister on the Lower Eastside, you don't wanna mess with her. Even the Black chicks kept their distance. She learned the neighborhood secret to survival: Be loud. Overcompensate for the fear of speaking out by screaming. Everything. Combined with moping. See Greenblatt's little sister in the street there, age nine, tough, sassy, and at home, a moper and a screamer. Tools of survival. And out-Blacked the Black chicks:

"Your Momma," one of them said once, a generic insult. Not "Your Momma wears army boots" or "Your Momma's a ho.'" No, just "Your Momma." How did Greenblatt's sister respond? She screamed so loud and so long that she scared the shit out of the Black girl: "MY MOMMA? MY MOMMA? NO YOU MISERABLE BLACK BITCH, IT'S YOUR MOMMA—YOU HEAR ME, YOU CHICKEN-SHIT WORTHLESS PIECE OF CRAP, IT'S YOUR FUCKING MOMMA." And so on. She had a mouth on her. She had to.

Greenblatt's sister was fiercely loyal to her family, particularly her older brother, Jerry. In a sense, he taught her everything she knew. He was a master moper and screamer and she molded herself in his image. But despite this social persona which, retained into adulthood is not such a great thing, the Greenblatts together in fact offered their friends a deep well of their own bare humanity—call it love—that lived just below the surface, but surrounded by a lot of screaming and tears, the emotional works. They loved and hated people and things with an intensity that would be frightening if not for the fact that in addition to being lunatics, they were also, each in their own way, brilliant comedians—geniuses of comedy—even if, as once happened at one of Jerry's stand-up open mike nights, I was the only one laughing. But I was really laughing. Maybe what some say about writing, that one should write to just one person, is also true for comedians. Greenblatt played to an audience of one. Me. And I was a damned good audience. The guy cracked me up.

But see her there—even then—in pigtails and morose eyes, being utterly unhappy. And with good reason: her Daddy was going to die and was an alcoholic in the meantime and a little daughter doesn't miss those things, not when your Daddy sometimes doesn't come home for three days and then when he finally does comes back, he just ignores you and passes out on the couch. That's the true secret to both of the Greenblatts' pain: It's real pain. It is not an act, or a tool for survival, or anything else; it just hurts. And they feel it. And if you get around them, you have to feel it too. That's why a sense of humor is so essential. Their ability to laugh as hard as they cried is what saved not only Greenblatt and his sister's souls, but, if you caught them on the right day, might save yours as well. But God help you if you made 'em mad. Easy to be with they weren't.

***

"Reb Miltie," I greet him, "There is no Mordecai."
"Then who am I?" he replies.
"You're Mordecai."

"Then there *is* a Mordecai."

"He's a fictitious character created by you."

"Mordecai is my Hebrew name. I am Mordecai. Reb Miltie is a fictitious character created by me."

"Huh?"

"And Norbert Wilner is a fictitious character created by you."

That was a real conversation stopper, so I just sort of shrugged and filed the information away, making a mental note to myself: *Find out who real self is and get back to me.*

"So," he asks, "do you enjoy Mordecai's poems in either case?"

"Yes," I said, "I like them a lot."

"Like isn't good enough. Like is good enough for God—you should like God. These poems have to pierce you to the core and change you. If you had a choice between breathing and reading one line out of that book, choose the book."

"You're so modest about your writings."

"It has nothing to do with boasting or modesty—I'm simply pointing out the correct response to all mystical ecstatic utterances. It's nothing personal. It has nothing to do with me. Here, I'll show you; pick a poem."

I flip it open and read aloud:

> *Sunlight and shadows disappear at night.*
> *Mordecai loves that Dark Place that goes on forever,*
> *littered with glittering stars.*
> *There, a soul can lay down her head*
> *and drift backward into a cool, delicious well.*
> *What seemed important in daylight is gone forever.*
>
> *Mordecai reflects:*
> *When Buddha said, "All is Impermanent,"*
> *he wasn't kidding.*

"Now, tell me what you learned from that."

"Well," I begin.

"WRONG!" he interrupts. "Your answer already stinks. Because if you had truly allowed the meaning of that poem to enter into you, you wouldn't even have an answer, you'd be dancing by now, or saving the world."

"So..."

"So you have work to do."

I left.

***

The Baal-Shem Tov knew the secret place, knew how to make the fire, knew the sacred prayer. Dov Baer knew the place, knew the prayer. Reb Moshe knew the place. Reb Rizhin knew only the story. And I only know *that* story, and my own. And it too shall be enough. Enough for what? Enough to avert the danger. And what is the danger? If you're alive on the same Earth as I am, the question is, what *isn't* the danger? The world as the continuous onslaught of bad news, of ominous signs and dark portents, life as ghost story, told at night to scare the little ones, only the little ones are us, and the ghosts have faces, and assault weapons, and weapons of mass destruction and terrorist schemes, and the ghosts are viruses and killer diseases, famine and pestilence, starvation and poverty, torture, oppression and execution, injustice and ecological suicide. It's as if all the newspapers everywhere had only one big, bad, daily headline:

DANGER
YOUR LIFE
AND EVERYONE AND EVERYTHING YOU LOVE,
CHERISH
AND HOLD DEAR
IS THREATENED
BEWARE OF LIVING

Our world is heartbroken. But telling the story shall be enough to avert the danger. To become the archetypal Rebbe is to sing a

lullaby to the planet earth, to soothe the troubled, sleepless soul of humanity herself, rocking her gently and making her laugh, telling the redemptive bedtime story to Man. It is to embody the power and the truth of the message in your every breath. And what's the message? The perennial one, the ultimate secret of the sages, the mystical revelation at the heart of all experience, in all times, in all places, and in all situations, now and forevermore, the other headline we're all waiting to see:

EVERYTHING IS OKAY

Or the variant,

RELAX

Or Weissbaum's classic,

CHEER UP

Imagine people everywhere waking up one morning to that headline in their daily paper. A bold banner across the front page of the *International Herald Tribune*, the *London Times* and *Washington Post*, the *Greenland Gazette* and the *Pago Pago Press*. The *Nairobi News*:

EVERYTHING IS OKAY.

In all the languages. Then the real irony: People all over the world reading their morning paper over coffee, seeing the lead story:

RELAX

and then saying to their partners, sitting across the table:

"What do you want to do today?"

and getting what could become known as the great Millennial Response:

"I don't know, what do *you* want to do?"

The "Marty" factor in contemporary post-apocalyptic life on earth, the existential trauma of finding meaning in a trouble-free world. Jean Paul Sartre finds the exit. Now what? Godot shows up. What becomes of Beckett? What to do when all is well? One thing, and one thing only, and this is why we need the Rebbe: celebrate. Life as sing-along, humans throwing a surprise party for the Divine, and boy won't God be shocked, walking in unsuspectingly and suddenly all His creatures jump out from behind their quivering mortal frames, singing "For He's A Jolly Good Fellow."

"For He," I silently muse, imagining myself delivering a great, cosmic sermon to the congregation of humanity, "is most certainly," pausing and staring fiercely into the eyes of the very soul of Human Being, the primordial Personhood of human life itself, "a jolly good fellow." The final resolution of the Great, Original Split, the Eternal Yearning for Union with the Creator, the Absolute Relief of Suffering and the end of the illusion of separated, egoic existence, is contained in this right-under-your-nose bare fact: the naked encounter with the Jolly.

"The Jolly," revealed as the Name for the next generation: Not my, but Thy Will be done, oh Jolly. The Jolly is my shepherd, I shall not be a miserable depressive. Our Father, who art in Heaven, Jolly be Thy name. Ascetics everywhere getting up, dusting off their ashes, putting balm on their wounds of self-flagellation, jaws dropping in astonishment as they hear the Divine Word:

"A funny thing happened to Me on My way into manifestation...you! Get it? You. You're the funny thing that happened to me. God, these people are so fucking serious. Hey listen carefully, for I say unto you: Lighten up, for chrissakes. Jesus! What happened to

you people? Couldn't handle a little incarnation? A little life and death? What is the big fucking deal? Get a life, friends."

For he is, as I indicated, a very jolly good fellow. And the Rebbe and the Jolly shall be as one. Listen to Mordecai:

> *Think of a shiny jewel*
> *in the bottom of a clear pond.*
> *Think of the sun causing a glare,*
> *and the jewel to sparkle.*

> *Now face the sun;*
> *now jump in the water.*
> *If the glare of your heart is too much,*
> *let others shade their eyes.*

> *Mordecai reminds you:*
> *The Wild One wears a crown of jewels,*
> *and that's some hat!*

CHAPTER SIXTEEN

Wilner

Wilner ran. Period. He skipped town. He bolted. That's the end of the big story. The kid ran like a motherfucker, like a scared rabbit. See him there, running his wet pants off, running for his life. And crying and mumbling to himself:

"I don't want to fight Grisatti, I'm scared, Daddy, I'm going home the back way, I don't care what anybody says, I'm not going anywhere near B'nai Shalom if it's the last thing I do. I'm going home, and I'm never going back to that school again as long as I live so help me God, I don't care what Philip thinks..."

The little boy never ran so hard and so fast for so long in all his scared, little life, running and panting, choking for air, desperate, literally running for his life. Wilner was copping out. Backing out. Pulling a grand no-show. Scared to death and without choice; his terror ran him home the back way without consulting him, with no thought to the consequences. And God help him there would be consequences. You don't chicken out of a major fight like that without major consequences. And the worst would be Philip. Philip, his guardian and protector, who had gone to such great lengths to assure his safety, who had bent over backwards to make sure Wilner wouldn't even physically have to move a muscle.

"Just show up," he had told him, "the easiest thing in the world."

In his wildest dreams, Philip never for a moment even considered the possibility that Wilner would pull a no-show, that Wilner would panic. And Wilner? Never in his wildest dreams did he, even for a moment, consider actually showing up. As soon as he got the note from Grisatti, his escape route had begun mapping itself out to him in his subconscious: I'll go one block up on Rt. 4, cut across 28th St—no, that's too close, I'll go all the way up to Plaza Road and circle around.

And circle around he did. He ran all the way up to Plaza Road and panted and huffed and mumbled and cried his way all the way back home, completely out of Grisatti's reach. He ran in a daze, a mind-befuddled fog, knowing only that he had to keep going, keep going, until he was safely inside his own house. He ran like a lone soldier through enemy territory, stripped of his weapons, bleeding from a bullet wound to the shoulder, running for his life. Wilner was running for his life, as fast as his little legs could take him, glancing over his shoulder, looking in both directions, afraid he would be seen by someone—anyone, from any side.

(Now leap out of linear time and see the adult Wilner running alongside, a few feet off the ground, running with the identical sense of urgency, just as anxious to get home, to be safe from the Grisattis in his life. The two of them, running. The two of them, scared to death.)

And boy was Philip ever mad. Mad Wilner could take. But Philip was contemptuous.

"Chicken," he spat out in disgust, when next he saw Wilner in school. "You make me sick. You make Moscowitz seem like Tarzan of the jungle, you big baby. I was the laughing stock of East Lake—are you happy now? Is that why you did it? You hate me? You betrayed me because you hate me and you wanted to see me humiliated? Is that it? Tell me, I'm asking you. You wanted to see Grisatti and Taylor laughing at me, me feeling like a complete idiot. Speak to me."

Wilner had no reply whatsoever. None. Couldn't explain it at all. Philip stomped off. Wilner was left in no-man's land. Everyone who was anyone at East Lake had heard about the disgusting little crybaby who snuck home rather than face Grisatti. Wilner was all but tarred and

feathered at East Lake. Ostracized and ridiculed. Laughed at or ignored when he tried to speak up about anything at all, both on the playground and even in the classroom. Little girls snickered behind his back, as if his fly was open.

He never told his parents. They had no idea why their son, over-night, suddenly seemed depressed, seemed to sit around a lot, staring into space. Seemed unhappy. No understanding why his friends seemed to come around a lot less than they used to. Something was definitely wrong with their boy Norbert, but they hadn't a clue as to what it was. His grades began to drop. The bright and cheerful, giggling Norbie had become the somber and morose Norbert; the energetic and excited child had become a listless and lethargic adult. And he was only eleven.

But ruined. Truly. Absolutely. Washed up. Finished. No good. Depressed, for years to come. Afraid, for years to come. Ashamed, for years to come. He was a failure and a coward, and the whole world knew it, and he hated himself for it and he vowed never to forgive himself as long as he lived.

He would never let himself forget that run home, the back way, the name Grisatti chasing him like sprayed bullets, his life at stake. He had no way of knowing he had been a machine, acting automatically in response to a perceived threat to his survival. All he knew, and all everyone knew, was that Norbert Wilner chickened out.

CHAPTER SEVENTEEN

Mrs. Bernstein

"Reb Miltie?" Once again I'm standing in the hall, outside #6H.

"Good Shabbes, come in, sit down, take off your shoes, I'll make you some nice tea with a nice piece sponge cake, we'll talk, we'll *shmooze*."

"I have a problem."

"No problem."

"Seriously."

"You're never going to quit with the metaphysical anxieties? I have problems of my own, believe me: Ethel Bernstein wants to marry me."

"Mrs. Bernstein? You? Get out of here."

"She was zonked on coke at the time, but I think she meant it."

"When did this happen?"

"Five minutes ago."

"Five minutes ago?"

"I'm a liar?"

"Sometimes."

"Five minutes ago. She called to thank me for lunch yesterday."

"What did you have?"

"What's the difference?"

"None whatsoever."

"Egg salad on white toast, a cup of creamy tomato soup."

"Yeah, so get on with the story, I don't need every detail."

"That's the story. At our age you don't need more than one egg salad. It's lunch, then marriage."

"So what are you going to do?"

"What *can* I do? Marry her. An *alter kaker* with diabetes doesn't get offers everyday."

"You have diabetes?"

"No, knock wood...anyway, she'll be a good Rebbetzin, she makes a dynamite *latkeh as* you know, and Bernstein will be my stepson, and probably my dealer if I'm not careful."

"You?"

"You don't turn into a funny-looking old man with a baseball hat calling himself a rabbi with no training whatsoever from *not* doing any drugs. In my hey-day I was the King of the Beatniks, I taught Allen Ginsberg the meaning of Bohemian, I was the prototype for the Maynard G. Krebs character on Dobie Gillis. I picketed outside the theaters the night they opened *Reefer Madness*. I been around, this old Rebbe of yours, I ain't no Johnny-come-lately..."

"This is all true?"

"No, none of this is true. Do I look like a character from Greenwich Villitch? I'm a little Jewish guy. Beatnik, schmeatnik, when all my friends were smoking weed I was home playing Pisha Paysha with my Papa, may he rest in peace."

"Pisha Paysha?"

"It's a rare card game that only Jewish kids played with their fathers in the old country. The *goyim* kids went hunting and fishing, we played Pisha Paysha."

And we went to the Garden State Plaza, I thought. But in those days it wasn't a covered mall, it was wide open to the elements, shopping was an adventure, risky. Now it's all closed in and

protected—the Native Americans would never have shopped in an indoor mall—we're so removed from the earth.

"So if you get married, could you do me a favor? Could you have some of those little hotdogs wrapped in dough at the reception? Which brings me to what I need to talk about..."

"Hors d'oeuvres?"

"Marriage. I'm scared of women. Especially single Jewish women looking for husbands."

"I don't blame you."

"What do you mean?"

"They are absolutely disturbing creatures."

"So why did you tell me to go find one?"

"Because you are an absolutely disturbed creature, and you could use a little disturbing of your disturbance."

"Who made you the Relationships Expert?"

"God. It's a knack. Don't ask me why, but when I arrange marriages, they last forever and the kids get a good home. Why do you and all your cronies need this? Because you all came from good Jewish homes. You all went to synagogue, got Bar Mitzvah'd, ate chicken every Friday night. You saw your fathers wrap *tefillin* in the morning, the rabbi blow the shofar on Rosh Hashanah, you found the *afikomen* every *Pesach*, you waved *groggers* around in *shul* every time they mentioned Haman's name on *Purim*, you kissed the Torah with the tip of your *tzit-tzit*, you sang *Kiddush* in the *sukkah*, played *dreydl and* ate *latkehs*, listened to your relatives speak Yiddish and German, you eat at Carnegie Deli, you watch Woody Allen films a dozen times each, you *look* Jewish."

"So?"

"So trust me."

"But I'm afraid I won't have the time I need for my creative pursuits. I'm afraid I'll be unattracted to her from the git-go, let alone three years down the line. I'm afraid I won't feel that sense of freedom and autonomy to do as I please, to go where I want, come home when I want to, eat what I please, spend money however I choose. What about all that?"

"History."

"HISTORY? HOW CAN YOU SAY THAT TO ME?"

"Because what you're saying is, "What happens to my being single when I'm no longer single?" And the answer is, "You're no longer single."

"Oh." I felt a dullness in my head, as if my soul were surrounded by a haze of grey smoke. I had come to Miltie for help, and I somehow didn't feel helped this time. I felt worse. I needed a new rabbi, maybe. No, I knew that wasn't it. Something about women. About giving up independence. About responsibility and commitment. All the things I hate. Mature adult life. Supporting a family. A job. A house. Kids. The whole catastrophe, as Zorba the Greek said. I felt I was way out of my league. And the one person to whom I turned for help was the very source of the problem. I felt backed into a corner with no escape.

"But Miltie, suppose I don't *want* to get married?"

"Oh no problem—then forget about it."

"Forget about it?"

"I never said a word."

"You never said a word?"

"Not a single word."

"I don't have to get married?"

"Of course you don't have to get married."

Immense sense of relief poured like liquid through my whole body, like fresh air.

"So now you're saying I *shouldn't get* married?"

"No, now I'm still saying you *should* get married."

"I *should* get married?"

"Absolutely."

"But I don't *have* to."

"Of course not."

"Is this an Abbot and Costello routine? I-don't-have-to's on first, I-should is on second?"

"You-should is on first."

"I don't get it."

"He's pitching."

I left, repeating like a mantra, "I don't *have* to, but I *should*." I went home and immediately called Bernstein:

"I double-checked everything with Miltie," I say.

"What'd he say?"

"He said we don't *have* to get married, but we *should*."

"Bingo!" says Bernstein, "We're free men, big guy, let's go out and celebrate. Gather the troops. Carnegie, be there."

An hour later:

"Who had the Zero Mostel?"

"Have no fear, over here," says Moscowitz.

"Listen fellas, I have an idea," says Bernstein. "Let's face the music, *boychiks*, none of us sitting here is a great prize..."

"Speak for yourself," Finkelstein interrupts.

"Okay, with the exception of this asshole who does all my plea-bargaining for me so I'm supposed to feel indebted to him the rest of my life—let me rot in jail next time, do me the favor—none of us is prime husband material, especially for Jewish women. So let's face it, this Miltie character means well, but he doesn't understand who he's dealing with, what we're up against, he doesn't grasp the extent to which we are all, each in our own way, completely demented. So, here's what I suggest: we do a test case. Why should all of us have to *hock* ourselves to death with this woman business? We pick one guy here and send him out ahead, on his own, like a scout, to test the waters, explore the terrain, report back. If we get the all-clear sign, the rest of us advance to the front lines. The question is, which one of us is man enough to do it? How do we choose?"

"We draw straws," says Greenblatt.

"We do it by height, tallest wins," says Goldberg, the midget-shrimp.

"Best of seven," says Weissbaum, going into automatic play-offs mode.

"Best of seven *what*? " I ask. Weissbaum shrugs.

"How about we just arbitrarily select Wilner for no reason at all and let him do it," says Bernstein.

"Great idea!"

"Perfect!"

"It's settled."

Everyone seems agreeable and happy with this choice. I am the lucky winner. By default, by natural selection, by survival of the fittest, my job is to get married.

"Now," Bernstein says, "the jewel within the gem of the diamond core within the essence of the center of the plan...where does Wilner find Ms. Right? In the personals? Out of the question. Too random. Too much left to fate and external circumstances. No, we appoint a search committee that compiles the demographics, interviews prospects, arranges the marriage. Wilner takes what we give him, no questions asked, the way they did it in the old country. Who knows what's best for him? Certainly not him! Who knows him better than his own mother? Clearly, gentlemen, we do...so who wants to serve on the search committee?"

"Is it a salaried position?" asks Finkelstein.

"Will there be refreshments at the meetings?" asks Moscowitz.

"We should have a first round draft choice and move on from there," says Weissbaum, "and no free agents, nobody on waivers."

"How do we screen out the fat ones?" Greenblatt inquires.

"So who's in?"

"I am," says Breshman, Finkelstein, Weissbaum, Greenblatt, Bernstein, Moscowitz and Goldberg. And Marvin.

"We need a woman for balance," notes Breshman.

"I'll call Mrs. Bernstein," says Bernstein, and gets up to go to the pay phone.

"Of course I'm on the committee," says Mrs. Bernstein, on the phone, "What am I, chopped liver? I'm the *chairman* of the committee. I'm the president. You don't make a move without consulting me. I have veto power. No woman goes near Norbert unless she gets past me first. Do I want to be on the committee...what kind of question is that? You should be asking instead, 'Mrs. Bernstein, is it all right with you if *we* can be on the committee with *you*, your Royal Highness, oh Queen of Sheba. *That's* what you should be asking. Now all of you

stop stuffing your faces like there are no children starving in Africa and get your *tuchi*—(her plural of *tuchus*)—over here for a meeting."

"What'd she say?" we ask, when Bernstein returns to the table.

"She said yes," he replies.

"Pass the Carl Reiner," says Goldberg.

"The Danny Kaye gave me heartburn," says Greenblatt.

"A bunch of comedians," mutters Marvin.

We pay the bill and hit the streets, a *minyan* in search of a generic wife. We take the hearse over to Ethel's. I decided that white was too tame a color for the hearse, so I had invited the gang over for a spray-painting party earlier in the week. We each had a different color and simultaneously sprayed until it had that late-60s-day-glo-psychedelic-paisley-summer-of-love-graffiti-Merry-Pranksters look.

"When do we inaugurate this thing?" Weissbaum asks.

"We need to find a dead person," I say. "Everybody keep your eyes peeled."

All of us clamber into the Hippie Hearse. We make Moscowitz lie in the empty coffin.

"You may as well get used to it, Moscowitz."

"You're not the healthiest guy in the world."

"Kiss your ass good-bye, buddy."

"Your life sucks anyway."

"Yeah, I suppose you're right," Moscowitz says sheepishly, and climbs into the casket. We drive around Washington Heights looking for a dead person. We don't see *any*.

"OVER THERE" exclaims Greenblatt. "The guy next to that bench."

"He's *alive*, Greenblatt," I say, realizing he doesn't quite grasp the concept. "By dead, we mean *no longer alive*."

"Maybe my mother can give us some leads," Bernstein says, and we head down the Harlem River Drive towards the home of Ethel Bernstein, the future Empress of Matzah Ball, the future Rebbetzin Gelberman.

Bernstein knocks.

"Who is it? What do you want? Go away."

"It's Bernstein."

"Bernstein? Which Bernstein?"

"Me your son Bernstein."

"BERNSTEIN" she proclaims, and opens the door. "Why didn't you say it was you, come in, come in. You know the old saying, '*Zolst farlirn ale tsyner akhuts eynem un der zol din veyton.*' "

"Thanks Mama."

"What'd she say?" we ask him, and he translates:

"You should lose all your teeth except one, and that one should ache."

"So," she continues, "you brought all your good-for-nothing *meshugeh* friends with you? My house is a soup kitchen for big Jewish babies? Come in everybody, come in."

One by one we file past Ethel like Sneezy, Doc, Grumpy and the rest. Ethel has something to say to each of us:

To Finkelstein: "The stationery maven with the Jesus fixation. Maybe you should design a crucifix-ballpoint pen, integrate your fragmented personality for once. How's your lovely wife? I never liked her. I never liked *you* too much either—come in, *tattala*."

To Breshman: "When you die and they try to reincarnate you, tell them 'I did that already.' How are you *bubbela*, you're wasting your life."

To me: "You're killing your mother. Get a job."

To Greenblatt: "The borderline psycho-comedian; they should lock you up."

To Weissbaum: "Mr. VCR—you think you can fast forward through life? You think you can press pause for even a second? Eject! Eject!"

To Moscowitz: "I heard you were dead, may you rest in peace... you know what everybody says, '*Er zol vaskn vi a tsibele mit dem kop in drerd.*'"

We look to Bernstein for the translation:

"He should grow like an onion with its head in the ground."

And last, she greets Goldberg: "Philip, *mein shaineh kind,*

how are you?" Phil is the only one to escape her tongue, because throughout his life, Phil was good with parents. Even as kids, he was our front man. He did the talking. I used to make him eat dinner at my house on big family occasions just so someone would talk at the table. He would go to great lengths to please parents, to identify:

"Norbert is so different from his father," my mother once said to him.

"Yes," Phil replied, "well, his generation was quite different in many ways from your husband's and my generation." Phil Goldberg, the brown-noser with parents, or, as Ethel often put it,

"Philip likes to blow sugar up my behind; don't think I don't know."

We all feel at home with Ethel. By the time she closes the door and joins us in the living room, our shoes are off; Weissbaum has helped himself to a turkey sandwich with lettuce, mayo and mustard, and has the camcorder set up on a tripod; Greenblatt is sprawled out on the floor; Moscowitz is in the shower; Bernstein is smoking a joint. Finkelstein is glancing through Ethel's cabinet drawers. Goldberg, Breshman and I just sit there, like dummies.

"Don't stand on ceremony with me boys," Ethel says, "make yourselves at home. Nobody's a stranger here. Now, let's get down to business, what's the *gantse megila*?"

"We need a woman for Wilner, Mrs. Bernstein," Bernstein says.

"But we also need a dead person," I interject, "if you happen to know anybody..."

"How about a dead woman?" Ethel says, "kill two birds with one stone."

"You have a dead woman?" Breshman asks.

"Not quite, but you know the old saying, '*Abi gezunt, dos lebn ker men zikh ale mol nemen*'...'As long as you're healthy you can always kill yourself.' And the way Mrs. Friedman in 4D looks lately, with her high blood pressure and retaining water and the arthritis and the diabetes...what isn't wrong with her? I give her two months, tops."

"Fifty bucks says she makes it through August," Bernstein says.

"You're on, Bernstein," says Mrs. Bernstein. "Weissbaum, you're eating me out of house and home, doesn't that Sally cook?"

"Why is it always 'that' Sally...why not just 'Sally'?" asks Weissbaum.

"That Sally is starving him to death," Ethel says to the rest of us, "the *goyim* eat like birds. Now, you want a woman, I'll get you a woman, I know people, I wasn't born yesterday. Mrs. Silverman in 5E has a single daughter who does nothing but *potchkey* around all day. She's nothing to look at, a little *zaftig*, but who do you think you are? The Clark Gable of the century? Burt Reynolds maybe? You're Fyvesh Finkel, and you'll take who I give you. What, you can afford to be choosy? Forget about it. Someone get that Moscowitz character out of my shower, he thinks water grows on trees?"

"MOSCOWITZ, GET OUT OF THE SHOWER!" several of us yell in unison. A few minutes later Moscowitz joins us, stark naked.

"This I have to look at?" Ethel says. "But why not? You think I never saw a pecker waving in the breeze before? Believe me, the things I've seen...someone make him get dressed, he's making Weissbaum uncomfortable."

"I'm not uncomfortable, and I'm not gay," Weissbaum protests.

"He's in denial," Greenblatt says.

"Latent," says Finkelstein, searching under the couch for something.

"Listen fellas," I say, "Are you all sure that I'm the man for this job? I mean, this Silverman girl is up for grabs, it's truly anyone's ballgame."

Dead silence. You could hear a pin drop. Okay, I admit it, my friends and I weren't really ready to make a commitment. We weren't quite ready to settle down. What's the big rush? Some of us hadn't even hit 40 yet. The bottom line? We were terrified of women.

"I hate that feeling of contraction I get when I'm in a relationship," Greenblatt says to Ethel, apologetically. "My chronic muscular armoring gets too intense."

"I don't breathe right. I start thinking I'm supposed to be loving," I say.

"Women always try to make you communciate. I hate communicating," Greenblatt says.

"I don't like to be touched," says Moscowitz, dressed.

"Too time consuming," says Breshman.

"Why not give the girl to Bernstein," I try, feeling trapped.

"Because Bernstein is a celibate ascetic Hindu drug fiend and my only son. Okay, not celibate. Okay, not ascetic. Okay, not really Hindu. But a drug fiend, and my only son. Okay, not my only son, but a drug fiend. You think I want the Silvermans in 5E to know all my business? I have my hands full without a *shlumpy*-looking daughter-in-law poking her nose in here all the time."

"*Shlumpy?*" I ask, timidly, feeling ill. Weissbaum zooms in for a close-up.

"Did I promise you Natassia Kinski? Suddenly you're Mr. Handsome? I'll give you the number."

I take the number. Finkelstein finds what he was after, rummaging through Ethel's sock drawer. He does a few lines with Mrs. B. and we parade back out of her apartment and down to the hearse.

"Every one of you is no good," she calls out as we're leaving, and then mumbling to herself "they're good kids," she shuts the door.

Back in the hearse, we make Moscowitz lie in the coffin. We drop Finkelstein off at his office and the rest of us accompany Greenblatt to a therapy session with Myron Spotnick.

CHAPTER EIGHTEEN

Rachel

I start rehearsing for my blind date with the Silverman girl:

"What do you *do*?" I imagine her asking, my most feared first-date question.

"What do I do...funny you should ask, I was just doing something today—strictly a coincidence I'm sure—just kidding...well, let's see, I find I need to spend a certain portion of each day handling the basics—bathing, eating, dressing, private bathroom matters, plus sleep and laundry and dishes, and a certain amount of spontaneous conversation with friends and neighbors who phone or drop by, and I try to get some daily exercise, and preparing my nutritional spirulina psyllium husk shake is time consuming because it's not such a quick job to clean a blender, and yes I'm 37 years old now and I can't exactly say that I have found exactly what I might perhaps do with myself in this world to, uh, uh, well, I guess *work* is the word I must be looking for, in terms of earning a living, or certainly the idea of supporting a family would be a bit difficult for me at this time although I actually, it turns out, have fairly well-to-do parents who have set me up for a sizable inheritance at some point, may they live to be 120, but in the meantime, well I have this part-time job, well it's about four hours a week, and..."

Panic. This will never do. I have reached the age of 37 and I completely forgot to get a life. Who would want me? Certainly no Jewish princess with eyes for Saks, Lord & Taylor.

"Well, I'm not exactly a materialist consumer, I like to shop at thrift stores on the general principle that if I spend four dollars on a used pair of jeans instead of forty, somehow someone somewhere will be a little better off. I know the logic is a bit abstract, but when I see the emaciated children on TV I just can't bring myself to shop in peace, and I do so love shopping, that sense of exchanging currency for goods, of bringing something home that I didn't have before and for a short while thinking that the mere *having* of something or other will make some sort of qualitative difference to my bottom-line existential experience of being human on this planet at this time, in these troubled times, I should say, or perhaps these end times, it seems to me, so you see, I really don't think we should go out if you're looking for a dentist kind of guy who will furnish your house in Long Island, because basically I uh, well, I guess you'd have to classify me as living sort of on the fringe of things. Did I say lunatic fringe? Well, no, that would really be a misnomer, for to live on the fringe of this world's lunacy, in my view, is to be part of the sane fringe, if anything..."

Disqualified. Celibate for life. My personal ad? "SJM—Undesirable." Or, "SJM, 37: You wouldn't want to know from me." Or, "SJM: HELP ME! LOVE ME! WANT ME! (But don't *hock* me to death.)"

"Jerry, you gotta help me." I went over Greenblatt's, desperate. "Let's role-play the thing—you be the Silverman girl."

"No problem."

"Okay, I just picked you up, we're in the elevator of your apartment building. She's in 5E—that gives us five floors worth of conversation—ready, go!"

"So tell me, Norbert, what's your line of work and how much money do you make?"

"Jerry, we're not even down to the fourth floor yet, give me a break."

"You're almost forty years old and your parents still support you?"

"Jerry, please, a little mercy, we're not even on three."

"What kind of man are you?"

"Jer," I'm sobbing, "the second floor for God's sake. Don't do this to me."

"I had a lovely time, thank you very much, watch your step getting out...WORTHLESS FAILURE!"

I tumble in a heap on the ground floor, wasted.

"Was that helpful?" Greenblatt asks.

"Very helpful. Have I ever told you that I think you were a Sonderkommando in a previous life?"

"That probably explains my recurring sexual fantasy of being tied up and whipped by Ilsa of Buchenwald."

"Jerry, in all honesty, be serious for a minute, do you think there's any chance whatever that any woman anywhere would ever want to be with either of us?"

"Absolutely not."

"No, but seriously..."

"Not even a remote possibility."

"Jer, I mean it..."

"I have no self..."—it suddenly occurred to me that I had turned to the wrong person for support—"and my whole life is a sham."

"Yeah, yeah, I'll see you later Jerry, feel better."

"There's a black hole in the center of my being, and I'll never fill it up."

"Later."

"I live in a constant state of pure dread."

I got out of there. But not unscathed. I was scathed. With dread. Greenblatt's dread was my dread. His black hole my black hole. No self, no self. We should go to Spotnick's together. Double trouble. Maybe he'd give us a joint ten-minute session. I desperately needed cheering up. I walked over to my favorite topless bar in Chelsea, had a shot of whiskey and stared at three

naked women dancing on the platform. Who *were* these girls? Did they have parents? Childhoods? Or did they just spontaneously appear in lewd positions, fully grown? Is this what they wanted to be when they grew up? Is this where *I wanted* to be when I grew up? Watching them?

Something felt really wrong. My soul itself was in exile. I was a walking Diaspora, urgently yearning to return again to the Holy Land. I felt "*tefillitic,*" the Jewish disease of the soul stemming from the failure to put on *tefillin* for too long. Worse than my failure to floss for so many years. Everything was catching up to me. I craved Sabbath. Family. Challah and my mother's Friday night chicken. Manischewitz. My great-great-grandfather Hirsch Kahn, with his long grey beard and his ancestral *davening*, the quiet walks on Saturday afternoon with no money in his pockets, the friendly German neighbors in a world before Nazis:

"Good afternoon Hirsch Kahn, going for a walk?"

"Yah, yah, good *Shabbes*, good *Shabbes*, beautiful day, no?"

"Yah, Hirsch Kahn, a beautiful day for a walk."

'Dem were da days,' I think to myself. Now my Sabbath is spent alone in New York City, in Ray's Topless Bar.

"Can I get you something else?" asks the barmaid, wearing a black leather halter-top and mini-skirt, black heels.

"You wouldn't have Manischewitz blackberry wine, would you?"

"Sorry."

"Concord grape? Mogen David?"

"How about a red wine with a little *shpritz*? It'll calm you down, you look *shpilkehs.*"

My mind stops. I am pulled from way back, from my German reverie of a century ago. I awaken. Startled from sleep.

"You know from *shpilkehs*?" I ask, incredulous, unable to believe my ears. Hearing the Yiddish word, in that place, is like music, like a soothing balm, a spiritual whisper in response to my deepest need.

"I'm from Brooklyn, I shouldn't know from *shpilkehs*?"

In spite of myself, I begin to weep.

"Oh boy, you *are shpilkehs*," she says, "Here, drink this."

I take the glass, and hold it before me, in the air, and intone the familiar chant:

"*Baruch atah Adonoi, elohenu melech haolam, borai p'ree ha gawfen.*"

"*Aw-mane*," she says, the Hebrew pronunciation of Amen, rhymes with chow mein. "Come on, let's get out of here." She grabs a purse and we're heading out the door.

"Hey Sweets, where you goin'?" some guy calls out.

"I'm quitting!"

"You can't quit on me today—Saturday's our busiest day."

"I don't work on the Sabbath. It is written."

And we're out the door. In New York City. Saturday. A sunny, fall afternoon. A beautiful day for a walk.

And her name was Rachel. And believe it or not, she was not Jewish.

***

See her there, at recess, little Rachel Lindstrom in pigtails, opening her lunchbox, the yellow one with Olive Oyl in the slinky bikini on it, motioning suggestively to Bluto, his eyes popping out of his head, staring at Olive's bare midriff. The sense of power Olive had over that big, bearded brute. Rachel wishes she could wield such a spell over bratty Jimmy Koogan, sick of his stupid tricks: the worms in her desk, the gum in her hair. The way he pretends to drop his pencil right by her chair just to have an excuse to look up her dress. Next time I'm gonna step right on his stupid hand, she tells her Mom, who proceeds to baffle her with a piece of information: "It just means he likes you, Rach; that's how boys show it."

After lights out, she quietly sneaks out of bed with her flashlight and stands before the full-length mirror and stares at herself, trying to affect Olive Oyl's pose, that sense of confident assurance. She tries jutting her hips out and puts her tongue between her lips like the women

in the underwear ads. She motions with her finger and imagines Jimmy Koogan's eyes popping out of his head.

And see her there—even then—in the cloakroom, taking her pullover sweater up and over her head, knowing full well from practicing at home that the swift motion will treat Jimmy and the others to a lightning flash of her bare stomach and the smallest glimpse of the bottoms of her newly budding, spherical breasts. She liked putting on the little show, and felt a tingling sensation between her legs when the sweater was off and her eyes met the leering stares of Koogan and his cronies. They liked her, her mother said, and armed with that knowledge, she felt as powerful as Olive Oyl ready to take on Bluto. And she understood those secret pictures her brother stashed under his mattress. At 12, she felt ready to grow up and "face a world of men," like the song from the Sound of Music said.

And face a world of men she did. Little Rachel Lindstrom, the top student in her Sunday School class who aced her confirmation and won the hearts of the congregation with her pulpit eloquence, her speech about "young Catholic women coming of age in this society," the importance of "creating a good Christian home for children," and finally, the big finish: "Our future as missionaries of the Good Word of our Lord Jesus."

But she had a double life, even then; even then, she was of two minds. There was light, the priest had said in her confirmation preparatory class, and there was darkness; and a good Catholic knows the difference and chooses the light. There was the evil inclinations of the heart—the Devil—and the good, pure motivations of inner sanctity and holiness, and a good Christian girl struggles her whole life to fight against the evil voice, hoping to be ruled by the desire to serve the Lord with purity and cleanliness of heart.

Rachel Lindstrom was divided, even then. Her "good self" would have her cheerfully kiss her parents goodnight, get into her favorite flannel 'jamies, and crawl into her soft bed with the down comforter and cozy quilt. Her pure self had her say her prayers every night: "Dear God, bless Mommy and Daddy, bless me, Rachel, and Brad, bless Grandma and Grandpa, bless all my aunts and uncles, my cousins

and teachers, friends and acquaintances, and P.S., don't forget to bless Scrappy, Amen." Scrappy was her favorite stuffed dog who slept right next to her every night, sharing the pillow, but who always liked to jump out of bed in the middle of the night to sleep on the floor, because that's where Rachel found him every morning, and she would scold him accordingly. "You silly dog, Scrappy, how come you never spend the whole night with me? Isn't the bed more comfortable than that hard old floor?"

But then once the lights were out, once all the goodnight kisses were over, the prayers said, Rachel's evil impulse would enter her room and take her over, and she felt powerless to resist. First there were the sessions in front of the mirror, the poses. Then it started touching her....there. The evil inclination made her get all wet and gooey, and it felt so delicious she couldn't stop. And sometimes, just as she was about to explode, the bad self inside her would make her think of Jimmy Koogan and all those other boys, watching her take off her sweater in the cloakroom. She imagined they were all in her room with her, seeing her standing there, naked in front of the mirror, rubbing herself in her private place.

And when it was over, she would get back in her good ol' soft 'jamies, hop back into bed and say to her favorite stuffed friend, "Now you must promise never to tell a living soul about this, Scrappy, okay? Now let's both forget all about it, and from now on the Devil is never going to bother us again, right Scrappy? Right? Sometimes she would cry a little, and knew that God would hear her tears and protect her.

And then one night, after one of her secret sessions, she noticed her hand was covered with blood! Her heart started beating a mile a minute. God was punishing her, she knew, with one of the ten plagues, just like the Egyptians in that movie, The Ten Commandments. She was terrified she'd find frogs in her bed, locusts. Nothing could calm her down, not even Scrappy. She thought she saw Koogan and his men pointing and laughing, Koogan himself dressed like the Pharaoh. Screaming, she ran out of her room, naked, into her parents' bedroom.

Who were making love. Screaming louder, she ran out of their room and practically knocked over Brad, who had gotten up to see

what all the commotion was about. He hadn't seen his kid sister naked since they used to bathe together as children; he promptly got an erection that popped out of his pajamas, as if to attack her. Screaming louder still, Rachel collapsed in a shuddering heap in the hallway, trying to cover herself with her arms, curled into a ball and sobbing.

That was the night Rachel Lindstrom learned the facts of life. Her mother stayed up with her for hours, drawing her diagrams of the fallopian tubes, talked about ovums and ovaries and the menstrual cycle. Tampons and sanitary napkins. Vaginal sprays and douches. About boys and penises, sperm and babies. And her mother told her it was all normal, *and that her body and its sexuality was* beautiful.

So convincing was her mother that Rachel soon forgot all about the evil impulse. Now she was a woman, a normal young woman, and as she grew into her teen years, she became more and more normal. No longer satisfied with providing the boys mere teasing glimpses of her beautiful body, she began creating even more exciting opportunities for them to look at her, to see her in all her normal, beautiful nakedness. In the girl's locker room, she discovered the slatted ventilator where the boys would peer in, thinking nobody knew. But Rachel knew, and nothing pleased her more than to stand with her back to the vent, and slowly remove her field hockey shirt and gym shorts, giving the spies a full view of her beautiful behind and then turning around to offer only a split second's eyeful of her growing, round pubescent breasts before dashing out of sight into the shower.

And then the games escalated. There were the Friday night dances, where the older, high school boys asked you to go "for a walk," and they took you back behind the custodian's shed and put their hands inside your blouse! And under the elastic waistband of your skirt! And Rachel knew it was all normal, even when, one night, not one, but three boys asked her to go for a walk, and right there, not four feet from her homeroom window, they all watched her take off her clothes, and then taught her how to make them feel good with her mouth. That night, she felt even more powerful than Olive Oyl and Marilyn Monroe put together! She now knew what it meant to be a woman, and she realized she was good at it.

Then one day in her junior year she walked into the girl's locker room and saw scribbled in one of the stalls, "Rachel Lindstrom is a whore." She just stopped and stared, and gazed numbly at the words. Something didn't compute. Something didn't feel beautiful and normal, all of a sudden. Suddenly she felt ashamed, and suddenly she remembered a figure from her distant past: the evil inclination. In a flash she saw her entire sexual history as a very bad mistake, a severe error in judgment, a sin. She felt defiled and ruined beyond repair. She had been seduced by the Devil and never even knew it, all those years. What her mother had promised her was beautiful and normal had turned out to be ugly and disgusting. She was ugly and disgusting, and to punish herself, she stopped eating.

And went off to Barnard College, a skinny, prudish, liberal arts major, gradually starving herself to death. Nobody knew what had happened to her—she was virtually unrecognizable, physically, and her bubbly outgoing personality had radically altered as well: She was a sullen, morose person with few friends and little enthusiasm for college life. She attended her classes, did her homework in the library, and slept in her dormitory room, all without interacting with a soul. For breakfast she picked at a slice of toast; she skipped lunch; for dinner, she would play with lettuce, have a spoonful of rice.

Only her sociology professor—Dr. Elizabeth Bentley—seemed to notice. "It's okay to call me Liz," she told Rachel after class one day, having asked her to remain behind after dismissing the rest of the young women. "Your paper was very disturbing, and brilliant...can I buy you lunch?" They went to a diner on 106th and Broadway, and Rachel ordered water and an English muffin, which she didn't eat. Liz Bentley noticed. Liz Bentley had done her doctoral dissertation on anorexia nervosa.

And Liz Bentley was a lesbian. She took Rachel under her wing. Over time, Rachel began to trust her. After awhile, Rachel began to laugh again. Eventually, they made love, and Rachel cried in her arms; soon after, she began eating. For her final undergraduate thesis, Liz suggested Rachel do a sociological study of the women who dance in topless bars. It would be, she thought, a healing for Rachel, given her sexual history.

It was. She befriended "Destiny" and "Violet" and "Desiree." Most of them were graduate psych students. Some were less educated, often single mothers, usually trying to support a kid. A few were drug addicts and hookers. The men who came to Ray's all looked like Jimmy Koogan to Rachel, and they mostly seemed very lonely and unhappy to her. But many of them were professional people, and just seemed to enjoy looking at naked women, and apparently felt no shame about it. They were very respectful of Rachel, and she often received offers to fly off with them to Barbados, or Acapulco. She never said yes to these offers, but as time wore on, she did begin to feel, yes, both beautiful and normal again. She received an A from Liz Bentley, graduated with honors from Barnard, and stayed on as a hostess at Ray's. Her relationship with Liz ended amiably when she realized that she was starting to be interested in men again.

***

It was demographics at first sight. Rachel was 28, never married, sexy and beautiful with long, dark raven hair, and had a body that passed the screen test to work behind the bar at Ray's. (Okay, she wasn't perfect: I like slightly rounder breasts, generally speaking; I'm generally not so crazy about those little pointy kind that are built according to the principles of a suspension bridge. I need soft and round, not too droopy. Certainly hairless. I once heard a female comic describe another woman as having "nipples like stacks of dimes." I'm not sure what she meant, but that's probably out, too. Is it my fault I learned my taste for women through the eyes of a youth-fixated, Hefnerized American culture, a land of Pepsi girls popping out of their bikinis playing volleyball, your Miss Julys and the "Girls Of The Ivy League"? My airbrushed taste for glossy tits is a disease I *caught*, not one I chose. What eighteen year-old can walk down 42nd Street, past "Topless Here" and "All Nude" there and look the other way? And then we grow up wondering from which hospital, which emergency clinic, they managed to find all those *Hot Vixen Nurses* advertised on the marquees, those *Lust-Maidens in Heat.*

Young boys can't help but do the arithmetic: "In this adult bookstore alone there must be thousands of photos and videos of naked women engaged in sordid sex acts—so they've got to be out there, somewhere. Just going by the percentages, some of these ordinary-looking women I pass on the streets of New York every-day have got to be either lust-maidens in heat or *Wet School Girls*. So Rachel's breasts aren't perfect, so what? I'm not some shallow guy who would rule someone out for something so superficial. Not me. Surely the striking radiance of Rachel's soul outshines any initial physical hesitation I may harbor in a very private and distant cranny of my awareness, a barely discernible voice somewhere deep within, stating quite matter-of-factly, the first time I see Rachel's bare breasts: too small, too pointy.)

Did she ever dance on the counter at Ray's? Once, to try it. And? She kept imagining her parents and grandparents kneeling at the bar as if in a pew, holding hymnals, singing to Jesus, and she was dancing where the altar and cross would ordinarily be. And? She couldn't get into it. She got dressed. She works the bar. Don't these other girls have parents? Yes but none of them come in here to pray. They go to churches. She was funny. She made me laugh.

(Okay, not funny the way Greenblatt's sister is funny. Not Jewish funny. I had to explain things I never had to explain to my Jewish cronies. Like when I was joking. Me: "I'm on a physical cleansing program; it's a dairy-only fast: lots of cheese, liquefied in the blender with butter and milk." Rachel: "Are you serious?" Me: "No." This oft-repeated "Really?"/"Only kidding" exchange was vaguely disconcerting to me, but for humor I have Greenblatt, I got Weissbaum, Goldberg, funny guys everywhere I turn, I could be a Borscht Belt booking agent. So what, I need my wife to be a comedienne, too? I need to marry Phyllis Diller, Joan Rivers? Sure I love Lucy, but who needs a slapstick spouse? Pratfalls in the bedroom are not a priority. Burns and Allen are not my romantic role models, I'm not about to Stiller-and-Meara myself out of this relationship. Instead, I fall in love. Sort of. At least to my way of thinking, falling in love for me anything more

enthusiastic than "I never want to see this person again as long as I live.")

"Can I tell you a story?" I ask her one day, perhaps the third or fourth time we have gotten together.

"Can you tell me a story?" Meaning, what else do I ever do?

"My friend Phil and I..."

"Is that Weissberg or Lipstein?" She was starting to familiarize herself with the players, still trying to keep all the characters straight.

"Goldberg; and it's Weiss*baum* and Lip*schitz.*" Breaking in a new woman is tough; there are a *lot* of stories to get through, a lot of basic training. But it has to be done; love me, love the *minyan.* Because I *am* the *minyan.* I do not exist in isolation from my community. I am merely a small figure in a larger social structure. Without knowing and understanding Bernstein, Weissbaum, Moscowitz and the rest, there would be no knowing or understanding me. Our collective stories make the man, the men. We are an interdependent species, created and configured as characters in our ongoing group *shtick.* And Rachel was starting to get it. Unwittingly, she had fallen in love with ten men, nine of whom she hadn't met in person, but was beginning to know intimately through their legendary stories. One of them, of course, was dead.

"So Goldberg and me are working at this Jewish resort in the Adirondacks; he's the waiter, I'm the busboy. We're working like dogs, sweating buckets in the non-air-conditioned dining room, hundred degree heat, a ton of people, obsessed with their food, ordering us around. There's barely time to breathe. I'm running all over, bringing out side orders, beverages, and trying to clear the tables. You gotta clear each course—the soup, the melon, the fruit cups, the salad, the gefilte fish, the main dish, you never saw so many courses. I just grab up the dirty dishes and pile them on a tray I keep stationed in my area.

"In the middle of all this chaotic, fast-paced, non-stop work in the heat of July, one of the other busboys—Barry Lembeck—finds

the time to sidle up to me; taps me on the shoulder, and with a conspiratorial twinkle in his eye, he says,

"Hey Norbert, notice anything *strange* about your *fruit cups*?"

Incredulous, I glance over at my tray of dirty dishes, and there are all my empty fruit cups, arranged to form a big "N" for Norbert. My fruit cups look like a marching band at half-time, standing in formation."

"And?"

"And what?"

"And so?"

"And so what?"

"And so what happened?"

"That's it. That is what happened. It was a funny moment. You had to be there. But you need to know this stuff. It's important, trust me."

"I trust you implicitly."

"That's a mistake...listen, if I really enter this relationship fully, make a co...co...commitment, does that mean I'll never sleep with another woman again?"

"Yes."

"Don't you find that a bit troubling?"

"No, what's troubling is that I won't ever sleep with another man again."

"Why should that bother you? I thought women were different, why wouldn't I be enough for you?"

"Why wouldn't *I* be enough for *you*?"

"Because a man needs variety, the cheap thrill of someone new, the ego strokes of another woman. We're basically very immature and insecure. Women aren't like that. You know who you are and who you love and you're faithful and loyal and understanding of our childish needs and our inability, in good conscience, to be faithful."

"Oh that's right. Okay, I will be faithful to you until the day we die, and you can sleep with as many women as you like."

"Wouldn't it be great if there was a planet where the women were really like that? You Earth Women are much too demanding."

In a funny way, I realized that although I had been celibate since Greenblatt's sister, I had technically been free, during those years, to sleep with as many women as I wanted to, and I slept with none. But my motivation for celibacy, far from a religious one, could more aptly be described as, "keeping all the possibilities of lust open." Now that I finally had a lover, the idea of one woman felt like a limitation of my freedom. Somehow, *none* had felt like more than one. After sleeping with Rachel the first time, I started to feel trapped, stuck with having sex with the same old woman-with-the-small-breasts-who-doesn't-get-my-jokes every night instead of being stuck home, alone, virtually celibate for years, but free as a bird to *consider* sleeping with anyone I wanted. I explained all this to Phil, who responded:

"You're probably safe in thinking of this as a frightening, pathological, mental illness."

"So you think I should keep seeing Rachel?"

"Let me ask you a question: What are you doing the next 40 years?"

So in spite of everything, I asked Rachel to marry me. Impulsively, it could be said. And in spite of a now formidable arsenal of inner voices screaming at me—"*Stop! Are you crazy? Marriage? Have you been paying attention? She may not be the one! Repeat: She may not be the one. All systems on alert. Do not rush into anything! These are orders. You are out of your mind. Do not do it. Do not open your mouth. Say nothing. Mums the word.*"

"Rachel?" ("*Stop!* ")

"Yes?"

"Can I babble to you about something for a little awhile." ("*No! No Babble! Pointy! Pointy!* ")

"No."

"No?"

"People usually cut themselves off when they realize they are babbling."

"Right."

Okay, so I don't get to babble my proposal. ("*Correction: You don't get to propose at all. Abort mission. Abort mission.*")

"Rach?

"Yes?"

"I have this idea, basically, about you and me, the idea of perhaps, like the two of us, both of us together, maybe being with each other, I mean, in the sense of two people, like a man and a woman, for example, actually choosing to spend their, uh, well, you know, in some way or other, in a manner of speaking, their lives pretty much in a similar time-space locus, you know what I mean? I'm not sure I'm being clear. I'm trying to say, maybe you, along with me, just the two of us, could agree to, how should I put it, hook up..."

"Are you asking me to go steady?"

"Yes, in a way I am. I am asking you to go steady...with *me*, of course, I think I neglected to mention that part, because that's a big part of this, an important part, that it be with me, and not just some fly-by-night floozy off the street. But I mean go steady in a bigger sense, like for a very long time, like basically for a real long time..."

"Til death do us part?"

"Exactly! You got it."

"So you're asking me to marry you...that was a proposal."

"Bingo."

"Just like that."

"Yes."

"Well okay then."

"Okay what?"

"Okay I'll marry you."

"That's it? That's how you accept a proposal? 'Okay I'll marry you.' Just like that?"

"Yes."

"Well all right then."

"Okay."

"Okay. I gotta tell you, though, I think you're making a huge mistake."

(*"You're making a huge mistake! Get out now! Say you were just kidding!"*)

"Listen, it's important to me that we have a Jewish household. I'm not demanding that you convert, but I need to raise the kids Jewish." (*"You don't need her to convert? You're telling her you want Jewish kids but you don't need her to convert? Hello?"*)

Her response was actually strangely comforting: "What *is* Judaism, exactly?"

"You say *shpilkehs* to me in a bar and you don't know what Judaism is?"

"*Shpilkehs* is Brooklyn, not Jewish."

"It's Jewish, believe me."

"Maybe, but nobody ever told us we were speaking Jewish... now I feel really *ferblungered.*"

I loved it, a Yiddish-speaking Catholic girl: It was the best of both worlds, like mixing milk and meat, the forbidden with the familiar.

"All we knew was that the Jews were those weird boys with the curly sideburns and the long black coats in the dead of summer. Whenever I asked my mother about them, she would just wave her hand at me and say, 'Shhh. Those are the Jews,' like we better not talk about them out loud. What did I know?"

"Not much, apparently."

"Do you still want to marry me in the *mitn derinen?*"

"Yes, you little *meshugeneh shikseh.*"

"Wait 'til you meet the *mishpocheh.*"

"No, wait 'til you meet *my mishpocheh*...you have no idea what you're getting into. Your parents aren't Nazis by any chance, are they? Because that would be difficult for my family."

"Are you serious?"

"Kidding."

"Oh."

"Is there anything I should know about you before we get married?" I ask, secretly looking for an out, an escape clause, some loophole in marital law that declares all proposals "null and void if aforementioned party withholds certain information, i.e., e.g., is dying of a terminal disease and has six months to live, or the like."

And my question elicits a response that so knocks me out even the voice of small-tits-and-other-considerations is temporarily silenced, so staggering is her reply:

"You don't know *bupkis* about me, babe." The combination of "*bupkis*" and "babe" in the same breath was, I believe, without precedent, and it gave me goose bumps, which I interpreted to be love.

***

My fantasy: Rachel converts and we get married, there is a joyous Jewish-style wedding with a few Gentile touches thrown in to appease the people from the pagan nations—the Lindstroms, basically—and a New Age shamanic multi-ethnic ecumenical religious overview to accommodate the bizarre assortment of spiritual no-goodniks such a gathering was bound to attract. In my mind's eye I see my mother cry as I dance a *hora* with my father and they even lift the bride and groom up on chairs like in the Chassidic weddings of the old country. Not the suburban wedding scene; something deeper than the decision to go with the Cornish hen over the prime ribs. A true wedding feast, like in *Fiddler on the Roof,* wild hearts dancing and laughing and joyous singing—in other words, a happy ending. Everybody happy, whole, healed and alive. And the world heals itself enough to let the Wilner newlyweds live happily ever after. To have children. To grow old. To die peacefully. I just want God to put off the End Times long enough for me to do my life, then let the whole thing crumble.

The Jewish way, Miltie said the day we met, is a way of joy. The legendary Reb Nachman of Somethingslov (Ok, Breslov) said that "G-d hates depression." (Why the dash? Because we were taught in Hebrew School that if we were to actually write the Holy Name on the paper, without the dash, it would make the paper sacred, and we'd kind of be stuck with it for life as ritual object. Can't throw that name around casually. The dash says, "This is serious, this word you're writing, and what it's supposed to stand for. So don't fuck around.")

So if G-d hates depression, I'm in big trouble. Better get happy quick before it's too late. Who knows how much longer I have to be happy. Today might be my last shot at it: a massive heart attack from too much Swiss cheese, maxed out on the quota. Everybody they send here gets rationed 650 8oz. packages of Kraft Swiss, go one slice over and they give you the heart attack. It's in the by-laws. I introduce Rachel to the troops:

"Rachel this is Bernstein, Bernstein this is Rachel."

"Rachel this is Breshman, Breshman this is Rachel."

"Rachel this is etcetera, etcetera this is Rachel."

I can tell that Bernstein's looking at her as if, when we do get married, he's gonna be very gentlemanly and say, "May I kiss the bride?" and then fiercely make-out with her in a hidden hallway and basically ruin everybody's life. That kind of look. The old saying: Never trust a drug dealer with your bride. On the other hand, I totally trust Bernstein to be exactly the way he is, and so in that sense, I can absolutely count on him never to betray me. He will always behave exactly like Bernstein, the low-life son-of-a-b. I spit on you for stealing my wife. Wait a minute, hold on. In honor of Bernstein, my Sadhu Hero, on his behalf, let it be said that no such incident ever occurred, nor will it, may it be blotted from the records.

(Whose side are you on, anyway? You're ready to turn on my friend Bernstein just because I have a moment's paranoid fantasy of him kissing my bride at my wedding, based on how I said he looked at Rachel when I introduced them, which I will now say, is *not* how he looked! Well, of course it was, but not in an offensive way. I'd be offended, truly, if he *didn't look* at Rachel that way, because the more my male friends find her beautiful and attractive or even lust for her, the more it confirms that I got a good deal, that I didn't make a biggggggg mistake.)

So I introduce Rachel to the troops, and Bernstein more or less looks at her with bedroom eyes, but it's okay. How about the others? How do they respond to my new companion? Watch:

"Raise your hand," I say to the guys when Rachel is in the

bathroom, "if you find her sexually desirable." All hands go up but one.

Guess who the odd man out is? I mean it...guess? Take a few seconds to think about it, and then I'll tell you if you're right. So who do you think doesn't find Rachel attractive? Goldberg? You gotta be kidding. You should know by now that Goldberg would go for her. Okay, you thought maybe out of fear of the wrath of his girlfriend, he might conceal his attraction, not only from us, but from himself as well. That's not bad thinking, actually. You're actually not completely off-base. But trust me, Goldberg is a sucker for Rachel's type. (What type? The attractive, shapely, under-thirty, Gentile type. Go figure.)

So who else? Who next? Finkelstein? Excellent choice, though not right either. Why excellent? Because you'd think that there'd be no way in the world he'd admit his attraction. You know he was putting Lilah up there in his mind next to Rachel and doing a taste test, comparison shopping, and it killed him that I had the more attractive partner. Irked the living shit out of him. But the only good thing that happened to the little irritating kid-Finkelstein in growing up to become the irritating adult-Finkelstein, is he knew we knew when he was lying, so he didn't insult us anymore by even trying. We had him nailed a mile before he opened his mouth.

Meanest thing we ever did to him, besides the famous "ditch Finkelstein" game was the famous black magic game. Finkelstein had to close his ears and eyes while the rest of us agreed upon an object. Then he had to guess it. We all agreed that he would be right every time, no matter what he said:

"That gray pebble over there by the fire hydrant?"

"Oh my God! How'd you get that on your first try? Unbelievable! Okay close your eyes again...okay."

"Ummm, that wrinkled terrycloth dish towel hanging out to dry on the neighbor's porch?"

"Oh my God, etc.," in this way convincing him of his extraordinary psychic abilities, and thus hopefully making him even crazier than he already was. To this day, when I try to tell him

the game was rigged, he thinks I'm making it up because I can't tolerate his Ultimate Power, albeit unrepeatable ever since.)

So it wasn't Finkelstein. Should I turn all the cards over, or do you want to keep playing? How do you know I'm not doing to *you* what we did to Finkelstein, only in reverse? No matter who you say, I'll say it's not it, until the end. Okay, I'll go easy on you: Try one more, if you don't get it, I'll tell you.

Weissbaum? Yo, wake up! Get a life! There isn't one reasonable justification for choosing Weissbaum. Anybody would know that either he would find her attractive, or he wouldn't but would say he did so as not to call his natural masculine responses into question. There is no conceivable scenario in which Weissbaum would not raise his hand. You lose the game. You didn't guess. So I'll tell you.

Breshman. You know I'm right, don't you? You can feel it. It just fits, somehow, that it would be Breshman. Am I right? Tell me, right or wrong? Of course right. For whatever quirky reason, Breshman neither found Rachel sexually attractive, nor did he feel compelled to pretend he did. What a guy. And probably the only one in the group whose lack of desire for my woman wouldn't be an out and out attack on my self-esteem. Later, after Rachel leaves, Greenblatt asks:

"What's wrong with this picture?"

"I'm happy," I tell him.

"Oh...I couldn't put my finger on it. But there's still something else..."

"I'm with a woman."

"That's it! You're happy, and, you're with a woman. That's a brand new concept. What's it like?"

"Well it's kind of like when you're miserable with a woman, except you're not miserable."

"Gees. I can't even conceive of it. Does Rachel ever say things like, 'You have some lint on you, honey'?"

"Not so far."

"How about, 'You're so self-centered, the world doesn't revolve around you, think of someone else for a change'?"

"Not yet."

"Gees."

For once, Greenblatt was speechless. I was presenting him with alien data, information from a new domain of experience outside his grasp; being happy with a woman as unusual as a UFO sighting.

Once Jerry was involved with someone for a few years and he told me he was still "on fire" around her, sexually speaking.

"That's unusual, for a couple," I told him.

"I know, we can't figure it out."

"Maybe you should get married, that will take some of the steam out of it."

"Yeah I've been thinking about that, because I want out."

Only in Greenblatt's warped system would marriage be considered as a way to get *out* of a relationship. Spotnick once told him that he only gets into relationships in order to end them, because he's addicted to that feeling of freedom when they are over. For Greenblatt, breaking up was the best part. He was a master at it. And he also enjoyed meeting someone new, the beginning stages of courtship. It was everything in between that he found intolerable. For a short time in his earlier days he had earned his living leading a workshop for men that were mourning the end of a relationship, called "Breaking Up Is Easy To Do."

"But what happens if you actually meet someone you like and *stay* in a relationship?" I once asked him.

"Then my career is fucked." For Greenblatt, ending a relationship was a good investment, a tax write-off, a business expense.

"So when you're with Rachel," he asks, "you don't feel a tight band of muscular armoring around your chest, cutting off your breath and life force?"

"Nope."

"A deep contraction of your energy making it impossible to express yourself?"

"Nah."

"Gees."

I could tell he felt betrayed. Neither of us were ever supposed to be happy. We had a Jewish misery pact, blood brothers of suffering. I had broken it.

"Listen Jer, I'm sorry...I didn't mean to do it, it just happened."

"Ah, it's okay."

"Look, I'm sure we'll be miserable together sooner or later. I have some questions about her sense of humor..." trying to give him hope.

"Yeah, I guess. Be seein' you Norb."

Poor Jerry...happiness killed him. Like holding up a cross to Dracula, it made him back away in fear for his life. To illustrate: after reading one of my earlier, depressive books, I asked him how he liked it, and he said,

"I loved it; it made me feel like putting my head through a plate-glass window."

When it came to emotional pain, he was a professional:

"I have 6000 years of Jewish guilt living inside me. I can't stand myself...what's going to become of a guy like us?"

And now there was no more "guy like us"; now there was only a guy like *him*, which must have been terrifying.

"Listen Jer," I say reassuringly, "I have a feeling that apart from Moscowitz, you're going to be the first one of us to die, so don't sweat it."

"Moscowitz isn't dead?"

"He was just here a minute ago."

"Well then he didn't look so good...what do you think I'll die of?"

"Probably a heart attack like your father."

"Yeah, I guess you're right. Thanks Norb."

"No problem."

***

"Next order of business," I say to the group, "is open discussion of our prostates. Gentlemen, I am now thirty-seven years old; the magazines say we don't have to check our prostates regularly

until we're fifty—that gives me thirteen more prostate-check-free years to enjoy myself. Breshman on the other hand, has already reported more frequent urination, and difficulty starting the stream, so go figure. When God created the universe, he made the glorious stars in the infinite heavens, the birds and the tulips, and for some reason he made prostates inside men that only work for a while and then kill them. You gotta trust that He had a plan, a prostate plan, it's written in, nothing to fear, don't worry, be happy."

Finkelstein: "All those in favor?"

("Aye aye aye aye" etc.)

"Opposed?"

Greenblatt: "Abstain."

Finkelstein: "Motion carried: seven for, none against, one abstention. There will be no prostate checks until further notice. Any other new business?"

"I'd like to conclude," I say, " with the reading of a poem, called God Speaks:

> *"Those who seek me, find me.*
> *Those who find me, love me.*
> *Those who love me, I love.*
> *Those who I love, I kill."*

"You're such a cheerful fellow," Goldberg comments.

"Excuse me," says Greenblatt, "I have to go put my head through a plate-glass window."

"Meeting adjourned."

***

Ten Jewish men, forming *minyans* all over the world, across time, in the Old City *shtibls*, small square rooms down forgotten stairwells in Polish *shtetls*, huddled in dark basements in the Ukraine, the Warsaw ghetto, *davening* in fear in 1938 Berlin, in underground Stalingrad, *davening* in Dachau, secretly, in the shad-

ows of barbed wire. I went to Dachau, I stood before the memorial shrine and I *davened* to free my soul, and as I prayed I heard the voice of a child nearby and a father saying, "Shhh, the man is praying," and I realized he meant *me*, that *I* am a man, *a man praying*.

Later in the states I experiment wearing a yarmulke when I drive cross-country, but only in the moving vehicle; no way will I keep it on when I go into Denny's in Kansas, or Kentucky Fried in Nevada. (Were there Jews in the Wild West? "Okay, hold it right there, drop your guns—*we're doing havdalah*.") As I reach for the car door to get out, I freeze. A simple fact smacks me in the face with stunning clarity: It's not safe to be Jewish. And the rest of the syllogism didn't need to be thought through: I am Jewish. Therefore, It is not safe to be me. Being myself suddenly revealed as a very dangerous proposition,

As a kid, this big guy once said to me, "Are you Jewish kid, 'cause I beat the shit out of Jewish kids," and I, not finding that an attractive offer, said, "No, I'm Catholic," and then ran home and told my family and they said I did the right thing. But then in Hebrew School we learned of the martyrs who chose to die rather than deny their God, and I had wangled my way out of merely getting the shit beat out of me. I was sure I'd hear about it when I met God:

"Catholic, huh? Why I oughtta..." God smacking me around upstairs, to fulfill a karmic debt. "I'll give you Catholic...right in the kisser."

And now? Now I'm at the head of the class, compared to my friends. Wait 'til He gets hold of Finkelstein:

"Jesus? I'll knock the everlivin' bejesus out of you...you're about as Christian as your poor cousin Sidney Freiberg, may he rest in peace."

And all the rest, denying their heritage like nobody's business. I tried to tell them. No one listened. The moment they die they're

going to hear a booming voice, saying, "NORBERT WAS RIGHT: DO NOT PASS GO, DO NOT COLLECT $200, ONLY JEW-ISH JEWS ALLOWED, ALL OTHERS HAVE TO SIT HERE FOR ETERNITY LIKE BUMPS ON LOGS."

"The problem with being Jewish," Bernstein once said, "is they make you *do* stuff."

It was true. A lot of stuff. Prayers upon rising, upon going to the toilet, upon eating fruit, upon smelling a new smell, upon seeing a deformed person, upon traveling; how and when to make love, three formal prayer services a day, how to bake challah, how to build a *sukkah*, prayers at bedtime, the midnight prayer of the Kabbalists, when to bend the knee, when to recline on a pillow, how to dip greens in saltwater, how to pass the potato salad. What wasn't covered? The Covenant was a full-time job, and I, while spouting off about the eternal secrets of the depths of wonder to be found in the heart of the Jewish mystical soul grounded in the holy teachings of Torah, did none of it. None. And neither did Reb Miltie.

"So I skip over a few things, here and there," he said once, then joyfully tapped his chest, "but it's a Jewish heart, through and through."

"What makes it a Jewish heart?"

"When it's broken by the world. When the entire world completely breaks your heart, tears you apart, and yet you're filled with joy...that's a Jewish heart."

Miltie masterfully diagnosed my soul-problem and assigned the Baal Shem project as radical surgery: not only show up in the world as Jewish, but do it ecstatically! Shout it from the rooftops! Take it to Broadway! Let your broken Jewish heart burn for G-d in a song and dance! With top-hat, tails, and *tzit-tzit*. ("Blessed art Thou, Lord of the Universe, for commanding us to tap dance.")

And what *does* break my heart? The sight of my mother, standing in the kitchen, preparing a High Holiday meal of chicken, pot roast and kugel, when I know that someday I'll be packing up her pots and pans and selling the house, eating a kosher hotdog alone at Nathan's on Rosh Hashanah for my festive meal. And the sound of

my father's car leaving on Sunday mornings breaks my heart, off to buy the *Sunday Times* and bagels, getting the coffee brewing before any of us are awake, when I already know the terms of his "living will," when to pull the plug, how much of the inheritance will be taxed, the possibilities of second-to-die life insurance, and I've even seen the empty cemetery plots, waiting, my father handling the business of death as efficiently as he did life, an estate executor's dream. They'll give him a plaque on the other side: "Affairs Most In Order: Noah Wilner."

So my parents break my heart. That's easy. But the whole world? Yes. To see every person as if they are a beloved, slowly fading from sight in the window of a train as it pulls out of a station, perhaps never to be seen again. Every person as your only child, in grave danger. Every person a dying friend. That will break your heart. The world as one big broken home, life as mourning, loss.

Sounds grim. Where's the joy?

> *Dancing in the moonlight with your shadow in the valley of death.*

***

I'm walking in the dark, down a steep dirt path in Safed, pronounced "Sfat," in the north of Israel. Safed is where nearly all the Kabbalistic greats gathered centuries ago, and where they are all buried. Here, in this graveyard I am wandering in after dark, most of the tombs are big and boxlike, and blue, many with candles burning, and covered with Hebrew writing. Nearby is the underground mikvah, or spring, icy cold, that the greatest of the great—the Reb Yitzhak Luria, known simply as "The Ari"—used to take his daily ritual ablutions. It is said that all who dip in these waters are guaranteed liberation in this lifetime, or your money back. I do it, can't afford not to, dipping in the frigid dark underground waters of the great Ari, connecting my soul to the circle of mystics sitting by candlelight in 1568, before the burning white fire of the Hebrew let-

ters of Torah, transfixed and transmuted into holy truths channeled through the Ari.

I find his tomb, I lie down on it and I lie there in the dark for an all-night vigil, praying to the soul of the Ari that I be released from this prison of mind, released to the ecstatic mystery of my holy Jewish soul.

Reb Miltie is with me now. It is dawn, and in the golden light of early morning in the Holy Land, we wear our tefillin, *our* taleisim, *and gently rock back and forth, swaying in the cool breeze of true* davening. *Not the mindless repetition of liturgy, but the ecstatic yearning prayer of the heart. In the presence of Abraham, of Sarah, I feel the deep tradition of my ancestors, as I intone the* "Kidusha":

"Kadosh, kadosh, kadosh"—"Holy, Holy, Holy," each repetition of the word holier than the last.

"Adonoi tzvaot"—"Lord of Hosts."

"Melo kol haoretz kvodo"—"The whole world is filled with Your Glory."

And in that moment the world is ablaze, flames leaping from all the tombs, trees turning crimson, exploding, the sky a bright white, and across the sky Hebrew letters form of flame, blue on orange, then suddenly white on black, and I understand the mystery of all creation hidden in Kabbalistic scramblings of the sacred word, the single letter Aleph looming larger now in multi-colored fireworks, drawing me in and back to before the beginning. Then the pieces of ashen letter fall and fade and my very soul follows, disappearing into the ocean of G-d, the tears of mothers blending with the sound of the wind and the Ari's laughter, and when I regain consciousness, Miltie is there, eyes burning with a ferocity I've never seen before, and he says, "You are dust and ashes." And as the horror of that begins to penetrate my awareness, he adds,

"And for you was the world created," and I am no longer teetering on the edge of some great abyss, but am walking, sure-footed, on a narrow bridge between Heaven and Hell, singing, with Miltie,

> *The whole wide world, is a very narrow bridge,*
> *A very narrow bridge,*
> *A very narrow bridge.*

The whole wide world, is a very narrow bridge,
A very narrow bridge.

But the main thing to recall,
is to have no fear, have no fear at all.

But the main thing to recall,
is to, have no fear at all.

I awake from the dream happy, and feeling like there's something I need to tell the boys, something alive in me I desperately need to convey. I realize I'm ready for the performance, the big finish: "The Baal Shem Tov, Live at the Fillmore."

There is a time for you to walk slowly
and hum along with the
black bird's song.

Or to sit in the back seat of
the Wild One's limousine,
pouring mixed drinks.

Mordecai says:
"Bottoms up!"

CHAPTER NINETEEN

Silverman

Ol' Jerry Greenblatt, getting fat, got the Silverman girl by default. Mrs. B. had already made all the arrangements and, as she put it, "What do I care if she gets the nice guy or the *shtunk*? It could be The Man From TUCHUS for all I care. Just make sure somebody shows up at her door Saturday night like I promised her...just do me a big favor, don't send Moscowitz."

Judy Silverman had a ghostly-pale Addams family look about her and a prematurely aged voice that sounded like it had escaped from someone's elderly aunt in Miami and attached itself to Judy. A minor form of demonic possession, manifesting not only in a Flo Greenblatt-like loud, nasal tonal quality, but also in the things she *said*. During an R-rated movie, for example:

"I DON'T HAVE TO SEE WHAT GOES ON IN THE BEDROOM. I HAVE MY OWN DIRTY LAUNDRY." Which was basically out-of-character for her, given what Greenblatt eventually confessed to us about the variety of kinky sexual favors she was eager to provide, literally upon command, in addition to cleaning his house and doing *his* dirty laundry. So it was as if she were at times channeling some discarnate, Jewish mother.

The only thing missing in the relationship, Greenblatt would tell us, was love; but "What do you need that for?" he said, quoting his own mother who once set him up with a neighborhood girl and later asked how it went:

"SO?"

"So I didn't find her sexually attractive."

"SO WHAT DO YOU NEED THAT FOR?" Flo Greenblatt had replied, in her own original loud, Brooklyn nasal voice. In fact, it occurred to the rest of us that Judy Silverman was in fact channeling the voice of Jerry's own mother, a situation we were sure would simply have to do him in eventually. ("JERRY, TAKE AN UMBRELLA, IT'S BETTER TO BE SAFE THAN SORRY.")

Believe it or not, at the same time, completely dissociated from her voice and the things she said, Judy was performing outrageous sex tricks for Jerry—acrobatics involving ropes and lingerie, a suspended chair, illegal acts she learned in Bangkok, the Japanese dipping technique, the African knotted handkerchief, the Balinese *Pas de Deux*—the woman was an exotic, a United Nations of eroticism, fulfilling Greenblatt's wildest fantasies on the one hand, then bombarding him with her verbal outbursts on the other:

"BE CAREFUL, YOU'RE GONNA GET A HERNIA. YOU'RE NO SPRING CHICKEN YOU KNOW."

Bernstein had a theory:

"Don't you get it? He's handling the Oedipal thing. It's a perfect set-up—no wonder he's so turned on. The voice is part of it, he *needs* the voice…Jerry Greenblatt, forgive me for saying it, is *shtupping* his own Mama."

Greenblatt also had a theory:

"Bernstein can stick it where the moon don't shine."

The rest of us began referring to Judy Silverman as "The Voice," as in, "Greenblatt and The Voice are coming over later," or, "The Voice is giving Greenblatt head."

Ironically, at the same time he began dating The Voice, Greenblatt also met another woman. ("WHEN IT RAINS IT POURS.") She was the complete opposite type of woman: not

Jewish. A blonde, blue-eyed, soft, New Age, vegetarian yoga instructor. She was bright, pleasant, sexy, and seemingly every Jewish man's dream. When I looked at her brochure and saw her picture, read her bio, I asked Jerry,

"How can a beautiful, hip, blonde sexy New Age yoga teacher be attracted to a middle-aged fat Jewish *shmuck* like you?"

He just shrugged. "I don't know. It's a great mystery."

A mystery he can't really tolerate, apparently, because despite all appearances and probable outcomes—even Nick the Greek bet on the blonde— he drops the yoga teacher and stays with The Voice.

"See?" Bernstein said.

We saw. There was something to it, Bernstein's theory. The Voice had a powerful hold on Greenblatt, and instead of destroying his libido, every utterance seemed to increase his desire, no matter what she said:

"JERRY, DON'T BE A DOORMAT, YOU'RE A GROWN MAN." It was the equivalent, for Jerry, of talking dirty.

"JERRY, SAVE YOURSELF A TRIP AND TAKE THE GARBAGE OUT WITH YOU." Like whispered sweet nothings. In any event, like I said, Greenblatt wound up with the Silverman girl.

Meanwhile, Weissbaum and Sally finally have a kid (which throws Weissbaum into a mild homosexual panic) and I'm on the phone with him during the last three minutes of the NBA playoffs, incredulous that he's willing to be on the phone and not glued to the set, and what do I hear on the other end of the line? "Say hello to your Uncle Norbert, Boo-Boo." He's kutchy-kooing his kid during NBA playoffs and I can't believe it.

"Weissbaum," I say, "are you aware that the Bulls are down one point in the last game with two minutes left on the clock?" Me, who knows and cares nothing about it but got pulled in by the sheer drama and intensity.

"Norbert, how old are you?" he says.

"Thirty-seven."

"And you mean to tell me that you have nothing better to do than to sit around watching a bunch of grown men throw a ball through a hoop? Grow up."

So I hang up, thinking there's hope for humanity.

When I eventually meet the baby, Weissbaum's giving him a bath, saying over and over, "Who's my best boy? Who's my best boy?" He looks at me watching and says, like a coach explaining the fundamentals to a rookie,

"You know the key thing about giving babies a bath? The most important thing?"

"I'm tired of being on a quiz show when there are never any prizes."

"The prize, son, is a sense of satisfaction and pride at getting it right, learning the ropes from a Master Parent, winning one for the Gipper. Now think, what is the most important thing about giving a baby a bath?"

Most people would be dying to tell you the answer to their own riddle and at some point would say, "Give up?" Not Weissbaum. I guess wrong a few times:

"Don't get soap in his eyes?"

"Nope."

"Say 'who's my best boy' in that funny voice?"

"Close, that's second."

And finally I give up and beg him to give me the answer, just to relieve the psychic tension and get the torturous game over with. But he will not relent, just shrugs his shoulders and says "Okay" in a tone which means "Your loss, you're the one missing out on vital information. I'm a little disappointed in you, I have to say, that you're not more motivated, but forget about it, no problem, maybe it's not the time for you yet, maybe you're not ready." All that in the way he says "Okay," going up in pitch and wavering on the second syllable, leaving me feeling totally ashamed and defeated, and now genuinely wanting to know the answer, and then suddenly, it's there:

"Don't let the baby drown."

"Bingo!" Weissbaum says, and now that I understand the game, the rest of his Master Parenting maxims come quickly and easily: The most important thing when holding a baby?

"Keep the head up?"

"Nope."

"Say 'who's my best boy' in that funny voice?"

"Close."

"Don't drop him on the floor!"

"Bingo!" Weissbaum, the rocket scientist of fathering.

I'll tell you what I think about when I see a newborn child: you don't want to know. But I'll tell you: that poor thing has to live a human life? Those poor parents have to watch their baby try to exist on planet Earth? Is there anything possibly more sad and heartbreaking than to give birth to a new human and know that it has to endure an entire lifetime? Is this a depressive attitude? I don't think so. I've had experience. I've *lived* here.

And how many parents check their babies at night, to see if they're still breathing? Most. And they never stop checking. To this day, all my parents' concerns for me, all their worries, all the phone calls, the money...it's all a huge, lifelong extension of a single concern: "Is our baby still breathing?" The answer in my case, so far, is yes. *Keyn eyn hora,* knock wood. The answer for the parents of Finkelstein's brother Jake, is no.

And the child returns the favor to the parents: "Are *they* still breathing?" I have been consciously asking this question internally on a daily basis since I was about four years old, nearly four decades, painfully aware that every "Yes" response is a temporary reprieve, a delay. I know, because Greenblatt and his sister told me about their father—Ed, still dead. One night they go to bed with a father, the next morning, poof, no father. Heart attack in the middle of the night. I know because of Weissbaum's mother, and Bernstein's father, and my father's father, and my mother's, and their mothers, and Uncle Izzy—everybody dead. I'm afraid to have a family because they would all die on me or I would die on them. We would all stop breathing eventually. For me life is simply *grief waiting to happen.*

So this is what I think when I meet Weissbaum's baby. The most important thing? Don't let it die. Ever.

***

I asked Reb Miltie to meet me in Greenwich Village, in front of the Waverly, 10 a.m., rainy day, people sloshing around with three-dollar umbrellas, plastic tarps over all the newsstands. Miltie's standing there in a bright yellow raincoat, the kind you had in fourth grade, flirting with old women walking by, old women alone in the rain, alone in the world, widows in lonely New York apartments with *yuhrzeit* candles burning every other night in memorial for some loved one or another, most everyone dead, and children scattered everywhere. Not like the old days in Europe, in Poland, when the kids and the parents and the parents' parents and the kids' kids all lived together forever in one little village, one house, and told stories on porches in the early evenings while someone played a concertina nearby. Now it's the old ladies of rainy New York mornings, limping and breathing hard, carrying shopping bags, wearing bulky black coats. Even their best friends, their peers, long gone, passed over—"May they rest in peace, God willing I won't be dead and buried by *Shavuous*." Now they talk only to the doorman of their apartment buildings, the super, the deli man behind the counter at Balducci's, their "family" now down to these few strangers, these goyim, and Miltie can see it all at once, and knows no one has flirted with these women in thirty-two years, so he says,

"Sweetheart, what's in the bag? Dinner for me? Such short notice, I can't make it tonight, can I take a rain check?"

"Ah, who are you kidding?" she gets out between deep breaths, the weight of giant sagging breasts, the swollen ankles.

And to another one, with a walker, taking two hours to go a block and a half, he says,

"Slow down, lady, you're gonna cause a big commotion racing around like there's no tomorrow...am I imagining things or did you make a pass with me?"

"Ah, what are you talking crazy? Leave an old lady alone."

"Alone? Give me your phone number and you'll never be alone again."

"Go on, I'm old enough to be your mother, young man."

"Young man she calls me," Miltie says, poking me with his elbow, "Look who I have to hit on to be called a young man. Good-bye darling, you should live to be 120."

"Who needs it?" she says, and goes on her way, an inch at a time.

Miltie and I walk south on Sixth to Bleecker, cross over and continue east to MacDougal, turn right and wind up sitting at a table in the Cafe Dante.

"There's more to cappuccino than meets the eye. You called me here for a reason, I know, but let me tell you something: We are creating history, you and I...your history, to be exact, because now one day you'll remember and even write about that rainy morning in the middle of your life when you sat in Greenwich Villitch and had a café au lait with Reb Miltie and talked about nothing in particular."

"But there is something particular I want to talk about."

"Even better."

"I'm getting married."

"HA!" he laughs/yells. "The Silverman girl? Mrs. Bernstein told me..."

"Not the Silverman girl."

"Not the Silverman girl?"

"Ix-nay on the Ilverman-say irl-gay," I say.

"Who then?"

"Her name is Rachel. I met her saying *kiddush* in a topless bar."

"I like it! This I like!" And then, an afterthought, "But what will happen to the poor Silverman girl? She had her hopes up, her heart set, her mind made up..."

"We funneled her over to Greenblatt, she'll never know the difference."

"I like it! This I like! Uh, this Rachel, she's Jewish? A *yiddela*?"

"Not exactly, not completely."

"What, the father's not Jewish?"

"Right."

"So okay, it's the mother that counts."

"Her mother's not Jewish either."

"Not the father or the mother?"

"Right."

"So she's not Jewish at all."

"Exactly. Ukrainian Catholic. But both of us had borscht in our background."

"That's important...so let me ask you something. When I told you to go out and find a nice Jewish girl and get married, what did you think I meant?"

"That the woman I marry should be Jewish?"

"That's the conclusion you jumped to?"

"Yes."

"That's not what I meant."

"That's not what you meant?"

"Okay, that *was* what I meant, but I'm changing it."

"To what?

"To a non-Jewish woman."

"So I'm doing the right thing?"

"More or less."

Ding ding ding ding ding: Miltie taps his water glass with a spoon to get everyone's attention.

"Ladies and gentlemen sitting at Cafe Dante in New York City on a damp fall day where no one ever talks to anyone else, I'd like your attention for just a few minutes, long enough to announce that my son ('makes a better story,' an aside, to me) just told his old father he intends to marry. The angels in heaven are smiling on me, may all your souls be blessed. Please join me in the traditional cheer of our people: Chip chip..." (Not "ch" like chocolate chip. The hard, throat-clearing Hebrew "ch," as in *chupeh*.)

"Chooray," the crowd responds.

"Chip chip..."

"Chooray," a whole cafe, like a congregation.

"Chip chip..."

"Chooray," like Jewish cheerleaders. Everyone laughs and applauds. I'm red, they go back to their separate, isolated New York cappuccino lives and I'm alone again with Miltie.

"Now," he says, "when's the wedding?"

"When are you free?"

"I'm free now."

"Not so fast, Smith," (alluding to the old joke about the insensitive sergeant who was told to break the news gently to Smith that his mother had died, and greeted the morning line-up with "Everyone who's mother is still alive, please step forward...not so fast, Smith.")

"When then?"

"In a few months."

"A few months? In a few months I could be dead...okay, a few months."

(And speaking of *chupehs*, the canopy under which a Jewish couple stands during a wedding ceremony, I once rescued Weissbaum from a serious *chupeh* crisis. He and one of his ex-wives were invited to contribute one small square to what was to be a collective, patchwork quilt of a *chupeh*, all the wedding guests sending in one piece to be sewn on. His wife left Weissbaum with an appropriate aphorism by Gibran and instructions to stencil it on with fabric paint. He got as far as "May the winds of chan" when he realized the "n" in "change" was backward. In a panic, he managed to erase it with alcohol and redo it correctly, and finished the word, at which point he looked over at the aphorism and discovered that the word "change" wasn't even part of it: It was "May the winds of *truth* something something something."

As he started to panic, I jumped in and created a "*chupeh* chotline": called Greenblatt who called his sister who called her aunt who looked like Moe from *The Three Stooges*; called Goldberg who called his clothing mistress who called customer service at

Saks; called Bernstein who called Mrs. Bernstein who called Mrs. Fleishman in 7B; called everyone, to try and come up with a new phrase that would work, getting entries which ranged from "May the winds of change not give you a *loch en kopf*" *from* Greenblatt's sister, to the one they actually used, "May the winds of change be gentle with your love." Weissbaum was saved, and I was the *chupeh chero*.)

So I pay the check and my Rebbe and I head back down McDougal towards Houston. About two buildings in from the end of the block, this big guy with a shaved head and an Ivan the Terrible t-shirt steps casually onto the sidewalk, facing us with arms crossed, smiling and blocking our path. Reb Miltie looks him over, then looks at me. My heart is pounding, I'm scared out of my wits. My mind races in a panic as I look over my shoulder praying I'll see a cop. The street is empty. The next sequence of events happens so quickly I can barely recount the order. The guy grabs Reb Miltie around the neck with one arm, takes out a switchblade with the other hand, and says:

"Doesn't look like such a good day for your Jew, does it?"

He laughs, as I stare, frozen in horror. Miltie doesn't struggle, but stares back at me as if to say, "I'd give you some advice about how to proceed, but as you can see, I'm a bit indisposed."

My heart pounds louder as I realize the next move is mine and mine alone. *In my mind I see Butch Taylor, I see Grisatti, waiting for me on the corner of 30th and Pine. I see Philip, Lipschitz, Bernstein in the shack. Ivanovich, on all fours. Finkelstein, leaping through the air. Moscowitz and his schoolbooks. I see* myself, *running.* I look back over my shoulder at McDougal, and know I could run to the corner if I just take off. But I am paralyzed. There is this problem of Reb Miltie with a big tattooed arm around his neck and a switchblade at his throat. Then I have an idea:

"Do you like money?" I ask the man. "We have *lots* of money, 'cause we're both Jews, you know. Rich Jews. Maybe we could give *you* some money. You want any money? How about if I give you lots of money? I'd be happy to...it would be my pleasure." I have

my wallet out, showing him the wad of bills. "But you'll need to have your hands free. I think you need to let go of my friend first, if you wouldn't mind..."

He throws Miltie toward me and lunges forward to grab the wallet from my hand, but I toss it back over his head, landing about twenty feet away. He turns and runs to retrieve it; Miltie and I turn and run up McDougal. A police car drives toward us. I frantically wave and point to the man in the street. The squad car zips up to him and the officer holds a gun out the window, pointing at the man's head. He drops the wallet and puts his hands in the air.

Reb Miltie approaches and says, "No, no officer, put your gun away. You misunderstood: We were trying to wave you on to Houston where some guy just tried to rob us and is running away with my briefcase. Go, go, maybe you can still catch him."

He peels out and disappears up the street. Our friend with the switchblade, looking incredulous, hands me my wallet. He is speechless. I take out twenty bucks and offer it to him: "Here, I promised you some money."

He stares at my hand in disbelief, looks up at Miltie and me, starts to back away from us, still looking, then turns and starts walking away, picks up his pace, and takes off running. *In my mind I see Grisatti running. I see Butch Taylor. I see myself, standing tall and proud, walking home from school the direct way, via 30th and Oak.*

Later I tell Phil about the incident. "Well," he says, "you did good. You didn't run. You saved Miltie. You got your money. Today you are a man."

"Who made you in charge?"

"You did. Twenty-six years ago."

"But wouldn't a real man have delivered a high karate kick to the guy's arm, knocked the knife into the air, caught it with one hand while kneeing him in the balls, and then pinned him to the ground, holding the knife to *his* throat?"

"What are you a Jewish James Bond?"

"I'm not?"

"No."

" But what would Butch Taylor have done?"

"Screw Butch Taylor."

"Grisatti?"

"Screw Grisatti."

"I didn't chicken out, did I?"

"Today you are a man.

"You forgive me, then?"

"Unconditionally absolved."

"Now what do I blame my fearful, guilt-ridden life on?"

"How about the fact that you've squandered your talents and opportunities?"

"Yeah, that's good, thanks."

***

Once a group of us had dinner with a friend who was to become a celebrated author of profoundly deep works of fiction. But at the time he was still merely a young genius. He wrote a poem describing that dinner, in terms of how each person at the table experienced love. For me, he wrote that it's as if I greet new love saying, "Oh damn, she's making me feel that thing again."

Rachel is making me feel that thing again. We walk to Washington Square Park and sit on the grass and eat Jarlsberg and a baguette from Balducci's. She gives half of her sandwich to a neighborhood derelict, the sort of intrusive stranger most picnickers ignore or send away hungry. Don't tell me she's a good person, I think. What are the implications? What will happen when she finds out who I am?

"I'm no saint," she says, reading my mind.

"That's a relief; saints don't usually approve of me."

"But I do prefer trying to relate to people in a loving way when I can."

"Absolutely, excellent policy—I'm all for loving ways."

She laughs and feeds me a bit of cheese, follows with a kiss. Most of the kissing I have done in the past, I participated in as an observer, standing at some mental distance, thinking, "It's certainly a bit odd to have this person's face all jammed right up against mine like that...what is she doing there? And too much tongue. I don't like too much tongue. If things start getting too wet I'm outta here, wipe my mouth on my sleeve, start over."

Kissing Rachel, however, swings a little too far in the other direction: her lips are too dry. "Moisture, moisture" I'm thinking, and silently file this oral humidity issue in a mental back drawer somewhere, out of consciousness. Other than that, my mind is pleasantly silent. When I look into her eyes I can actually imagine not minding having it be *her*, Rachel, that looks back at me. This was progress.

"There's someone I want you to meet," I tell her. Several days later we are in apartment 6H eating bagels with Miltie.

"Miltie Rachel, Rachel Miltie."

"Enough already," Miltie says, "How long can you spend on introductions? Now Rochela,"—he uses the Hebrew name for Rachel—Rochel— adding the familiar "ah" sound at the end, as in "bubbela"—"tell me, do you know how to keep a kosher home?"

"Well, two sets of dishes..." I had been prepping her for the meeting. For my life. For my wife.

"Wrong! That's kosher for the small-minded and big-kitchened. Do you think I have room for two sets of dishes in this place? Do you think if a chicken touches this plate today and a spoonful of cottage cheese tomorrow, they won't let me in upstairs? No, a kosher home is a home where everyone loves each other...and that's the woman's job."

"Excuse me, " I interrupt, protesting.

"Sha! Suddenly I don't know anything? Overnight I'm talking through my hat? Listen, *kindela*, children, a man is hardened by this world, afraid. He can only love when a woman makes it safe for him to love again. A man doesn't think right, feel right, love right. He's always fighting to win, survive, avoiding humiliation

and loss of face. He's up against big shots who know and do everything better." (*Finkelstein*, I think bitterly.) "He lets down his guard, opens his heart, he's a dead man, or so he believes. It's up to you, Rochela, to keep a kosher home, teach my Norbert Wilner to love."

Rachel takes my hand.

"So what do I teach her?" I ask, unwilling to be a full-time student of marriage.

"How should I know? I've never been married—what am I, the answer man all of a sudden?"

"Just be willing to let me see the shape of your soul," Rachel says. The poetry of it silences Miltie and me. In my mind, the ever-adjusting scale (of heads-I-go-through-with-this/tails-I-need-a-disguise-and-a-plane-ticket, this constant I-love-her-I-love-her-not like a stock report, a ticker tape across the bottom of my mental screen, a Dow Jones of Eros) tips again toward Rachel. This one line from her lips like the very waters of life cancels out the dry lips problem as I weigh things, the checks and balances of love. Then Miltie, nodding gravely, says,

"A *neshama* from the angelic realms. A poet. You shalt be a good husband to her."

"We shalt leave now."

"Go *gezuntaheit*...but tell me one thing: the ceremony, you want the regular or the deluxe?"

"What's the difference?"

"The regular is dull and boring, the deluxe is fun and meaningful."

"Deluxe"—me.

"Deluxe"—Rachel.

"Deluxe!"—Miltie, and closes the door.

***

I had to break the news to Greenblatt's sister, who though married with a child now, is still incredibly possessive and jealous.

I hesitated to tell her about Rachel but figured it would be better if she heard it from me.

"So I met a woman..." I begin, cautiously.

"What, she's so much *better* than me? I wasn't good enough? She's Miss America? Marilyn Monroe? What?"

"Her name is Rachel..."

"What, she has some kind of *biblical* act? A matriarch complex? A regular name's not good enough for her? Why not Mary, Linda, Jane? I don't like her already."

"We're getting married."

Silence. Then, "So mazel-tov, *kish mein tuchus.*"

"Thanks for your support."

"Support schmort, you never should have left me."

"But we fought like cats and dogs."

"Fought schmought."

"Our sex life was terrible."

"Sex schmex."

"Look, I gotta go, I'll see you, okay? Good-bye?"

"Bye schmeye."

Funny woman, Greenblatt's sister.

***

I take Rachel for a spin in the Happy Hearse.

"You're not serious about this funeral business?"

"No, that would be counter-productive. I'm light-hearted about it."

"Have you actually *done* anyone yet?"

"Well, not exactly. We tried Moscowitz but he ultimately resisted. Nothing ventured, nothing gained. It's tough to do funerals freelance—the death business is dog-eat-dog. But truthfully, I feel satisfied just driving this thing around. People see it, get the flavor, the idea unconsciously seeps into their awareness. I don't actually have to do it. It's more like performance art on wheels, the Good Humor Death Man. Come to think of it, maybe I *should* sell ice cream out of this thing."

"You're not exactly sure what it is you should be doing with yourself, are you?"

"This line of questioning could provoke a major anxiety attack."

"Sweetheart, you met me in a topless bar...anything above a pimp is progress for me. I just didn't like the idea of having our wedding in a morgue."

"I wasn't serious."

"Oh."

"Anyway, I'm only thirty-seven, I have my whole life ahead of me. I need a little time to find my niche, come into my own, figure out what's what...you really danced naked on a bar in front of strange men?"

"Just that once, I told you."

"Why does that idea turn me on?"

"Because, like most men, you're basically perverted."

"Absolutely not true," I say with finality and end the discussion. Later I tell Greenblatt about it:

"Why do you think the idea of her dancing naked in front of strange men turns me on?"

"Because like most men, you're basically perverted."

"True, absolutely."

But this was Greenblatt talking. This was the pot calling the kettle black. This was my brother in perversion. This was Jerry Greenblatt, the sinner. He was allowed.

"You didn't tell your parents where you met her, did you?" Goldberg had asked me.

"Of course I did...I mean sort of...I mean I tampered with the truth a bit, a little white lie, but basically I told them."

"Yes?"

"I told them she's a graduate student at Columbia and I met her at a Hillel function."

"Close enough...can't hurt me with that," Goldberg's pat response, dating from the time he was conversing with a stranger on a bus—a tough-looking guy with cowboy boots—who asked him

what he did, and when Goldberg replied, "I write music, classical music," the man thought it over and said, "Classical music? Can't hurt me with that."

Which is true. You can't hurt someone with classical music, unless you are Greenblatt's sister and you smash a recording of Bach's *Brandenburg Concertos* into a million pieces and then attempt to use one of the sharp, jagged edges to gouge someone's eyes out. No, she never did that—smash, yes, gouge, no. She was a smasher, not a gouger.

"Rach," I say, sitting now in her one-bedroom in Park Slope, "are you fully aware that you're marrying a depressive guy who has no positive feelings about living?" I need to get her to see the light.

"Yes dear."

"I don't want to bring children into this world and force them to contend with their own existence. Childbearing should be temporarily outlawed until further notice. Do you want to have children?"

"Yes dear."

"Well then you be responsible. I'm willing to throw the ball around, play with the Lincoln Logs and pay for the polio shots, you tell them who they are, why they're here, what's going on around them, where it's all heading, and that their pet rabbit and their mommy and daddy are going to die."

"Okay."

Rachel was easy—didn't take my philosophical difficulties to heart, thought life was just a difficult phase I was passing through, as indeed it *is*.

"Well then, let's talk about sex." I just kept bringing up subjects like a salesman in reverse, trying to sell her on dumping me, convince her she was getting a bad deal, talk her out of this product: me. "It's bad enough I have to live with me, why would you want to?"

"Because I, unlike you, love you."

"Well, I don't like ordinary lovemaking. After a few minutes, missionary position bores me. I have a predilection for dominance-

submission fantasy games, both ways. Plus, I prefer coming outside a woman where there's a little breathing room, not all jammed up inside a dark, black canal. I like to be passive sometimes, not always working to run things smoothly, orchestrating everything. In addition to which, in many ways I feel like I'm a woman in a man's body and will probably go to my grave wondering if I was secretly gay the whole time and just too repressed to know it. Also, I've an appreciation for tasteless pornography. And the last woman I had an affair with told me, and I quote, 'You're the only man I've ever been with who managed to make sex a completely miserable experience."

"Let's make love."

"Not tonight, dear, I have a headache."

And then little Catholic Rachel from Brooklyn pulled out all the stops: She confessed her own dark, quirky sexual nature, showed me all her black leather outfits from Ray's Topless—the halter tops, the pumps and black nail polish—showed me her handcuffs, the video camera. She promised to out-kink me, heal my s with her m, my m with her s, to animate my anima, dominate my animus, talk dirty, and in short, turn me on. (Leather halter top or no, the breasts could be a problem, I'm thinking. The questionable sense of humor. Those desert lips.)

And she was equally able to revert back, like Catwoman to business clothes, to Rachel of home and hearth, who could wear white and was willing, she said, to learn how to light Sabbath candles, to intone the Hebrew prayers, as if God and sex really *could* live together in relative harmony under one roof, in one woman, in *me* for Christ's sake, for God's sake, for Pete's sake. So any doubts I had about marriage certainly receded somewhat after that conversation. In some way, she had called my bluff, I had met my match. A "worthy adversary" is how they put it in martial arts—someone who'll give you a good game, go the distance, give you a run for your money.

So finally I said it, and at times I think I may have also meant it:

"I love you too." *Too*, the operative word, wherever *too* are gathered in love's name, there a relationship will be formed.

"However," I would pontificate privately, later, entertaining myself, making speeches in my bedroom, "as D.H. Lawrence put it, 'Let love be enough then, I'm bored with the rest.' The I-love-you/I-love-you-too as struck bargain, as firm deal, the romantic handshake like corporate merger, joining of assets—love's equivalent of 'you bring in your clients, we'll use our mailing list, together we'll get a bulk mail rate.' It's all 'my amp and your speakers, my turntable your deck, my *milshedik* plates, your *fleishadik*.' The sheer wheeling and dealing of it all: 'I'll give you Mantle and Maris for your Mays, McCovey and Marichal'—marriage as all-star team. I love you *too*, as in *also*, and you *also* love me, therefore let us Brady Bunch our fates, 'my futon your bureau, I got a juicer and coffee grinder, whattayou got?' The two-way dowry of shared goods, the pre-nuptial arrangements: 'Do you promise to love and cherish my microwave 'til divorce do us part?' But all this notwithstanding—the pettiness of love's complications, the utter *smallness* of it all (gone are the days when 'shacking up together' was a simple matter, required no moving men, no monthly storage unit, no putting Con Ed in one name, no printers incompatible with your hard drive, no marriage today without converting, only it's not to Judaism, it's your floppys on Word-Perfect to my Microsoft Word, it's love as software)—I love her *too*. *Also*. We each love one another—back and forth, two-way, bi-directional, give and take, table tennis love, tea for two, two for tea."

"Too schmoo, you never loved me too," Greenblatt's sister would have said.

***

Tonight the full moon fell in love with
Darkness and began writing
anonymous love letters:

"I fall off the edge of my self and
find You everywhere.

Minyan

My round white body floats in Your
Great Sea of Black.
No human lovers know
about this position!"

Mordecai suggests:
When you marry the Tender One,
send out invitations to
the whole world.

CHAPTER TWENTY

Wilner

Finkelstein's got files. On all of us. Dating back thirty years. The kid had been a six-year-old district attorney, showing up at my backdoor, saying, "My client has a little matter he wants me to discuss with you."

"Your client?"

"A Mr. Philip Goldberg."

"Yes?"

"It concerns a bit of real estate—a trespassing charge, late payment..."

"I don't follow."

"Does the name Park Place mean anything to you, mister?"

"I see. Won't you come in?"

The day before, we were involved in a serious Monopoly game and I was sitting on Marvin Gardens, Goldberg had hotels on Boardwalk and Park, my mother called me up to dinner just as I rolled a fateful eight. Now he was sending his lawyer to collect.

"I'm sure, Mr. Wilner—or can I call you Norbert?—that we can come to some sort of settlement out of court. Perhaps a one thousand dollar handicap in our next game? Or tithe ten percent of your two hundred dollars every time you pass Go? Arrange-

ments can be made, I'm certain, to everyone's satisfaction...and now, if you'll excuse me."

The six-year-old psychotic attorney. But Finkelstein had his files. To this day, there's a card in my file saying, "October 3, 1958: Wilner lands on Park Place. Owner: Goldberg. Runs up a $2,000 tab. Still owes $1500." He's got a copy of my bar mitzvah speech, the clipping from the B'nai Shalom Bulletin where it says, "Norbert Wilner enjoys magic and playing the piano." He's got the computer print-out with my SAT scores, an expired library card, the program from my senior year Thanksgiving assembly, photos of three ex-girlfriends in various stages of undress, the little plastic pool tag from the local beach club, the combination to my high school locker.

Finkelstein kept tabs. He had his hand in, his eyes out. He was informed. He knew how many points I had on my driver's license, my blood type, Xeroxes of a ten-year-old EKG. He had his finger on the pulse, my very heartbeat part of his dossier. He had my ticket stubs from Expo '67, my letter of acceptance from NYU, my shoe size and an old eyeglass prescription.

And it's not just me: He had Bernstein's police record, Goldberg's clothing receipts; Moscowitz's caloric intake, Greenblatt's voice on tape; he had Weissbaum's total at bats and a bootleg video. He had nothing on Breshman.

"How'd you stay out of his files, Breshman?" I asked him once.

"I ordered an expungement. Basically, I went over to his house and took my file."

"What was in it?"

"Three lift tickets."

"Slim pickings."

"Still."

"Still."

Finkelstein; you had to hate him.

I drove out to his place the morning of my bachelor party, got there early.

"Wilner, Wilner, my good man, good to see you. Would you be so kind as to step into my office for a moment?"

I follow him into a room with a big desk, a few bookshelves, half a dozen plaques, and lots and lots of files. Mentally I'm surveying the layout, the placement of windows, where he keeps the keys. I'm Haldeman, I'm Erlichman, I'm G. Gordon Liddy. Finkelsteingate.

"*Shnapps?*" he offers. I decline. It's 10 a.m. "This, uh, Rachel you're seeing..." he says, rummaging through a file drawer.

"Marrying."

"Huh?"

"I'm not seeing her. I'm marrying her. Tomorrow."

"Yes, yes, of course...Rachel Lindstrom is it?"

"Yes."

"Ah, here we are."

I just can't believe what I'm seeing: Finkelstein is pulling her file. He's got Rachel.

"You know of course that from July of '89 until only recently she was employed at an establishment of somewhat ill repute, a Ray's Topless on..."

"Finkelstein, tell me this isn't happening."

"A husband should know...attended Bard College briefly—a real party school I'm told...involved in a minor possession thing—misdemeanor, no priors...small potatoes—hey, she was a kid, gotta give her a some leeway. Who didn't experiment in college? Nobody ever accused me of being a saint, I can promise you that, hah hah... hey, what are you doing?"

What I'm doing is grabbing Rachel's file out of his hands and ripping it to shreds.

"Hey you can't, that belongs to me, it's classified, give me that..."

I have wrestled him to the ground. "Fake fight," he whispers. I get the file and stand up.

"Norbert, it's Top Secret stuff. Code 301. Special services. Classified. You can't walk out of here with that."

"Finkelstein," I say slowly, deliberately, "let me tell you what is classified: You are classified. A delusional, paranoid, arrogant,

prying asshole. And, I want you to know something: I've got files of my own, big guy. I've got affidavits from Mrs. Bernstein regarding her unusual way of paying you for your services, I've got a photo of Lilah by the pool last fourth of July, stuffing her face and popping out of her bikini and it's just not a very becoming shot, and I've got, Finkelstein, your sixth grade report card from Mrs. McQuicksand where it states: 'Doesn't get along with the other children, has an attitude problem.' Am I being clear? Are you getting the picture?"

"I was just trying to help. A husband should know."

"You have an attitude problem, Finkelstein. You do not get along well with the other children."

"Okay, just don't come crying to me four years down the line, saying, 'Why didn't you tell me there was high blood pressure on her mother's side, an affair with her English professor."

"FINKELSTEIN!"

"Say no more. My lips are sealed and locked. I'm throwing out the key. I'm a mute, I'm Marcel Marceau. You couldn't make me talk if you put a gun to my head. Case closed. The prosecution rests. Go in peace. Praise Jesus."

Finkelstein had an attitude problem.

***

"Friends," I begin, my marital acceptance speech, standing in the pool at Finkelstein's, the big shot's, looking like a wet Chassid, at my bachelor party. Goldberg is tending the barbeque, sweat dripping onto the all-beef hamburger patties, the Hebrew Nationals, the Empire thighs and breasts. Even Weissbaum, in his prime considered the Master of Barbeques, has to stand back and watch Goldberg handle a spatula with the sureness and dexterity of a balding short-order cook behind a counter somewhere. And memorizing orders with nothing written down, repeating it back to you:

"Two burgers rare, one medium no cheese, how many dogs?" Weissbaum looking on, like a retired army colonel looking at the

new young recruits, like Bob Hope watching Billy Crystal host the Academy Awards. Oh Weissbaum had his day in the sun, his golden tongs and mesquite briquettes, his way with the lighter fluid. Even Goldberg, today, still defers to Weissbaum in matters of subtle barbeque etiquette, questioning him in the respectful tone a prospective son-in-law might use to ingratiate himself to his fiancé's white-haired chairman-of-the-board father:

"Uh Sir, excuse me, but would you, in this case, keep these rares off to the edge a bit longer while letting the medium wells catch up, or uh..."

"Serve 'em right up, Son," Weissbaum replies with sureness, the certainty of a seasoned veteran, then actually stepping in himself for one last flip, the feel of the spatula in his hand like Willie Mays holding a bat at Oldtimer's Day—he's still got it.

Me, they won't let near the stove. My history with noodle puddings. And on Weissbaum's wedding day—one of his ex-marriages, this one to Carolyn, a woman who was a staunch pro-thisist and diehard anti-thatist, demonstrating against animal experimentation, nuclear power—you name it—abortion rights, El Salvador—make a list—whales, Native Americans. By the time she had been married to Weissbaum for six months, she had pretty much dropped all of it and was mostly into cleaning the house and watching videos. Two years into the marriage she briefly considered becoming a lesbian.

"That's really a bummer," Bernstein had said, "when your wife stops being heterosexual."

She got over it. Once, before she had dropped her political activism, when she was still *active*, she had half a dozen women over from her Boycott G.E. group, to discuss strategies. General Electric made huge financial contributions to the nuclear power industry, and Carolyn's group intended to convince consumers nationwide to stop using G.E. products, posting themselves outside supermarkets and appliance stores. During their meeting, I would casually walk through the room carrying a toaster oven, or a light bulb, and then later, after they had gone, would say to Carolyn,

solely to infuriate her nearly-lesbian politically-correct feminist sensibilities, "You girls are just so *cute* with your little placards and petitions."

She would laugh, and gradually relax her right-to-choose hard line into more of a right-to-snooze position, curled up next to Weissbaum, watching videos.

So on their wedding day, they put me in charge of picking up the cake—a huge, flat, sheet affair, impeccably decorated by a local baker. As I stand by my car, balancing the cake in one hand and opening the door with the other, it slides off its cardboard base right onto the sidewalk, causing significant damage, but not complete destruction. My first impulse? I start grabbing up scattered mounds of whipped cream off the sidewalk and eating it, thinking, "It shouldn't go to waste." (Reminiscent of Mr. Leibowitz at Twin Oaks who returned from the hospital after his morning heart attack in order to have the dinner to which he was "entitled." We were entitled to that whipped cream.)

I hid the episode from Carolyn and Weissbaum, saying merely that the cake had gotten "a bit jostled" from the ride home. This was not a jostled cake; this cake now had written across the top, "Congratylllmxxms followed by even more illegible markings and heiroglyphics that would require an archaeologist of icing to decipher, a curator in a baker's museum maybe, could tell this had once been a wedding cake. (The baker's museum is an idea worth exploring: In the next display we have several cookies from the Paleolithic Era; some Metazoic rugelachs from Mesopotamia; Babylonian *shnecken* that used to make Nebuchadnezzer *kvell*.)

So Carolyn takes the cake back and has it repaired and resurrected and only later, on video, do I confess that I had had a slight mishap with the cake, attributing it to "a problem with gravity, with physics—inclined planes and levels."

"Friends," I was saying, my bachelor party, Miltie floating on an inner tube, smoking a cigar, wearing his Mets cap and a "My parents went to Miami and all they got me was this stupid t-shirt" t-shirt and sunglasses, talking to Moscowitz, lying on a raft:

"You're going to burn and get skin cancer, you need cream... SOMEONE BRING MOSCOWITZ CREAM...I'm going to send you to the *Mezuzah* Rebbe. You bring him your *mezuzah*, he takes one look at it and tells you everything."

"I don't have a *mezuzah*."

"Ah hah!" Miltie says, holding one finger up in the air, as if to say, "My point exactly," and looking, also, like the customer in the old joke who tells the waiter to "Taste the soup."

"Why?"

"Taste the soup."

"It's the same every day, why should I taste it?"

"Taste the soup."

"You've been ordering it for twenty-five years, we make it the same every day, I already had some..."

"Taste the soup."

"Okay okay...where's your spoon?"

"Ah hah!"

Moscowitz is hooked. "But if I buy a *mezuzah*, doesn't it have to live on my doorpost for awhile before the *Mezuzah* Rebbe can read it? You know, to gather my vibes?"

"Vibes schmibes. This is not a murder mystery where you give the dog a pair of underwear to sniff, the psychic a handkerchief. It's like the *I-Ching*, synchronicity, whatever *mezuzah* you should happen to choose will tell him all he needs to know."

Moscowitz is a sucker for divination games—palms, tarot cards, dowsing rods, trance channels. Once he was arguing with Greenblatt's sister about the fact that he was on anti-depressants. She kept telling him to "get off the medication," and he argued that she didn't understand the full biochemical picture. Back and forth they went and then finally gave it up, and then Greenblatt's sister says, "I've been doing some channeling lately..." (This during that unique period in the late 70s when everyone and their mother was channeling...but Greenblatt's sister's mother, Flo, was not) "...you want a reading?"

Of course he does. She pulls the shades, lights a candle, some incense, they sit cross-legged, close their eyes, her voice deepens

and she says, "I AM THE COMTE DE ST. GERMAIN...MOS-COWITZ, GET OFF THE MEDICATION."

So Moscowitz would certainly go buy a *mezuzah* and it would eventually set him back about fifteen hundred dollars—$35 for the *mezuzah*, plus plane fare to Israel to find the *Mezuzah* Rebbe who would tell him:

"Too much cholesterol...eat less, exercise more." And to justify having gone to such an expense, he took these instructions in as sacred gospel, holy teachings, Jewish mantra, and came back repeating it to himself like it was big news, revelation:

"Eat less...exercise more! Eat less..." pausing to think about it, turning over the words in his mind, "and exercise more!" like solving a riddle, getting to the punch line.

"Friends," I say, at the party—I keep getting distracted, just trying to give you a picture of the goings on: Goldberg *shvitzing* onto the chopped meat, Miltie and Moscowitz in the pool; Bernstein is high, naturally, face down in the pool, snorkeling—pops his head up once in awhile with something like,

"You guys don't know what you're missing. Coral reefs, bluefish."

Finkelstein and Breshman sit in lounge chairs, talking business:

"Mr. Breshman, you come in with me, we do strictly phone orders, 800 numbers, distribution centers in the Pacific Northwest. You've been wanting to move out there—you're my local man, my Johnny-on-the-spot. The White Supremacists in Hayden Lake didn't get their ballpoints, you're there. The clinic in Boise ordered 3x5s and got the 5x7s, bang, you're on the scene. What do you say? You're my Pacific Northwest sales rep, you *represent* my sales force."

"I know what sales rep means."

"So?"

"Nah...I did that already. I wore the tie and the blazer, the chinos, shook hands with the supplies people, presented the slide shows, the film strips, gave out the free samples, threw in the extras, got the perks—the company car, the junkets—shmoozed with the

stock boys, talked shipping and handling, first name basis with the UPS man, accounts receivables, payables, calculators, changed the paper in the adding machines, the Xerox machines, the fax machines...I quit. Too many machines."

Weissbaum has stepped away from the grill and is tossing a ball back and forth with Greenblatt:

"Pop the ol' pea right in there, that's the baby," Weissbaum's saying, "Toss me the ol' rawhide, slip me the ol' golden nugget, hum that ol' mother-of-pearl, nice and easy, gotta warm up that arm slowly Greenblatt, it's early in the season...you want to see my knuckler?"

"I'm going to give you a knuckle sandwich if you don't shut up," and then to the rest of us, "This guy is a non-stop sports cliché, and I can't turn him off, someone help me."

"No batter, no batter..."

"HELP!"

"And he's in the stretch, here's the wind-up, and the pitch...change-up, high and away, it's 2 and 0."

"Weissbaum, how's your baby?" Trying to distract him.

"Youngster's coming up...keep your eye on that boy, scouts are watching. Looks to me from the way he handles a spoon that he'll be an opposite field, spray-hitter, a line-drive man like his dad, a number two in the line-up kind of kid..."

Greenblatt: "I'm gonna kill myself."

"Friends," finally I get a word in, "I have traveled all over the world trying to find myself. Where haven't I been? What haven't I done? Didn't I climb Mt. Sinai on a camel, sleep alone at the top freezing my *tuchus* off, begging God for a little feedback? I wasn't asking for bolts of lightning, no tablets, just some advice—the kind I probably could have gotten from Breshman at his bar, and in fact, while I think of it, in my own private heart I am beginning to feel very strongly that Breshman *is* God.

"And did I not pray at Abraham's tomb, stuff notes in the Wailing Wall? I did the Holy Land, I went back to the source, the center, I bought my *lulaf* and *esrog* in Mea Shearim, I went to

Nazareth and Bethlehem and Gethsemane just to cover my bases. I snuck onto the Temple Mount where no Jew goes, to pray to Allah with the Muslims at the Dome of the Rock. What didn't I do? I dipped in the Ari's *mikvah*, I walked all thirteen stations of the cross, I swam in the Red Sea and the Dead Sea, I sang at David's tomb, Rachel's tomb—whose tomb didn't I sing at? Where haven't I been?

"Over to India, to this temple and that shrine and the other stupa, to visit Baba this and Ram that, met your Sri Gurudevs and Bhagwans left and right, I meditated with the Tibetan lamas at the top of the world for chrissakes, I met His Holiness the Dalai Lama himself, in his own living room. Who haven't I met? What's left for me? Just like Bernstein, I smoked the *chillums* in Rishikesh, I sat at the burning ghats in Varanasi, the funeral pyres, I watched legs sticking straight up out of the flames, dogs munching on leftover skulls rolled off to one side, children running between cremations to gather coals in buckets for cooking fuel, bodies of the too-poor-to-be-burned floating down the Holy Ganga River.

"I walked through death's waiting room. Literally. The building next to the funeral pyre, the antechamber of the Other Side, filled with decrepit ancient sickly people lying on hard stone floors in damp dark rooms waiting their turn. I stumbled past lepers with their stubs and open wounds, the blind. Friends, what haven't I seen? The smell of the bodies, the sound of crackling bones, and suddenly the piercing sad eyes of an Indian man and someone says to me in English, pointing to one of these human bonfires, "That was that man's mother," and suddenly it's no longer some spiritual experience I'm trying to have, some death meditation practice, suddenly I'm at a man's mother's funeral and I back away, I go back down the narrow alleys of Benares. Friends, I have gone to great lengths to find out who I am, is it not true?"

"It's true," Greenblatt calls out over his shoulder, hauling down a pop fly on the run.

"Sea anemones, yellowtail," from Bernstein.

"Friends," I continue, "I have been to the Primal therapists, the Reichians, the Gestalt people, the Rogerians with their uncon-

ditional positive regard, the Behaviorists, I've been Adlered and Junged, Mick Jaggered and silver daggered, done my sand trays and Rorschachs..."

Greenblatt has started interjecting "Me too, me too," after each item.

"...been Rolfed, shiatsued, acupunctured, Alexandered, Feldenkraised..."

"Me too, me too."

"...took *est*, Actualizations, Life Spring..."

"Me too."

"...and every hallucinogen known to man: peyote and hashish, mescaline and opium, traveled to Brazil to take ayahuasca and psilocybin with shamans of the Amazon, I've been hypnotized, exorcised, depossessed..."

"Me too, me too."

"...and today I stand before you—I've known some of you for thirty years—and how do I feel after all this? After all the Polarity Therapy, the Zero Balancing, the herbal tinctures and Holotropic Breathwork, the Rebirthing...how do I feel? Goldberg, you tell them, you've known me the longest, what do you see?"

"Ah you haven't changed a bit Norb...you want your burger well done no cheese, right?"

"Then I'll tell you how I feel after all I've done—and what haven't I done? After all I've seen—and what haven't I seen? And after all I etcetera, and what haven't I etcetera? I'll tell you: I feel a little better."

"So *mazel-tov*, you feel a little better, so *kish mein tuchus*," Greenblatt's sister says, just arriving, "You should be marrying *me* tomorrow, you big moron."

"You're already married," Weissbaum reminds her.

"So?"

"I feel a little better."

And that's what I said at my bachelor party, to my old friends, the *minyan*, my war buddies, the day before I was to marry Rachel.

CHAPTER TWENTY-ONE

Greenblatt

The morning of the wedding I found Goldberg in bed with me. (Phil Goldberg, not Mrs. Goldberg of the baked potato incident.) We had slept feet to head and he told me he woke in the middle of the night to my pounding his feet furiously with my fists.

"What are you doing?" he had asked.

"The feet were coming dangerously close to the head," he said I said.

"Phil?"

"Yeah?"

"Was there something I was supposed to do today?"

"Get married?"

"Yes, that was it. Thank you."

"You're welcome."

"Is it Ha-*va*-ii or Ha-*wa*-ii?"

"Havaii."

"Thank you."

"You're velcome."

"We still got the old one-two punch, we can still knock 'em dead...why are you in my bed?"

"It just seemed right. Your last night and all. There was no hanky-panky."

"Phil, I have one very small concern about this whole thing that I need to talk about."

"I'm all ears. I'm Mr. Ears. I'm the Earman, ears are my bread..."

"Okay, I got it."

"So what is it?"

"Well it's nothing, really...it's just this little voice in the back of my head that thinks maybe I'm not really in love with her, that I'm not really turned on to her, that she's not Jewish, that maybe this is absolutely the wrong way to spend my day today..."

"But are you having any second thoughts?"

"Seriously, I could still *not* do this, I still have a shot at being lonely, single and alone, if I seize the opportunity."

"Hard to pass that up."

"So you're saying?"

"I'm saying, we need to get dressed."

"Okay. I'm getting married."

"Exactly my point."

"Okay. But should I tell Rachel I'm heterosexual?"

"Break it to her gently, after the wedding."

"You're a very funny fellow...are you comfortable?"

"I make a living."

Bitti boom boom bing—rim shots after every line, we were pulling out all the old one-liners for a last run-through.

"Do you want to sleep with Rachel?"

"I only want what's most convenient for you."

This referring to Mrs. Schneiderman at Twin Oaks—the "older" Schneiderman sister, I called her.

"How do you know she's older?" Goldberg had asked me that summer, incredulous, since both women were quite elderly in appearance.

"She's taller," I replied, applying the logic of schoolchildren.

When Goldberg offered her a choice of sponge cake or honey cake for dessert, she had said, "Whatever's most convenient for you," to which Goldberg had replied, "What would be most

convenient for me, Mrs. Schneiderman, is if YOU MADE A CHOICE!" almost losing it. Ah, stories about Goldberg…I could go on all day, I could keep 'em coming, but I got a wedding to go to. Mine. But there's time, maybe, for one more. Nothing big and dramatic, but a real slice of life story. Goldberg *verité*. Goldberg *in situ*. Quintessential Goldberg. Goldberg *ad nauseum*. You get the picture. I'm talking about the famous boiled beef story. For this story, even my wedding can wait.

We're at Twin Oaks. The schizophrenic general manager has called a meeting of the dining hall crew. All the waiters and busboys. He's mad. Guests have complained that we smell, that our clothes look soiled. "From now on, every one of you assholes hits the shower everyday, and you show up with clean white clothes. I don't care if you have to do a load of laundry at 2am, you show up smelling good and looking clean. Or you're out of here. Finished. Gone. I'll fire your ass if you show up looking like a slob. Am I making myself understood? Any questions?" We're all cowering, looking down at our feet, mumbling "Yes Sir" and "We understand Sir" and "It won't happen again Sir." Only Goldberg cautiously raises his hand—a finger, really.

"Yeah Goldberg, what the hell is it?"

"Well I was just thinking," Goldberg replies, "I don't think it's too late in the season to start a boiled beef embezzling ring. I figure if each one of us sitting here can get one flanken out of here every other day or so, that's about 230 nice cuts by September 1. We row them across the lake to Camp Timlow, where our connecting man…"

"ALL RIGHT QUIT FUCKING AROUND GOLDBERG." None of us could believe our ears. Goldberg was our hero, a living legend in our midst, an Al Capone of the Catskills. The story had to be told. And now, so does this one:

The ceremony is to be held in a small social hall in Paterson, New Jersey. Miltie made all the arrangements; he has connections. The hearse is parked outside, all decked out with ribbons and balloons and tin cans. Written on the windshield in soap is, "Just

married, not dead." (Reminds me of the time one of my girlfriends wrote "Just Dating" on my car.)

I arrive with Goldberg, feeling mildly nauseous, while he keeps repeating every two seconds, "Take it easy sweetheart, take it easy." Finkelstein and Lilah are there; Goldberg's Dorothy dressed to kill; Weissbaum and Sally; Bernstein and Mrs. Bernstein; Moscowitz and Myra; Breshman is standing with a strange woman I don't recognize, but who looks familiar.

"Do I know you?"

"I'm Rachel's friend...Lizzie."

"I don't recall meeting..."

"I was dancing on the bar the night you and Rachel met."

"Right! Of course...your face, you have a face...I mean, in addition to everything else..."

Miltie is milling around pinching girls, dressed, of all things, like a rabbi. And I notice he made all my *boychiks*, the *mensches*, the *minyan*, wear yarmulkes. Goldberg gets out his accordion—he'll play the processional; Miltie has connections. What, Goldberg and I never played weddings? We didn't play the social halls in Paterson? The Sisterhood fundraisers, the Purim parties and Hadassah Award nights? We knew our rumbas, our merengues. We could pull off a bunny-hop, the alley-cat, an "Anniversary Waltz" to bring tears. Who else should play at my wedding? (Goldberg does a medley from *Man of La Mancha* with the big finish on "The Impossible Dream," he brings the house down. He came in first place at a talent show with that number, in Bolton Landing, New York, summer of 1971. Second place went to a harmonica player. There were two entries.)

Once, we were hired by the Temple Emanuel Ritual Committee to play for their annual *Simcha* Social and our usual drummer was unable to come. We were forced to hire a kid from a local rock band, the Dark Devils. He showed up wearing all black, including boots and a cape, and agreed to play the gig only if we allowed him to read his poetry aloud. And so sometime around 9 o'clock, between a cha-cha and "Chosen Kalle Mazel-Tov," he took center

stage, and using a timer, made it ring into the microphone and began:

"Eight o'clock, time to feed the baby. Putting food into baby's mouth, so baby grow up big and strong."

Then the timer again:

"Nine o'clock, time to feed the baby. Eat, baby, eat. Burp, baby, burp."

And so forth, ending with one last ring:

"Twelve o'clock: Baby dead, overfed."

My Uncle Nat, who helped get us hired, commented to me later, privately,

"You boys did a wonderful job...but your drummer's a strange young man, isn't he?"

Ah, forget about it, only to say that of course Goldberg would play his accordion at my wedding.

But with Moscowitz walking around with trays of little hotdogs wrapped in dough, and Goldberg handling the music, I say to Miltie:

"This is the deluxe?"

"You want country clubs you should have gone with Finkelstein. You want the real thing, you want heart, you made the right choice. Now where is Marvin with those platters...and Weissbaum, get over here, I need an usher...Goldberg, give me an A...is this a wedding or what? At some point we'll need a bride...where's Greenblatt with the ring?"

Suddenly something is wrong. We all look around, at each other. Greenblatt, and his sister, are missing. His sister would have opened up the place, leaves the bedroom two hours early to get to the kitchen. When she had to be somewhere five minutes away, she'd be dressed and standing at the door, ready to go forty-five minutes early, saying, "By the time you get up, you put on your coat, you go to the door, you go down the stairs, you start the car, you go over, you get out, you go up, you gotta stay, you gotta be, you gotta go, come back, everything takes time."

She would never be late, and Greenblatt was coming with her. I run to the pay phone in the hall and call her. No answer. I try

Greenblatt. No answer. On a whim, I try their mother's house. A strange voice answers.

"Who's this?" I ask.

"This is Mrs. Rosenbaum, the neighbor. I'm the one who found them...it's a terrible thing. A terrible, terrible thing."

"FOUND WHO? WHAT?"

"The both of them, the mother and the boy...gone. The poor sister..."

"PUT THE POOR SISTER ON."

But she's a wreck, can't get two words out. My first thought, I admit: Greenblatt, you had to go and fuck up my wedding day? I race back into the hall, spread the word, grab Rachel, the guys, Miltie and Mrs. B. and we all pile into the hearse and head for Brooklyn.

We pull up in front of Flo Greenblatt's place on Avenue N. Neighbors are swarming about, Greenblatt's sister is hysterical:

"Dead as doornails," is all she can get out between sobs. The Silverman girl is hysterical: "I FINALLY GOT A BOYFRIEND AND NOW LOOK AT HIM."

Everyone is hysterical. From the neighbors we piece together the story: Jerry and The Voice had stopped by Flo's apartment on their way to our wedding to take pictures, and to meet Greenblatt's sister and give her a ride. Apparently Jerry was posing with his mother and sister on either side, and The Voice had screamed "SMILE, YOU LOOK LIKE DEATH WARMED OVER." As it turned out, Jerry *did* look like death warmed over. He keeled over, everyone started screaming, "CALL AN AMBULANCE, CALL NINE ONE ONE," running to phones, to neighbors. "PUT HIS LEGS UP, GET HIM SOME WATER." Jerry had remained conscious for a few minutes, long enough to say to his sister and mother, his last words, "I have no self." Flo had screamed back at him, "WHAT ARE YOU TALKING ABOUT? OF COURSE YOU HAVE A SELF. WHO DOESN'T HAVE A SELF? WHAT ARE YOU CRAZY?" and then collapsed herself, right on Jerry's chest, the impact too much for him, killing him instantly. At

which point The Voice had screamed at Flo, "HOW CAN YOU SCREAM AT YOUR SON AT A TIME LIKE THIS? NOW LOOK AT WHAT YOU DID, YOU KILLED HIM. NOW HE *REALLY* HAS NO SELF." And when the truth of her words sank in, Flo's heart gave out as well.

At which point Greenblatt's sister had attempted to strangle the Silverman girl to death, and was forcibly pulled off of her by Mrs. Rosenbaum, the neighbor, just in time, just as her face was turning blue.

"Rough day," Bernstein comments, as Mrs. Rosenbaum finishes telling us the story. The rest of us are speechless, broken. I hold Greenblatt's sister in my arms; she is weeping uncontrollably. Goldberg holds Mrs. Rosenbaum in his arms. Moscowitz holds Weissbaum holds Breshman. Bernstein embraces Finkelstein, tells him he loves him. Everyone holds someone, even though none of us likes to be touched, ordinarily. I feel numb, and vaguely annoyed, somehow, that after a lifetime of worrying about Nazis, Jerry's was a garden-variety death, with no bad guys to pin it on. Take out the SS factor and they *still* rip your heart out in this place. Love someone—anyone—and one of you gets left behind, wailing. If Hitler doesn't get us, our breaking hearts will.

***

When I was a kid, I had an odd fantasy I never told anyone, because for me it wasn't a fantasy. I believed it. It was this: Everyone in the world had clothing on except me. I alone was seen by all as stark naked—by my teachers, the kids in school, the crossing guard, everyone—and they were all in on it together, all agreed never to let on to me that they could see me. But I knew.

And today? I'm still naked, but I no longer believe anyone can see me. Now I see them—naked, all of them. And shivering in the cold. I want to make everyone warm. We should all build a fire and sit around it and sing sacred songs until the world ends. I want everyone to be there—my mother and father, and their parents, and anybody

who anyone has ever loved anywhere at any time should be there, reunited, all broken hearts healed. Tikkun olam: *"the fixing of the world." Shattered vessels everywhere once again able to contain and transmit the light of the* Ain Sof, *the Primordial Emptiness which is the Source of all form, the Original Fullness that is the great bosom in which all the dispersed and fragmented and separated ones at last rest their weary souls.*

In the heart of Jerusalem is the Old City, and in the heart of the Old City is the remaining ("Wailing") wall of the Second Temple, destroyed in 70 AD. And in the heart of that temple there had been one awe-ful place called the Holy of Holies and nobody could enter there or risk being burned alive by G-d. But once a year on the Holy Day of Atonement, Yom Kippur, the High Priest who prepares and purifies a whole year, a whole lifetime for this moment, enters the Holy of Holies and utters the unnamable, unpronounceable 72-letter name of G-d and then blacks out and is dragged from the outside by a rope tied to his leg.

Right beneath that spot in the temple is an underground chamber which is the very center of the world; the place of the very beginning of creation, where the soul of man is formed and given breath, G-d's hobby shop, the place where the dead return. And that is where I live, naked, surrounded by flames, calling out to friends and loved ones: Come home, it is Sabbath, sit at my table, share a meal, have some wine, say l'chaim to G-d and the Devil and dance, the men with the men, the women with the women. And sitting quietly watching, over in one corner, 192 years old, a white beard down to his navel, hunched over, smiling with his eyes looking like the Holy Baal Shem himself, is my great-great-grandfather, Hirsch Kahn, come to watch his descendents celebrate.

And Hirsch Kahn takes my hand and we dance in a circle, eye to eye, the men whirling and clapping around us, and from his eye a single tear of joy forms and slowly trickles down his cheek. I reach over and take it with my finger and taste it and it is not salty, but sweet. And as I swallow I am transported in a vision to a place on High where I see Greenblatt and Goldberg, Weissbaum and Finkelstein, Bernstein and Moscowitz, Breshman and even Freddy Lipschitz is there, all old

men with long gray beards, all dressed in black with long caftans and furry streimels, all wearing tefillin, taleisim, swaying and davening around a golden fire, eyes shining, ecstatic, saying the "Shema":

"Hear, oh Israel, you who struggle with G-d, the Lord our G-d is One," and as they intone the last word, "Achad"—One—they dissolve into the golden light of the flame in the center...and then the flame itself dissolves into an infinite vast dark void as big as the soul of man, as big as Hirsch Kahn's tear, as big as my very own heart.

***

The *minyan* carries Greenblatt and his mother down to the Happy Hearse. Miltie and Mrs. B. stay back with Greenblatt's sister, holding her up, still crying like a baby. The rest of us squeeze in.

"Our first gig, and we get two," Moscowitz says, a poor attempt at humor, but it makes me realize something as I pull away from the curb: the Happy Hearse only seemed feasible when all my friends were alive. Ironically, death has destroyed the whole idea. When push came to shove, I lost my sense of humor. Seeing Jerry's ashen face frozen into a permanent Jimmy Durante-like expression, looking like something from Madame Tussaud's, I decide I'm getting out of the funeral business. This is no fun after all. I imagine suing the Greenblatts, having to prove in court that they caused me to lose my sense of humor. The prosecution brings in Alan King to do a routine and make me laugh, and I just sit there, deadpan, and the defense rests.

Then I find myself imagining all of us, the whole *minyan* in a Jewish wax museum:

Me, bearded, holding a guitar, wearing a yarmulke, *tallis*, and *tefillin*—a 3-D Chagall.

Phil, sitting before a plate of food, his arm suspended in mid-air, with a forkful on the way to his mouth.

Weissbaum, reading *The Sporting News*, with a live video feed of Weissbaum, reading *The Sporting News*.

Moscowitz, lying flat on his back in a corner somewhere.

Finkelstein, with his attaché case, surrounded by a sea of files, genuflecting.

Bernstein, sitting on his feet in the crouched manner of the Indian street *babas*, smoking *chillums* out of a pipe.

Nearby is Freddy Lipschitz, shooting up.

Finally, Breshman, on a ski slope, laughing. Breshman, pouring a drink, laughing. There's a whole Breshman wing. Everybody comes out laughing. (The Wilner exhibit makes them cry.)

This morbid fantasy runs through my mind as I incomprehensibly contemplate Greenblatt's corpse, catching a glimpse of it in the rear-view mirror. I don't even want to see Flo.

Okay, so I never really got the funeral parlor thing off the ground. So all I did was buy a big car and spray-paint it. So sue me. As far as I'm concerned, with Jerry's help—and Flo's—I did do it. I didn't know any dead people until they came along. I didn't know how you break into the death business. I was a bit naive. But now with Jerry and his mom resting in the back, me driving along the Brooklyn-Queens Expressway with my buddies, the music playing "Toot Toot Tootsie Goodbye"—this was the fulfillment of my vision. How many friends do you have to bury to call yourself a funeral shportler? I'll tell you how many: One. Plus his mother.

The Minyan

Ed—still dead. Jerry—now dead. Flo—also dead. Greenblatt's sister: inconsolable. Me? I still can't feel anything. I'm in shock. I don't quite get it; in my experience, Greenblatt hasn't really gone anywhere. (Denial, the first stage of grief.) To me, he was, and is, a voice in my head, our minds fused in some way, seeing life as Cosmic Vaudeville together, a sense of humor the only thing that saved either of us. And his voice is still very present for me: I can call forth the spirit of Greenblatt in a flash, make you think he's in the room with you. In fact, who needs him? "There ain't room for both of us in this town, Pardner...if you ask me, you lived too long. Fuck you." (Anger, the second stage.)

Jerry and I always had a code word for death: "Petak's." If either of us began a conversation with that word, it meant somebody had died. Because whenever anyone we knew passed on, inevitably the two of us would wind up driving over to Petak's Deli to pick up the platters for the funeral gathering, for the *shivah*. And now Jerry himself, the Petak's king, is gone, and I'm left to go to Petak's alone, to shlep the potato salads, the smoked turkey breast. No one else knows the code, but I try anyway. It's futile:

"Petak's," I say to Bernstein.

"Yeah, what about it?" he says.

"Petak's," I say to Weissbaum.

"You buying?" he answers.

And meanwhile, Jerry Greenblatt's in heaven. (Everyone sitting around up there tired and bored, then Jerry shows up and it's all showbiz and glitz, he gets the folks splitting their sides, rolling, finally realizing they are in heaven, Jerry   knocking them dead.)

"PETAK'S JERRY," I call up to him, "PEE-FUCKING-TAKS GREENBLATT, WHERE THE HELL ARE YOU? COME ON BACK HERE, GREENBLATT, I'LL LET YOU RIDE SHOT-GUN IN THE HEARSE...PLEASE? I'LL GIVE YOU MY SIMON WIESENTHAL SWEATSHIRT." (Bargaining is third. Then finally, acceptance: My friend is dead. May he rest in peace. There are five stages; I'm forgetting one—probably the best one, too. Oh yeah: Depression. Goes without saying.)

When I spend the night sobbing in Rachel's arms, crying like a baby for hours, into the night, into the early morning, it finally occurs to me that I am sad. And I make the connection: I am sad because Jerry died. Grief is utterly simple. I am grieving the death of my friend, Jerry Greenblatt. I feel bad. I feel sad. My grief process reduced to a Dick and Jane primer: See Jerry die. See Norbert cry. Norbert is sad. Why is Norbert sad? Norbert is sad because his friend Jerry died.

Death is no laughing matter. Or is it? Maybe the Grim Reaper is really Dom DeLouise wearing a silly costume. Maybe the closest analogue in human life to the death experience is a Mel Brooks movie. Or maybe someone tickles you as you pass through. You enter the other side giggling uncontrollably. As God runs down your life with you, pointing out the good and bad stuff you did, you nod your head as if interested, but you keep losing it and bursting out laughing, annoying God, but then you tickle Him too and soon the whole place is filled with the sounds of uproarious laughter, echoing back through time to before the beginning and drifting forward to after the ending, Creation revealed as Primal Chuckle. For He's A Jolly Good Fellow.

So a funny thing happened to Jerry Greenblatt on his way to my wedding: He fucking died. ("Too bad I couldn't have died fucking," he says in my head.)

***

I did my whole grief process with Jerry in under twenty-four hours. I took the Evelyn Wood speed-grieving course. No, really. That same night that the Greenblatts met their untimely end, I went through it all and came out the other side by morning. It had to do with the most vivid and real-to-life dream I'd ever had. If I didn't fear ridicule, I would confess that I didn't really believe it was a dream at all, but in fact an actual visitation from Jerry's soul. In the dream, Jerry and I are walking the damp, dark, grey-blue streets of London on a chilly, drizzly night. I am clutching my chest, sobbing, and saying, "Oh Jerry, my heart is breaking," and I feel a wrenching pain; I am grief-stricken.

But then suddenly Jerry jumps up on a statue in Trafalgar Square and begins singing "If I Only Had A Brain," except he changes it to "If I Only had A Life."

"Get it?" he says. "I'm *dead*. I no longer have a life. Now I know what they meant when people used to say to me, 'Get a life.'" Then he laughs hysterically, doubling over, clutching his stomach with uncontrollable mirth. I wake up in the middle of the night laughing hysterically. Rachel turns to me:

"What's so funny?

"Jerry's dead," I say, and then crack up again. The pain in my heart goes away and I wake up in the morning no longer mourning.

***

Breshman and Finkelstein are already at the gravesites when we arrive at the cemetery. Miltie and Ethel are there, and Green-blatt's miserable sister with her miserable husband. Marvin, the waiter from the Carnegie Deli is there. And Myron Spotnick. Ra-

chel, Goldberg, Bernstein and the rest rode with me, in the hearse. We have a *minyan*. We gather around the graves and look towards Miltie, expectantly, but he gives no indication of doing anything. Finally he says to me,

"*Nu*, Reb Norbert, what are you waiting for?"

So okay, so I lied also about becoming a rabbi. I never promised I'd go to seminary. I never vowed. But I didn't lie. Ask Reb Miltie: As of today, I have my *smicha*, my ordination, from him. And it's kosher, legit, the old country way, the Master-Disciple way. It counts. (You can take a boy out of Judaism, but you can never take Judaism out of a boy. Never forget the bitter. I was young and I got old. Something is alive in me, what can it be? I will tell you: it is the Rebbe within.)

I start by singing a *niggun*. Most everyone joins in and we sing for a long time—ten minutes maybe. The melody is in a minor key, and as I hear everyone intone the *niggun*, I realize that the Jews are a minor key race, a sad melody in A minor, the song of a thousand years, of a grieving people clutching infants to their breasts, living in fear. The Christian hymns are celebrations, the exuberance of major keys, a rejoicing. The Jewish melodies are laments. (Name that tune? Jewish, in A minor.)

When we stop singing it feels like words would be superfluous, so I launch right into another *niggun*, this time an up-tempo number, a peppy one, the kind you might clap along with, stomping one foot, appropriate for a wedding. Joyous. We start slow. We start sad. But we keep going. We let the music take us along, gently, gradually, towards a lighter place in our hearts. It is very sweet to be singing for Jerry and Flo. Even Greenblatt's sister, for a moment, pulls up and out of her abyss and throws me a look, a look that tells me she's okay, she'll get through this, then plunges back down into the darkness and sobbing.

So it is a good opening, I have to say. I know how to warm up an audience. Then I try to say a few words but all I keep thinking is, This just isn't funny. I need better material. If I had half a brain I would have died first and let Jerry do *my* eulogy. He would have had 'em in stitches by now. Still, I try:

"To those of us whom Jerry and Flo Greenblatt have left behind, all those who have come here to mourn and pay their respects today, I greet you warmly from my heart. We all knew the dearly departed deceased so well it would be pointless to try and recap their lives and their wonderful qualities in a few words..."

"Pssst." Miltie gets my attention.

"Excuse me for one moment," I say to my congregation, and approach my mentor.

"While I think of it," he says, it's either 'dearly departed' or 'deceased,' not both."

"Right," I say, and return to my eulogy.

"Therefore, I can say only one thing on this sad occasion..." I realize I don't have anything particular to say at all on this sad occasion. I'm an actor going up on my lines. I need to stall for time. I fear that Miltie might be regretting having handed the reins over to me prematurely, that he should have started me with a bris or a sick call, not a funeral. But he gives no indication of this.

"Ah hem," I cough, looking desperately around at the faces for a clue, some assistance, a hint, sounds like. Weissbaum is standing in the rear holding his hands up in a "T" position; he is telling me to call for a time-out. I do. The guy is a lifesaver. "But before I continue, I'd like each of us to take a few moments to silently reflect on our memories of the dearly deceased..."

"Departed!" Miltie says, emphatic.

"Departed," I say, and quickly move through the crowd to Weissbaum, undoubtedly the man for the job, the job of bailing me out, steering me clear, pointing me in the right direction. Okay, I admit it: the guy to *coach* me.

He's down on one knee, drawing a diagram in the dirt with his finger. The rest of us huddle around him.

"Okay, now listen up: over here we got the two graves. Wilner circles this way, around Miltie and Ethel, and back to the front; we each approach from the sides, blitz to the front line and form a two-one-two zone defense, flanking the graves. We each say a few words in remembrance of Jerry and Flo and we get Reb Wilner off

the hook. When it's over, we zip over to Finkelstein's to eat Lilah out of house and home. Okay boys? Okay, now let's GO!" And we all break ranks and go to our positions.

"I'd like to take this opportunity to invite some of the departed deceased's loved ones to say a few words. Arnie? Can you get us started?"

"As you all know, Jerry worked with severely disturbed boys in special ed.," Arnie begins. "One day, the parents of Herbie, one of his Downs syndrome kids, report that Herbie had begun to soil his pants. A psychologist is consulted, and she speculates that Herbie is being sexually molested at school.

"A meeting is called, and gathered together in the principal's office are Herbie, Jerry, the principal, the psychologist, and a cop. The psychologist interrogates Herbie with a string of questions to which Herbie responds in his customary language of gibberish and mumbles. The psychologist takes copious notes. Jerry's standing there thinking, 'What is this woman writing?'

"Then she pops the big question: she asks Herbie to 'say the name of the person who touches your private parts.'

"Greenblatt's nervous as anything, because remember, this is the guy who felt nervous leaving a department store, couldn't look the security guard in the eye, afraid the guy would take one look at him and assume he had just stuffed the entire lingerie department into his coat pockets. Jerry was afraid when a police car drove by while he was checking his oil, afraid they'd arrest him for trying to steal his own car. And these are all *his* jokes. Afraid at a Ted Kennedy rally that someone would suddenly point to him and scream, 'GET HIM! HE'S GOT A GUN!' So remember who we're talking about when it comes to paranoia and guilt. The champion, ladies and gentlemen.

"So Herbie answers the woman:

"Ha-koo, ha-koo," he says, one of his pet phrases.

"Didn't that sound like 'Jerry, Jerry'?" the psychologist asks.

"With all due respect, M'am," Jerry says, "it actually sounded like, 'Ha-koo, ha-koo.'"

"So she changes tacts:

"Herbie, write down the name of the person who touches your private parts."

"Jerry's scared to death, excuse the expression, but of course, Herbie writes down the one and only thing that he knows how to write, which just so happens also to be the truthful answer to the question—he writes, 'Herbie.'"

(In my head I see Jerry, saying, "Man, that's *my* material, and when *I* tell it people laugh their heads off; it's all in the delivery, man, Weissbaum's embarrassing me out there.")

I motion with my hands, an invitation for others to speak. Goldberg speaks up:

"That reminds me of the time at the airport, when he was trying to check this big plastic bag and the lady told him, 'I'm sorry sir, you're going to have to get that re-packed, because it's flammable. So Greenblatt says, "With all due respect, M'am, if the plane catches fire, EVERYTHING IS FLAMMABLE!"

Mrs. Bernstein steps forward:

"He was a *meshugena*, they should have locked him up long ago; and she was nothing to write home about either, she should rest in peace."

"They could eat," is the best Marvin, the waiter, can come up with.

"No more breath, hello death." Moscowitz says.

Breshman offers,

"I gotta hand it to you, Greenblatt. You finally got me. In terms of this dying business, this keeling over with a heart attack in the middle of the day routine, I have to say, I never did that."

"Just a reminder to the family of the deceased," says Finkelstein, serving as their lawyer, "there still remains several outstanding bills to settle up, after the *shivah* period, of course. Naturally."

"Your time's up, your time's up," Myron Spotnick says.

"May your next incarnation be free of suffering," Bernstein says, exhaling marijuana smoke.

Don't think we weren't all torn up inside. But this was our way. This is how Jerry would have wanted it. He would have wanted his

funeral to be a *kibitz*-fest, a *shmooze*-athon, a *zetz*-capade. Truly, I mean it: he would have wanted it like that. He truly would have. Because Jerry Greenblatt was a real nut. A real dead nut.

"I have a story," I say. "It's about Jerry. Sort of. Not specifically. It's about all of us. It's about EveryJerry:

"There was once a young man who was very discontented. Inside he felt a glimmer, a hint of something goading him on to find deeper meaning in life. So he left the mainstream, the ways of his peers, and he abandoned traditional goals. Instead, he entered a monastery. They shaved his head, gave him robes and a begging bowl, and each morning he rose at 4 a.m. to meditate. In the afternoons he worked in the garden, and in the evenings there was often a brilliant discourse by their beloved Master, the Abbot.

"He remained for six months, when again he heard that inner voice of dissatisfaction, urging him on, saying 'no, this is not it, you must continue your search,' and so he left the monastery. His hair grew back. He put on civilian clothes. After some deep soul-searching, he decided to travel to India, to the majestic Himalayas, and bow his head at the feet of a great Sage. And he spent his days chanting the name of Ram and serving his Guru, helping in the kitchen, and doing whatever was required to help keep the ashram running smoothly.

"But again, after a relatively short time, he heard the voice: 'There is something to be found in this life, a higher calling you must respond to, an inner truth, and you haven't even begun to approach it in this place.' So he graciously bid farewell to the *Baba* and his people and knew not where to turn, but eventually chose to tackle his quest all on his own. He got himself set up in a modest, simple cabin, situated deep in the forest, next to a clear, running stream, far away from all other people.

"He stocked up on dried fruits and nuts and grains, and settled in to live as a hermit. With him he had brought the great texts of spiritual literature and scripture, from the *Bhagavad-Gita* to *Siddhartha,* the poetry of Kabir and the *Dhammapada.* He brought the Old and New Testaments, the *Mahabarata* and the *Koran,*

Walden and the Heart Sutras of the Buddha. And he read and contemplated, sat by the stream in meditation, talked and prayed aloud to the birds and flowers, became quiet of mind and heart for a little while.

"But then, as before, the voice was louder than ever, and said, 'Human beings are not meant to live in isolation. We are communal creatures and need the warmth of contact and loving friendship. Go back into the world—you cannot find God alone, you need the support of the *sangha*, or community of seekers.' And so, after nearly a year of solitude, he once again packed his few belongings and left for the city.

"There he sat in cafes, attended art openings and concerts, became briefly involved with a beautiful woman whose friends were all writers and poets and painters, and they would all sit up late into the nights discussing matters of great urgency, as they passed a pipe containing hashish and sometimes opium. But the glamour of this life wore thin very quickly, and he began to feel impure inside, worse than ever, and felt the need to abandon such worldly and wanton ways.

"On the very day he came to this inner conviction, as if arranged by Providence, an old Jew accosted him in the streets, saying, 'You—come in here, we need you for a *minyan*.' He followed the man down the stairs to a dim lit basement room where eight others stood with prayer books, waiting. Though completely unschooled in the Jewish way, he put on a yarmulke and *tallis*, took a *siddur*, and became the tenth man in their *minyan*. Inside he felt he had been guided there, that this might be the next step he was looking for.

"And so after the service, and after tea and sponge cake, he spoke with some of the men. One thing led to the next, and within a few days he was enrolled as a full-time, live-in student at a yeshiva. For two years he studied Torah and Talmud, recited prayers and *bruchas*, observed the Sabbath, wore *tefillin* each morning. He embraced Judaism with the same dedication he had once given other paths.

"And yet, though in some ways this life was closer to his heart than all the others, after two years, again his inner voice

was screaming: 'There is something alive in you...find out what it is. You must move on.' So he left the yeshiva, removed his *tzit-tzit* and skullcap, and commenced his wandering life once again, experiencing great despair, feeling that there was nowhere left to turn. He knew that wandering in itself had no particular advantage over staying put, in matters of the spirit, and so, weary of moving about, he eventually settled in one place—a small city. He got himself a room and a menial part-time job, helping out at a printer's shop. He made some new friends with whom he would sometimes sit for a beer at the end of the workday.

"And then one day, not too long afterward, he died."

Stunned by the abrupt ending, the group stands there, silently staring at the grave. Finally, Moscowitz breaks the silence: "What do you mean, he died? That's it? He just died?"

"That's it," I say, "he just died." Then, indicating the graves, I add, "Like some *other* people I know."

I conclude the service with an offering from Mordecai's *Book:*

> *In the beginning,*
> *and at the end,*
> *the lover of the Wild One says*
> *"Thank you."*

> *Nobody knows the combination*
> *to the safe,*
> *but the friend of the Laughing One*
> *knows it is unlocked.*

> *Mordecai has to smile:*
> *All weary travelers feel a soothing caress*
> *in the Tender One's back room.*

Epilogue

Rachel and I never got married: I couldn't make a commitment.

After the exhilarating first month when I thought I had met my soulmate, I gradually began to contract and stop breathing when I was with Rachel. After Greenblatt's funeral it seemed we hardly ever laughed anymore. Me, Mister Laugh-a-Minute, in a laughless marriage? I don't think so. I would spend time with my friends, being animated, alive, laughing it up, and then return to Rachel and instantly shut down. It was a familiar story, an old pattern of mine, material for about another ten years of intensive psychotherapy that I had no intention of undertaking.

I made up reasons why the relationship wasn't right, although the truth was plain from the t-shirt I started wearing: "Terrified of Intimacy." Nevertheless, I found myself wondering if I could ever feel truly at home with a non-Jewish woman, despite Rachel's Brooklyn-born Yiddish. I wanted someone who got my sense of humor. ("I get it," Rachel said, "It just isn't funny.") My post-coital bit about finding the human body disgusting didn't really fly either.

And yes, I also privately wondered if I needed someone with slightly rounder, fuller breasts. ("Needed?" Miltie asked, when I confessed. "You need food and water. *Wanted*, maybe. I want a lot of things, too. I just don't make important life decisions based on

them. I *wanted* Sophia Loren in her *gatkes*; I *chose* Ethel Bernstein in a corset.")

Yet I miss Rachel, and I do love her, and I secretly want her back, but I don't dare call her, because she might actually come back, and then where would I be? What would I do if she came back and the very next day the real woman of my dreams showed up, then what? (Love is a hedged bet: "I'll see your Rachel and raise you a Christina." I fold. I'm out of the game. Rachel called my bluff. Next time I propose to her, I should do it the old-fashioned way: get down on one knee, put my palms together in the prayer position, and say "Please say no.") I find it infinitely more exciting to be lonely and fantasize about whom I might end up with than to actually confront the daily challenge of facing the same person with our slew of emotional issues to work out, my habit of doing relationships-as-couples therapy, a marathon encounter group of two.

Fortunately, I was impossible enough to be with that when I finally broke it off Rachel was more relieved than heartbroken or angry. And I felt a perverse sense of satisfaction that I had convinced yet another woman that losing me was even better than having found me in the first place. ("Maybe it's a self-esteem thing," Bernstein had suggested.) I broke it off when we were trying to reschedule our wedding, and I accidentally said, "How about the 10th of Never?" which led to an "inquiry" on her part during which I convinced her that this wasn't a good time for me to get married to anyone, and that it was completely my problem. I had used that approach effectively in the past to extricate myself from attachments. ("Of course it's your problem, you idiot," Greenblatt's sister had said, when I used it on her. And "She wasn't for you," when she learned that Rachel and I had called off the wedding.) My other woman friends were not supportive of my breaking off the engagement: "Do you want to grow old alone?" they asked me. "Do you want to be a lonely, bitter old man?"

My answer? "Well...I guess not; no, I don't."

My male friends understood: "You were kidding yourself the whole time; you should never expect to be happy with a woman for

very long before the deep, neurotic patterns set in." I haven't given up. I believe growth is possible. Finkelstein advised affirmations:

"I, Norbert Wilner, am a real man."

"I, Norbert Wilner, am capable of love."

(*I, Norbert Wilner, am a child.*)

Not surprisingly, when we took the marriage pressure off and got through the broken hearts, Rachel and I actually became friends. "You're a much better friend than boyfriend," she told me, which wasn't big news. "Maybe we should move in together, have children, but never tell you you're in a relationship." She had some smarts, that girl. And who knows, we might trick me into a commitment yet. What I don't know won't hurt me.

But meanwhile, I continue to live alone, but at least I have a "kosher" home, Miltie-style: A place where people gather, and love each other, in a world that is heartbroken. Every Sabbath, I invite the gang over to sit at my table and drink wine, eat challah, sing songs and tell stories. Rachel comes early and helps me set the table, and she's always the last one to leave. As we were cleaning up together once, she said, "You know, you're getting the milk without buying the cow."

"That usually refers to sex."

"With a guy like you it's dishes."

I was starting to fall in love with her all over again.

Miltie and Mrs. B. usually come—they're living in sin, and Mrs. B. refers to herself in the third person now, as "the Rebbetzin": "Hello Norbela, give the Rebbetzin a nice cup tea, she's an old lady." Or, "Where should the Rebbetzin sit?"

"On your *tuchus*, Mrs. B."

"Such a mouth—that's the way to speak to the Rebbetzin? You know what they say, '*A geshvir iz a gute zakh bay yenem uintern orem*'...'A boil is a good thing as long as it's under someone else's arm.'"

Over time, Mrs. B, had started using her Yiddish proverbs indiscriminately, whether or not they suited the occasion.

"How's everything?" I might ask her.

"How can everything be? There's an old saying, *'Oyf a fremder bord iz zikh gut tsu lernen shem'...'* It's good to learn to shave on someone else's beard."

Reb Miltie has retired. "I'm old," he says, "I taught you everything I know, I think I deserve to soak my feet in Epsom salts for a few years."

Phil comes, alone—Dorothy can never find a thing to wear. He's decided to give their relationship one more decade, and if it still doesn't feel right, he's out of there. He feels committed to this plan and in his own way, given their history together, it represents what can only be termed "resolve." No more Mr. Nice Guy, Phil has taken a stand. Ten more years, and that's it. He's had it. Invariably, he tells the same pointless story every week:

"We were at my grandmother's once, when I was a kid. She was about 3'2", and weighed 240 pounds, a scary Russian woman with a husky voice. She comes in the room with an armful of pears and hands one to each person in the room, saying fiercely, 'EAT THIS PEAR OR I KILL YOU!'"

Everyone laughs, even though we're hearing the story for the hundredth time. "It just never gets stale, that old chestnut," Goldberg declares with glee. Weissbaum's usually in the other room watching a ballgame.

"You let him watch television on Sabbath?" Moscowitz's Myra asks. (Moscowitz, by the way, reports increased heartburn since dating Myra; she keeps him on antacids, carries Rolaids everywhere: "He gets terrible indigestion. He never chews his food," she tells us.)

"In this house, to have Weissbaum sitting at our table and *not* watching television when the Giants are on, or the 49'ers, *that* would be desecrating the Sabbath."

We make our own rules. We're not good Jews, but we have Jewish hearts.

Greenblatt's sister is almost her old self again:

"*I* should come to *your* house to have Sabbath with you and

your no goodnik friends? I'd rather walk barefoot on hot coals across Siberia...okay, I'll come, if you force me."

Finkelstein is busy every Saturday, taking Lilah to the malls, buying her things.

"What things, Finkelstein?"

"*Stuff*. Lilah needs more *stuff*, and those malls are filled with lots of *stuff*."

Bernstein's a regular, when he's not in jail. Sometimes he shows up with the Silverman girl, with whom he has been shacking up. When they started in together, I told him I didn't think he was being a good Hindu. "Maybe this religion's not for me," he had said, and began formally studying with Miltie—my only convert: "Hey, I never knocked the Jewish God—*Hashem*, *Ram*, it's all the same to me, all names of the Divine. Miltie's my new *Baba*, a *mensch* is a *mensch*. And you give good Sabbath." The Silverman girl had mourned Greenblatt for about two months, and then said, "I'M NOT GETTING ANY YOUNGER" and began dating Bernstein, who was then still worshipping Brahma, Vishnu and Shiva, which got The Voice all riled up: "WHERE DID YOU GET ALL THIS *MISHEGAS* IN YOUR HEAD? YOU'RE *MESHUGA*." And he was.

Breshman comes and just sits there. He has come full circle, back to how he was in high school, silent. But then it was due to shyness, now it is because he feels he has already said everything he has to say. In terms of dinner conversation, Breshman already did that. You couldn't get a peep out of him anymore. He just sits there.

And Greenblatt? May you rest in peace, *shtunk*-o'-my- heart.

But the rest of us live it up. We drink a lot of Manischewitz Concord Grape and Miltie tells us Kabbalistic fairy tales about the Baal Shem Tov in his magical chariot, arriving in distant villages the day before he leaves. And most of all, we sing *niggunim*, banging on the table the way the Chassids in their black coats do it in Brooklyn, the way their fathers did it in the old country before the war, our voices often rising in a mad frenzy of love-drunk sound,

an ecstatic emptying of all that we are into sheer melody. And for me it is in fact a secret transmission, a transgenerational gift that I am sending my grandmother's soul in the other world, from this world of "the Hitler." I want her to hear the message that I also need the world to hear: "I am Jewish, and I am here; the walrus was Paul, I am the Rebbe." I want her to hear, between the lines of our music, the message: "The Hitler didn't win, because we're here singing to *Hashem*, with joy and gusto, in Hebrew. The Hitler didn't win, because *I'm here*, singing...*and singing the song shall be enough.*"

Yiddish/Hebrew Glossary

NOTE: Is it *schmuck* or *shmuck? Schlemiel* or *shlemiel? Schmeer, schmear, schmeer or shmeer?* After *way* too much research and debate among self-professed Yiddish mavens, the author decided to make arbitrary choices.

afikomen: the ritual piece of matzah (unleavened bread) that is part of the Passover ceremony, customarily wrapped in a white napkin and hidden, later to be searched for by the children who then "sell" it back to the head of the household so that the service may be completed.

alter kocker: an old fart

balhabosteh: a housewife

bochur: student

boychick: affectionate term for a Jewish man

bris: the circumcision ceremony

b'ruchas: blessings in the form of prayers

bupkis: nothing; zilch; zip.

chazzerai: junk food

chupeh: the wedding canopy

chutzpah: nerve, audacity.

davening: chanting the Hebrew liturgy

dreydl: a spinning top with Hebrew letters on it used for a Chanukah game.

esrog: an oversized, lemon-like fruit used in the festival of Sukkos.

farbisener: embittered

farkrimpt: sour-faced

ferblungered: mixed up, confused.

flaumkuchen: a sweet, flatbread made with sour cream, sugar and cinnamon

fleishig/fleishadik: meat products

gantseh k'naker: a big shot

gantseh megila: the whole story, a big deal

gatkes: underpants

genug: enough

gezuntaheit: go in good health

goniff: a thief or mischief-maker

goy/goyim/goyishe: non-Jew/non-Jews/in the style of non-Jews

Havdalah: the ceremony that concludes the Sabbath on Saturday evening

hocking/hock me a cheinik: to badger, bug, and annoy incessantly

hora: a traditional circle dance, usually done at weddings and celebrations

kaddish: the prayer for the dead

keyn eyn hora: superstition meaning "No evil eye."

kibitzer: a joker, offering solicited comments

kichel: a fluffy, airy pastry

kiddush: the prayer over wine

kishkehs: guts, intestines

kish mein tuchus: kiss my ass

kneidlach: matzah balls

kvell: to well up with pride

lamed vovnik: one of the 36 legendary hidden holy people who "hold up the world."

landsman: countryman, compatriot

latkeh: a potato pancake

l'chaim: a toast, "To Life"

loch en kop: a headache ("hole in the head")

luchshen: noodles

lulaf: a leafy branch used in the festival of Sukkos

macher: big shot

mamzer: bastard

meeskite: an ugly little imp

mensch: a "real" man

meshugeh: crazy

meshugeneh: a crazy person

mezuzah: ritual object placed on a doorpost

mikvah: ritual bath for purification and ablutions

milshig, milshedik: milk products

minyan: the quorum of ten men needed to conduct a religious service

mishegas: craziness

mishpocheh: family

mitn derinen: in the middle of everything

neshama: soul

niggun: melody

nosher: one who likes to snack a lot

nu: Well? So?

nudnik: a pest

payis: the curly sideburns worn by religious Jews

pisher/pishiker: a nobody, a little squirt

potchkey: to waste time fiddling around

pupik: belly-button

Purim: the Jewish holiday based on the Book of Esther

putz: a shmuck

Shabbes: the Sabbath

shaineh kinderlech: beautiful children

Shavuous: the festival commemorating the Jews receiving the Torah

shikseh: a non-Jewish woman

shivah: the mourning period

shlemiel: an inept person

shlepper: an incompetent, hopeless person

shlof'n: go to sleep

shlub: like a shlump

shlump: a slob

shmateh: a rag; a shabby piece of clothing

shmeer: (1) noun: the cream cheese spread on a bagel

        (2) verb: to bribe or tip someone

shmegegee: a fool

shmendrik: an idiot

shmooze: to gossip or chat

shmuck: a putz

shmutsik/shmutzadik: dirty

shnapps: whiskey

shnecken: little pastries

shnorer: a beggar or cheapskate

shofar: a ram's horn

shpilkehs: nervous, anxious

shpits: peak, point; end

shpritz: spray; seltzer added to a drink

shportler: an athlete

shtetl: a small town

shtibl: a small room used as a synagogue

shtick: a comic routine

shtunk: a stinker

shtup: to have intercourse

shul: synagogue

shvank: to wash food down with liquid

shvants: person who behaves stupidly

shvitzing: sweating

siddur: a prayer book

simcha: joy

smicha: ordination

streimel: furry, black hat

sukkah: the outdoor hut constructed for the festival of Sukkos

tallis/taleisim: prayer shawl(s)

tefillin: ritual phylacteries worn in prayer

tikkun: to heal or fix

trayf: non-Kosher food

tsores: trouble

tuchus: derriere

tzimmes: a sweet dish made with raisins and carrots

tzit-tzit: ritual fringes worn as an undergarment

yeshiva: a Jewish school

yiddela: a Jew

yuhrzeit: the anniversary of someone's death

zaftig: chubby or fat

zei gezunt: go in good health

zetz: a verbal jab, a punch or blow

zeyde: grandfather

ABOUT THE AUTHOR

Eliezer Sobel is also the author of **Blue Sky, White Clouds: A Book for Memory-Challenged Adults.** Although there are over 20,000 books for caregivers of people with dementia, this is one of the only books aimed at the patient. **www.blueskywhiteclouds. com**

He is also the author of:

The 99th Monkey: A Spiritual Journalist's Misadventures with Gurus, Messiahs, Sex, Psychedelics and Other Consciousness-Raising Experiments, the tale of the author's hilarious and poignant 30-year journey that transported him from the sublime to the absurd in equal measure;

Wild Heart Dancing: A Personal One-Day Quest to Liberate the Artist and Lover Within, designed to awaken and unleash the reader's dormant creativity in a one-day, at-home, self-retreat;

Why I Am Not Enlightened, an e-book that should make anyone feel better about failing to be a Perfect Realized Master; and

The Manual of Good Luck, long out of print.

Eliezer Sobel has a blog on **PsychologyToday.com,** has led creativity intensives and meditation retreats around the United States, and is a certified teacher of the 5Rhythms™ movement practice developed by Gabrielle Roth. He is married to Shari Cordon.

NOTE FROM THE AUTHOR:

Minyan first appeared in hardcover in 2004 at the daunting price of $32. My own mother wanted to wait for the paperback, which never came. Although *Minyan* won first prize among 400 entries in the Peter Taylor Prize for the Novel, and was praised by several National Book Award winners, it was never properly promoted and quickly disappeared into the Graveyard of Literary Obscurity, a fictional realm of purgatory where many unsung gems languish unread. The present edition is the first time *Minyan* is available as a trade paperback. It is also now available as an e-book in the Kindle, Nook and iBook formats. If my mother could still read, she would finally have the chance. –E.S.

www.eliezersobel.com